"Better

Alli dodged ~~~~ ~~~~ ~~~~
she and Kevin made their way between the rows
of cars.

The van continued to prowl. Passing several
vacant spaces, it came relentlessly in their
direction.

When the glare of a lamp illuminated the
interior, she saw two men in the front seat.
Pairs of men didn't generally cruise around
swanky hotels in the middle of the evening,
passing up available spaces.

Unless they were looking for someone.

Kevin kept darting in a stop-and-go pattern,
homing in on his car. At last they reached the
sedan and he opened the door with a key.

"The next part's going to be tricky," he said.
"Keep your head down in case they start
shooting."

"Maybe we should call the cops...."

Dear Reader,

As a former newspaper and Associated Press reporter, I enjoy reliving the excitement—and the sometimes sharp mix of personalities—that one finds in a newsroom. I may lack Alli's disregard for danger, and I never suffered a backstabber on the order of Payne Jacobson, but if fiction didn't heighten our experiences, it would be dull indeed!

Kevin Vickers isn't based on any individual police officer or detective I've known, but in my single days, visiting the police station was the highlight of the morning. After reading the log, I'd chat with lieutenants and sergeants in the detective, patrol and traffic bureaus. Some of them definitely fit the bill as hunks! Most proved patient and quite helpful. I'm glad to say that, unlike the stereotype of the antagonistic reporter, I sometimes managed to repay the favor in my articles by encouraging witnesses to come forward.

So there's a bit of nostalgia for me in this tale, but Alli and Kevin ran away with the story and made everything fresh again. I hope you feel that way, too!

If you enjoy the book, please e-mail me at jdiamondfriends@aol.com and visit my Web site at www.jacquelinediamond.com.

Best wishes,

Jacqueline Diamond

THE *Baby* SCHEME

Jacqueline Diamond

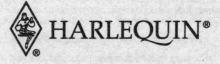

HARLEQUIN®

TORONTO • NEW YORK • LONDON
AMSTERDAM • PARIS • SYDNEY • HAMBURG
STOCKHOLM • ATHENS • TOKYO • MILAN • MADRID
PRAGUE • WARSAW • BUDAPEST • AUCKLAND

ISBN 0-373-75079-X

THE BABY SCHEME

ABOUT THE AUTHOR

A former Associated Press reporter, Jacqueline Diamond has written more than sixty novels and received a Career Achievement Award from *Romantic Times* magazine. Jackie lives in Southern California with her husband, two sons and two cats.

Books by Jacqueline Diamond

HARLEQUIN AMERICAN ROMANCE

Don't miss any of our special offers. Write to us at the following address for information on our newest releases.

Harlequin Reader Service
U.S.: 3010 Walden Ave., P.O. Box 1325, Buffalo, NY 14269
Canadian: P.O. Box 609, Fort Erie, Ont. L2A 5X3

For Kurt

Chapter One

Alli Gardner had just arrived at her newsroom desk on Thursday morning when she spotted the startling front-page headline. As she sank down and read the story, her feeling of shock shifted to outrage.

The allegation that the recently named mayor of Serene Beach, California, had run backroom gambling tournaments to benefit his computer stores didn't surprise her. After all, she'd done the research and written the story.

The problem was, it didn't carry her byline.

She read the first few paragraphs again. Those weren't only her facts—they were her words. Yet she hadn't quite finished the exposé the previous night and therefore hadn't submitted it, although the assistant managing editor had known she was working on it.

The byline belonged to Payne Jacobson, the assistant managing editor's nephew.

In her five years with the *Orange Coast Outlook,* Alli had never considered the possibility that someone might raid her computer. That is, not until Payne joined the staff six months ago.

After he'd twice written articles based on her research and quotes, she'd complained to his uncle that he must have found a way to access her computer files. But not only had Ned Jacobson sided with his nephew, he'd hinted that Alli feared competition.

This time, she'd deliberately kept all the notes on her personal laptop to prevent Payne from accessing them through the newspaper's networked computer system. She'd taken the laptop home at night, too, but she'd left it unattended on her desk several times during the past few days.

The jerk couldn't have read her files last night. That meant he must have installed spy software.

Alli felt as though steam were pouring out of her ears. If that weasel thought she was going to sit still over this, she had news for him—the kind of news he *wouldn't* want to steal.

She flipped open the laptop and typed in "You little thief!" then added a few more colorful insults for good measure. As she saved the file, she glanced across a group of desks to where the twenty-three-year-old sat smirking while typing on his keyboard.

His blond, designer haircut and trendy suit couldn't offset the thinness of his face or the deceitful cast of his small eyes. Of course, she wasn't exactly an unbiased observer.

As she waited for his spyware to steal her latest keystrokes, Alli reflected on how hard she'd worked to earn her reporter's job, while Payne had waltzed into it, courtesy of his connections. After completing journalism school, she'd labored for two years as a writer in a public relations office, then spent three years at a weekly before landing this position against stiff competition.

Even so, she wouldn't object if Payne were honest and did good work. But his writing—when he did any of his own— had a clunky, amateurish quality despite Ned's editing. In addition, according to his annoyed interviewees, he often misquoted them. Surely anyone other than a doting relative could tell that he hadn't written this exposé.

Across the room, she saw Payne's cheeks flush and his gaze flick toward her. Insult received. She'd proved her point about the spyware.

Beyond him, behind a glass office window, J. J. Morosco stood up and stretched. Despite the early hour, the short, rotund managing editor had been at work for quite a while.

A forty-something go-getter, J.J. had stepped on more than

a few toes during his first year at the *Orange Coast Outlook*.
Hired from a newspaper in the San Francisco Bay area, he'd re-
vamped the sports and entertainment sections, turning them into
showpieces that the publisher trumpeted in TV ads. The result
had been an increase in subscriptions and newsstand sales.

Alli hated to bother him with an intramural quarrel. But
how could anyone tolerate having stories stolen? Besides,
this act of plagiarism threw the newspaper's ethical stance into
question.

After unfolding her five-foot-nine-inch frame from behind
the desk, she marched across the linoleum. Reporters nudged
one another and turned to watch, probably expecting a show-
down. She'd made no secret of her allegations about Payne.

The sight of her reflection in the glass made Alli pause.
Where she'd stuck a pen in her shirt pocket, a telltale spot of
ink revealed that she'd forgotten to cap it. The way her skirt
had swiveled around her hips didn't improve her appearance,
either.

What a mess, and at only nine o'clock in the morning. She
lacked the patience to repair to the ladies' room, however, especially since she could do nothing about the inkblot.

After hiking her skirt into place, Alli realized she'd done
so in full view of the managing editor. With a sigh, she resumed her approach. She couldn't back down now.

When she stepped into his office, J.J. rose out of courtesy.
Noticing that she loomed over him, she quickly found a chair.

"I'm here about the story in this morning's paper," she
said. "The one concerning Mayor LeMott."

"Ned tells me you were working on something similar." J.J.
eased into his seat. "He says Payne warned him you might
have a complaint."

"It wasn't similar. This *is* my story," Alli told him. "Word
for word."

"But you hadn't filed it yet."

"I'd written it, but I was holding off so I could double-
check a couple of points," she explained. "And there's a sidebar I didn't have time to complete. Mr. Morosco, Payne's

planted spyware in my laptop. He stole every bit of that piece from me."

The editor's forehead wrinkled. He'd been putting in such long hours that he'd begun to lose his tan and had gained a few pounds, she noted.

"The two of you have never gotten along, have you? He'd only been here a month when you accused him of stealing your notebook."

"It disappeared from my desk right after he passed by, and the next day he turned in a story based on my research!"

"A guard found your notebook outside that afternoon, right next to where you usually park," the M.E. replied.

"I didn't drop it. I'm not that careless." Alli hated being put on the defensive. "Look, you can talk to any of the people I quoted in today's story and they'll confirm who did the reporting."

"Except that most of your sources spoke anonymously," he pointed out.

"I was going to identify them to Ned when I handed in the piece!" That was standard procedure. "Also, since when does this paper assign two people to the same story?"

She'd heard of a few big papers that ran their operations in such a cutthroat manner, but the *Outlook* couldn't afford such a waste of staff time. Besides, that kind of competition did horrible things to morale.

"He says Payne asked if he could pursue the same subject. He decided to let the kid show what he could do, and he beat you to the punch."

How could she win when the assistant managing editor was stabbing her in the back? If she were in J.J.'s seat, she probably wouldn't believe her accusation, either.

"Give Payne his own assignment, something he can't steal from anyone else," she said. "He'll blow it."

"As it happens, he's going to have plenty of chances." J.J. fiddled with some papers. "I'm sure you're aware that I've streamlined two other sections. In the meantime, the publisher and Ned and I have been tossing around ideas for the news operation. I'm about to put those proposals into effect."

Why was he telling her this? Allie wondered uneasily. And why was he avoiding her gaze?

"The publisher believes we've got too much duplication and dead wood," he went on. "Some of the older staff members will be asked to take early retirement, but I'll have to cut deeper. After careful consideration, I'm afraid we have to let you go."

"What?" Alli stared at him in disbelief.

Until six months ago, she'd been one of the *Outlook*'s stars, a feat she'd accomplished through hard work, drive and an instinct for news. Despite her abilities, she knew as well as anyone how few jobs opened up in the newspaper business. Being laid off might mean banishment from the career she loved.

"I was going to wait a few more days, but this seems as good a time as any," J.J. said. "It's best if you clean out your desk and leave immediately. Naturally, you'll be eligible for unemployment, and we'll give you two weeks' severance pay."

"You can't—" She stopped. Of course he could lay her off if he wanted to. But it was so unreasonable! "Was this your idea, the publisher's or Ned's?"

Ignoring the question, he began to talk about issuing her last paycheck. Alli didn't ask again because she was too busy trying to absorb the awful news that she'd just been fired.

A minute later, when she emerged into the newsroom, a hush fell over the place. Even through the glass, people must have realized what was happening. Payne buried his face inside that day's paper.

Alli ignored him. Obnoxious as he was, he'd never have gotten away with this thievery if his uncle hadn't condoned it.

She walked over to Ned Jacobson. Swiveling in his computer chair, he peered at her from beneath a shock of graying hair.

Keeping her pitch low, Alli said, "I always respected you. You had high standards and you taught me a lot. I don't understand why you don't apply those standards to your own family."

She strode away with her head high. There was a lot more she wanted to add, but hurling insults would reflect worse on her than on him.

After reaching her desk, Alli couldn't think what to do. She'd never been fired. She had no idea where to start.

The newsroom secretary scurried over with an empty box. "I guess you'll be needing this," she said. "I'm sorry."

Alli nodded in response and bit her lower lip. Thirty was too old to cry, and besides, she prided herself on her toughness.

From the drawers, she scrounged a few personal items and discarded an assortment of candy wrappers, sandwich boxes and plastic spoons. A clipping fluttered to the floor. When she picked it up, the dark, brooding eyes of Detective Kevin Vickers seemed to fix on her.

The article, which dated back three years, announced that he'd left the police department to start his own agency. She couldn't remember why she'd saved it, except that he was probably the hunkiest guy who'd ever booted her out of his office.

She and Kevin had butted heads frequently when he worked for the PD. Unlike larger police departments, Serene Beach's didn't restrict reporters to dealing with a public-information officer, unless that reporter proved unreliable.

Most cops had cooperated once they got to know Alli, but not Detective Uptight. He'd refused to answer all but the most obvious questions about his cases, and she hated taking no for an answer.

She'd been relieved when he left. Well, not entirely. The picture captured his intense gaze and thick brown hair, reminding her how much aesthetic pleasure she'd taken in their encounters. She'd imagined they might run into each other again after he went out on his own, but so far that hadn't happened.

And, obviously, it wasn't going to. If she did land a new reporting job, it would have to be somewhere else. Maybe another state.

Without thinking, Alli tossed the clipping into the box,

then added some documents she'd dug up about the mayor. Not that she had any use for them, but she wasn't going to leave them for Payne's follow-up.

He had to sink or swim on his own now. She wondered when he would realize that and what he'd do about it. Probably steal from somebody else.

Larry Corman, a young photographer Alli hung around with, approached with a glum expression on his round face. "I can't believe what I heard. They laid you off?"

She nodded.

"It stinks."

"You're not kidding." The rasp in her voice embarrassed her. Alli had always been the strong one in the family, bucking up her mom after her father left them and whenever they hit rough financial waters. "I'll survive."

"Everybody knows Payne's a lousy reporter," he muttered. "This is going to hurt the whole paper."

Hearing him say so made Alli feel better. "Guess what he did? He bugged my laptop."

Larry pushed his round glasses higher on his nose. "Take it to the High Tech Emporium, their main store near the mall. There's a guy named Brett who can clean it up."

How ironic, Alli thought. The emporium chain belonged to Klaus LeMott, the man whose shady dealings and political ambitions she'd been investigating. "I'm not sure I'd trust anyone there."

"I went to high school with Brett. He's okay," Larry said.

"Thanks." Right now, Alli wasn't sure she could afford to pay anybody to do anything. How much did unemployment compensation pay, anyway?

"Just because you're leaving doesn't mean we can't still be friends," he added.

She would have hugged him if so many people hadn't been watching. "Of course."

"I've got your phone number. And you've got mine. And you'll probably land a job in no time…aw, phooey." He hurried off, his eyes misty.

When her phone rang, Alli nearly ignored it, but her instincts wouldn't let her. Besides, the call might be personal.

"Hi. This is Alli," she said into the mouthpiece.

"Allison Gardner?" a woman asked. "My name's Rita Hernandez. You don't know me, but I read your articles all the time. Something's happened that I think you should look into."

Alli hated to explain that she didn't work here anymore. Why not hear the woman out and, if it proved to be a nonstory as so often happened, at least let her down easily?

"Go ahead." Alli listened, at first out of politeness and then with growing curiosity. From habit, she almost began typing into the computer; then, remembering the lack of privacy, she pulled out a notepad, instead.

As the source talked, she scribbled rapidly. Rita Hernandez had stumbled onto something interesting, all right, and Alli didn't intend to hand it over to Payne or anyone else at the *Orange Coast Outlook.*

The woman had become the victim of a crime she didn't dare report to authorities. Alli made a snap decision to investigate on her own, no matter how impractical that might seem.

"I appreciate the call, Mrs. Hernandez," she said when the woman finished. "I'll work on this and get back in touch. Let me give you my cell-phone number. It's the best way to reach me."

"Thank you so much!"

After she rang off, she saw Ned regarding her curiously. "What was that about?" he asked.

"Wrong number," she responded, and was pleased to hear a few chuckles. Before he could quiz her, an intercom query from the back shop distracted him, and then a woman from Accounting showed up with her check.

Alli pocketed it, grabbed the box and her laptop and scooted out the door. Maybe she'd sell the story to a magazine, or she might use it as leverage to find a job at a bigger paper. One way or the other, she was going to help Mrs. Hernandez and her career at the same time.

Let Payne Jacobson dig up his own stories. She hoped he dug his own grave while he was at it.

ON FRIDAY AFTERNOON, Kevin Vickers drove slowly past a two-story house, noting the fresh paint job and elegant landscaping. The location, just off San Michel Way, in a neighborhood only a step down from a nearby row of mansions, was pretty much what he'd expected for a well-to-do retired obstetrician.

A few days earlier, a young widow named Mary Conners had arrived at his office after receiving a blackmail demand for twenty thousand dollars. She couldn't pay, she'd told him in tears, and she didn't want to lose her little boy.

She and her late husband, unable to conceive, had tried in vain to adopt a child in the United States. Agencies had rejected them because of a drunk-driving arrest on her husband's record.

It had seemed like a miracle when her gynecologist and his partner had offered to help them adopt a baby through an orphanage they knew of in the Central American country of Costa Buena. Three years ago, they'd joyfully welcomed their son.

Now, less than a year after her husband had died from an aneurysm, an unidentified phone caller had informed Mary that the orphanage illegally bought and sold babies and falsified documents. If she didn't pay up, she'd be reported to the authorities, who might deport her son.

Mary had confirmed via the Internet that the orphanage was being probed by its home country. She'd spotted Vickers Investigations in the phone book and asked him to find the extortionist. At first, she'd only wanted to persuade the man to accept a lesser amount because of her financial status, but he had pointed out that if she yielded once, more demands might follow.

He'd suggested contacting the police and putting a trace on her line, but she'd refused, even though he'd assured her the police had neither the authority nor the desire to take away the baby. She'd become so distraught that he hadn't pressed the issue. Besides, the blackmailer, who'd been smart enough to scramble his voice, would almost certainly be using an untraceable phone.

Instead, Mary had begged Kevin to try to track down the blackmailer by other means and threaten him with prosecution. He'd agreed, although he'd warned that if the call had originated from another country, there wasn't much he could do.

The extortionist had allowed her until Friday to come up with the funds. That made for a week to catch him.

Kevin had quoted Mary the lowest rate on his pay scale; he always gave people a break if they won his sympathy. He'd also been known to bill a little extra on occasion for a bad attitude.

She'd insisted that under no circumstances should he notify the authorities. Kevin had agreed, as long as he didn't have to violate any laws.

He'd decided to start his fieldwork by paying a surprise visit to Dr. Joseph Abernathy, now retired as a gynecologist, to ask about his still-practicing partner, Dr. Randolph Graybar, and their involvement in the baby ring. He hoped to find out how the blackmailer might have gained access to information about adoptive families.

He circled the block, alert for any suspicious activity. Even in an apparently peaceable community, taking heed of details could mean the difference between life and death.

Kevin had no illusions about the potential for danger. Thanks to California's stiff restrictions on concealed-gun permits, he was about to walk unarmed into a meeting with a man who might be either an innocent bystander or a blackmailing baby seller. He hadn't even been able to arrange for backup. Although his agency was profitable enough to bring in a second detective, he'd had no luck finding anyone qualified.

As he made a second circuit of the block, a gray van passed him going the other way. The bright June sunlight showed two shapes in the front seat, but Kevin couldn't make out any details.

He parked half a block beyond the house to avoid attracting attention. His midpriced white sedan contrasted with the expensive models around it, but at least he'd had the car washed and detailed.

When he got out, he could smell the ocean less than a mile away. He heard a dog barking and noted that it was too far off to pose a threat.

On the short walk to Abernathy's house, a red sports car with a bent antenna and a back seat crammed with junk caught Kevin's eye. He guessed it belonged to a kid home from college, although not the doctor's. According to his bio on the Web, his two children had long ago reached adulthood.

The walkway that bisected Dr. Abernathy's lawn ascended in a series of steps past flowering bushes to an entrance secluded beneath an arched cover. About to mount the porch, Kevin froze at the scraping sound of the latch opening. He'd come too close to duck out of sight. He'd have to brazen it out.

"I'm grateful to you for talking to me and I'm sorry if you took it the wrong way," said a smoky female voice that stroked his sensibilities like black velvet. He'd heard the voice before. "I assure you, I have no intention of printing anything until I learn all the facts."

Onto the porch emerged a willowy figure he had no trouble identifying even though he hadn't seen her in several years. A breeze fanned her chestnut hair and, although she was glancing back at someone, he knew her eyes appeared slate-colored indoors but jade in sunlight.

Kevin's mouth twisted at his foolishness. Alli Gardner had always irritated him with her refusal to lay off when he didn't care to discuss a case. As far as he was concerned, her eyes might as well be mustard yellow.

Before he had time to wonder what brought her here, she stumbled into him. As his hands closed around her upper arms, he felt the pressure of her thigh against his and caught a flash of mirth on her generous mouth.

"Well, well," said the reporter, "if it isn't my favorite dick."

Behind her in the doorway appeared a man in his seventies. "Who are you?" he demanded.

"Kevin Vickers, private investigator." Setting Alli firmly away from him, he dispensed one of his cards. "I'd appreciate a few words with you, Doctor."

Abernathy's frown deepened. "I'm not talking to you and I shouldn't have talked to her. Whatever you think is going on, it doesn't involve me."

"I'm here on behalf of one of your former patients," Kevin said. "I'm sure you'd be concerned if you knew…"

He halted, registering the sudden acceleration of an engine on the street. Before he could react on his instinctive sense of danger, a sharp *crack!* rang out.

"In!" Grabbing Alli, he pushed her and the doctor into the foyer and slammed the door. The last thing he observed was a gray van disappearing around the corner.

"Is somebody shooting at us? Nobody's hurt, are they?" The reporter spared a glance at both men before adding, "That was amazing! Like something out of a movie!" Her face had the feverish look he'd seen on rookie cops whose adrenaline rush overwhelmed their common sense.

He'd been wrong about Alli, Kevin reflected. She wasn't just a loudmouthed annoyance. She was a pain in the neck who would likely get killed.

"A car backfired," the doctor said, although he sounded breathless. "I'm sure that's all."

Did he believe that or was he trying to avoid summoning the police? "Sir, it sounded like a gunshot to me," Kevin replied.

"Serene Beach doesn't have drive-by shootings," the doctor insisted.

Kevin could hardly argue, since he didn't intend to call the police. As for Alli, she stood observing the two of them as cheerily as if she were watching a sitcom.

He returned to his purpose for coming here. "Doctor, you may have information that could help one of your former patients, a woman who's already suffered more than her share of tragedy."

"As I said, I'm not interested in talking to you." Sharply, the doctor added, "I don't wish to be disturbed again, by anyone."

This seemed like a strong reaction for a man convinced he'd only heard a car backfire, Kevin thought sardonically. "Suppose I told you that a child's future depends on it?"

"Some people will say anything to get what they want." The man regarded him stonily. "Both of you—out of here, now!"

Alli quirked an eyebrow without commenting. The doctor's hostility didn't faze her. It didn't inspire her to move toward the door, either.

Kevin knew how it felt to be on the receiving end of her persistence. His sympathies lay with the doctor.

"Please keep my card." He would have liked to mention his client's name, but Alli's presence dissuaded him. "Whoever fired that shot—and it *was* a shot—knows where you live. They could come back."

"I'm not going to waste time worrying about someone with carburetor problems, and, unless you're a mechanic, you shouldn't, either." The doctor opened the door, but, Kevin observed, he stayed clear of the gap. "Don't bother me again. And that interview was off the record, young lady."

"Too late to change your mind!" she sang out, and scurried away.

Kevin kept his voice low as he put in one last plea. "My client is a widow, she can't afford to pay blackmail and she doesn't want to lose her son. Think about it." He followed Alli onto the porch.

As the latch clicked behind them, he noted a black-and-white cruising along the street, apparently on routine patrol. Even if the officer hadn't received a report of gunfire, his presence made the shooter's return unlikely.

Kevin surveyed the front of the house for a bullet hole and examined the ground for a casing, without success. He would have liked to retrieve some evidence, even if he couldn't make immediate use of it, but either the bullet was buried somewhere or the shooter had fired a warning shot, trying to frighten rather than injure.

Regardless, he wondered how the assailant had found them and how far he—or they—would go to stop this investigation. Kevin hoped the doctor had been right about a car backfiring.

Alli waited for him on the walkway, her head cocked and

one hand on her hip. A silky pantsuit skimmed her body. "Looks like we're working the same case, Detective."

"I wouldn't count on it." As he moved past, she fell in beside him. Had he really expected her to give up that easily? Kevin mused.

"Illegal adoptions and blackmail. Sound familiar?" she asked.

"I'm looking for missing medical records," he improvised. "They're for a lawsuit against an insurance company."

"Yeah, sure." She paused beside the red sports car, then apparently thought better of it and kept pace with Kevin. "We ought to share what we know. It might help us both."

"My work is confidential." He clicked open his lock.

She produced a creased business card, crossed off the newspaper's name and wrote a phone number on the back. "I'm freelancing these days. Here's my cell number."

He made no move to take the card. "What happened to your job?"

"It didn't give me enough scope." She proffered the card again. He ignored it.

"I'm about as likely to call you as Dr. Abernathy is to call me," he told her.

Reaching past his jacket lapels, she tucked it into his shirt pocket. Through the fabric, her fingers left a warm imprint against his chest. "Exactly my point, Detective. I've got a half-hour taped interview with him, and that's your best chance of hearing what he has to say. Think about it."

With a wave, she headed to her car. Stopping beside it, she mouthed the words "Call me!" before slipping inside.

Kevin gritted his teeth. He had other people to contact. Maybe he'd get back to her…but only if he ran out of leads.

And assuming someone didn't put a bullet through one of them first.

Chapter Two

Transcribing the interview with Dr. Abernathy took most of the afternoon. Until now, Alli hadn't spent much time working in her studio apartment, and the noise from the pool outside proved distracting.

Also, she kept pausing as she mentally replayed the interview and, especially, the scene at the end, which wasn't on the tape. She still couldn't believe someone had shot at her, but the more she considered it, the less she bought the idea of a backfire.

In retrospect, too, that gray van struck her as familiar. She must have seen it near the office earlier without paying much attention.

She wished she had someone to discuss this with, but the only person who came to mind was Kevin Vickers. In fact, he came to mind a little too often.

She had to admit he was sexy. A woman couldn't help admiring a tall, dark, moody kind of guy, one with a freshly laundered scent and a muscular build, could she?

Alli pictured herself grabbing him by the tie, tumbling him backward across a bed and ripping off those starched garments. Breaking down that prickly exterior and transforming him into a lusty male animal would be much more fun than arguing with him. However, it didn't appear she would have the chance to do either.

At last she finished the transcription. She had to write on

her laptop because it was all she had, but she didn't dare dial up to the Internet to look for a job or check out Dr. Graybar's background because Payne would be able to trace her every move. Just thinking about him made her blood pressure soar.

First chance she got, she was going to take her computer in to be debugged, Alli resolved. In the meantime, she didn't plan to let fear isolate her in this small apartment.

She dug through papers strewn across her thrift-store desk. Surely somewhere in the pile lurked a coupon from the local copy shop, which rented computers with Internet access. Although the library also had a few, they were almost always busy.

The coupon eluded her. Alli did find a half-price sandwich deal from the Black Cat Café, a nearby hangout. It was after five o'clock and her stomach sounded a warning growl. Okay, she'd make the sandwich her first order of business and then she'd draw on her limited funds to surf some job-related Web sites at full price.

Besides, she was feeling stifled in the bland unit with its worn carpeting and tiny kitchenette. If she'd bothered to do more than hang a few posters on the wall, that might have helped, but a used foldout sofa, a tired bureau and a scarred coffee table didn't exactly brighten the place.

As she drove, Alli's thoughts returned to the phone call she'd received yesterday morning. Rita Hernandez had sounded angry and frightened at the same time as she'd described how a caller had tried to extort twenty thousand dollars from her to keep silent about the supposedly illegal adoption of her four-year-old daughter.

"I don't even know if it's true!" she'd protested. "But how can I go to the police? I've read about cases like this. If there's anything hinky about how a baby was acquired for adoption, even though the person had nothing to do with it, sometimes immigration insists on sending the child back to complete strangers."

Although only thirty-nine, she had chronic health problems that precluded a pregnancy, she'd explained. She and her husband had been turned down by adoption agencies because they feared her ailments would interfere with parenting. However, that hadn't proved to be the case.

"We love our daughter and she loves us," she'd said tearfully. "Then this jerk calls and demands twenty thousand dollars. We're struggling to pay the rent and health insurance. He's given us a week to come up with the money, but it's impossible. What are we supposed to do?"

Alli had jumped at the chance to help her. Also, she saw a story here that went beyond Rita's personal situation. The doctors who'd arranged for the adoption must have helped lots of other couples. Were they being blackmailed, too? If so, by whom?

During the interview, Dr. Abernathy had appeared dismayed to learn that the orphanage might be operating illegally and seemed horrified about the blackmail. Although Alli wasn't thrilled at the way he'd clammed up at that point, she tended to believe in his innocence.

She wished Kevin weren't so pigheaded about pooling their resources. It simply made sense, from her point of view. But he'd always had a hardheaded attitude toward the news media.

Inside the Black Cat, Alli's senses took a moment to adjust to the dim lighting and the chatter bouncing off hardwood surfaces. Once she could see, she spotted a couple of familiar faces. The café was popular with the *Outlook* staff.

People nodded in her direction, but no one waved her over to a table as they might have done a few days before. The reason was obvious: J. J. Morosco and Ned Jacobson sat in one corner, having drinks.

Judging by the printouts and charts littering their table, she guessed the two editors were reviewing plans for the news operation. The other staff members must be afraid that their jobs, too, would go on the chopping block.

Luckily, she didn't have to worry about supporting a family, Alli reflected as she waited at the take-out counter. That was one of the many advantages of staying single and child-free.

She was ordering pastrami on rye when Larry emerged from the café's back room with another photographer, Bob

Midland. Noting the editors, he muttered, "I'll wait for you outside."

"You got it," Alli said. As the counterman rang up her bill, the managing editor glanced her way. "Hi, J.J.," she called breezily. "How's it hanging?"

The entire room fell silent. Ned averted his face.

"Fine," the M.E. answered politely.

"See you around." After paying for her order and collecting the takeout sack, she strolled outside.

Alli had learned long ago that the best way to handle an awkward situation was to tough it out. During her school days, her cocky attitude might have alienated some teachers, but it had rallied her spirits while she moved around the country with her mother, a graphic artist whose jobs were often temporary.

She found Larry leaning against her car. "What's happening with you?" he asked. "Any job prospects?"

"Not yet." She pushed a strand of hair out of her face and realized she'd forgotten to brush it. She hadn't put on lipstick, either, but what was the point? It would only smear on her sandwich. "Need a ride?" she asked as she unlocked the car.

"Actually, yes. I rode over with Bob. I'm on duty tonight. Do you mind dropping me at the paper?"

"Doesn't bother me." She didn't see why she should be ashamed about having gotten the boot. It was Ned and Payne who ought to be ashamed, and J.J. for not paying closer attention to her accomplishments.

During the ride, she inquired about the mood in the newsroom since she'd left. "I'll bet you could cut the tension with an X-Acto knife."

"Yeah. It's miserable. Everybody's afraid of getting the ax." He pushed his glasses higher on his nose.

"I'm sorry to hear it." People couldn't do their best work when they had to keep looking over their shoulders.

"This morning, a couple of reporters brought laptops to work," Larry added. "I think they're scared Payne will steal their stuff."

Although each employee had an individual password to the paper's networked computers, Payne had begun stealing Alli's notes almost as soon as he'd arrived. She assumed that either he had a talent for hacking or he'd found the passwords in his uncle's desk, in which case nobody was safe.

"You'd better warn them not to leave their laptops unattended," she replied. "He loaded spyware onto mine."

"I already put the word out."

She drove another block before asking, "What's Payne up to? Don't tell me he's doing some actual reporting."

"Did you read this morning's paper?"

"I'm afraid not." Accustomed to receiving a copy at work, she'd never subscribed. If she were to start taking a paper now, she'd prefer to study one of the larger papers where she might be applying.

"He wrote a follow-up to the exposé," Larry said. "While Ned was editing it, he kept yelling about risking a libel suit."

"Payne must have used the stuff I was saving for my sidebar. I'm sure he didn't bother to track down anything on his own. Obviously he didn't write it very well, either." Alli took some satisfaction in that.

One of the reasons she hadn't turned in her story a day earlier was that she wanted to take extra care with the allegations about Mayor LeMott. Payne must have slept through his libel class in journalism school, or perhaps he was too lazy to care.

She made a left on Bordeaux Way. "It's good to know the other reporters believe my version of events."

"Sure they do. Besides, they recognized your style in yesterday's article," Larry told her.

"I'm surprised Morosco didn't. I know he's relatively new, but surely he's read my work."

Larry shrugged. "Madge Leeky thinks he's trying to impress the publisher by putting his stamp on the paper. She says he wants to believe in Payne because he likes the idea that he hired a 'star.'" Madge had written for the *Outlook* since before Alli was born.

"I don't think that star's going to twinkle for very long. At least, I hope not." She pulled to the curb in front of the boxy, three-story building. It felt weird not to be parking in back as usual.

Larry sat glumly in place. "We all miss you. It isn't the same since you left."

"It's only been a day and a half."

"It seems longer."

It did to Alli, too. Then an idea hit her. "You could help if you're willing. But I wouldn't want to land you in trouble."

His face brightened. "Tell me how."

"It would be great if you would access the paper's library and look up Dr. Joseph Abernathy and Dr. Randolph Graybar," she said. "I'm working on a freelance story about them, kind of a showpiece. It's a secret."

"Graybar? Is he any relation to the former lieutenant governor, Aldis Graybar?"

She hadn't made the connection. "I'll try to check online, but I still can't use my laptop on the Internet."

"I'll get on it right away."

She made sure he had her cell number. "If anyone acts suspicious, don't do it," she warned. "One person being fired because of Payne Jacobson is already one too many."

He opened the car door. "I'll be careful. Thanks for the ride."

"You're welcome. I really appreciate whatever you can find out."

As she drove off, Alli hoped she hadn't done the wrong thing by making the impulsive request. Well, she'd advised Larry to back off if things got touchy. And she knew he would respect her request for secrecy.

The copy shop had a Closed sign on the door. The hours read 10:00 a.m. to 6:00 p.m. and it was a little past that.

Alli headed home. Inside the apartment complex, she was nearing her unit when her pulse rocketed into high gear.

In a visitor's space across from her building sat a gray van like the one in the drive-by shooting. Despite the late hour, lingering June daylight revealed two man-size silhouettes in the front seat.

Tapping the brake, she backed out of sight behind an SUV. Had they spotted her? She sat trying to listen past the rush of her blood for the roar of the van's engine or the slap of running feet, anything to indicate they were in pursuit.

She heard nothing.

It might not be the same van. But she didn't intend to run any foolish risks.

Common sense warned her to call the police. If she did, however, she'd have to tell them about the incident at Dr. Abernathy's and why she'd been there. Someone from the *Outlook* would read the report and discover what she was working on.

As Alli sat mulling over what to do next, it occurred to her that she must be on to something big for these men to spend their time stalking her. Unless, of course, the men weren't connected to the adoption ring. She'd also been investigating Mayor LeMott who, before going straight as a businessman, was rumored to have been involved in loan-sharking and racketeering.

He'd escaped prosecution because witnesses against him had a nasty habit of disappearing. The thought sent shivers down Alli's spine.

He knew she'd been working on a story about him because he'd granted an interview after his election as mayor in April, expecting a puff piece. Even though her name wouldn't have appeared on today's article, it had probably quoted from the interview.

Oh, the heck with it. She wasn't giving up her investigation, regardless of the danger. What would happen if reporters let themselves be intimidated into silence?

First necessity: to rescue a few essentials from her apartment. Second requirement: to locate another base of operations, preferably one that cost nothing and came with a computer.

Her mother would welcome her, but Mom lived in Texas. Larry shared a tiny beach pad with four buddies, so that put him out of the running.

An image sprang to mind of a glowering man with muscular shoulders, intense physical presence and access to In-

ternet databases. The fact that Kevin Vickers wanted nothing
to do with her was, in her view, a mere technicality.

After slipping out of the car, Alli traced a circuitous path
toward the back of her apartment unit. A glimpse around the
corner showed the two guys sitting in their van, staring in the
direction of the main entrance.

She'd met the mayor's bodyguards, Dale and Bruce, a few
times. The fellow sitting on the near side had cropped hair and
a beefy nose, just like Dale. The other fellow's bleached orange hair matched Bruce's.

Caked mud obscured the license plate's number. Considering that it hadn't rained in months, Alli figured the men had
hidden it on purpose, but now she knew who they were—for
all the good that did.

Quietly, she withdrew. Adrenaline powered her up the rear
stairs to her apartment, where she made short work of packing.

She'd completed the first step of her plan. Now came the
hard part.

JUNE WAS A TIME for fresh beginnings: weddings, graduations
and a new baseball season, during which the Anaheim Angels
might just possibly, if heaven smiled and fish learned to fly,
win another World Series.

It was also, Kevin had learned during his three years as a
private eye, a time when spouses cheated and people on disability leaped about reshingling their roofs with the spryness
of mountain goats. Cynicism firmly in place, he arrived at his
office after a long day, his camera brimming with evidence.

Sometimes he wondered why he'd left the police department. He'd liked his position as a robbery-homicide detective
and he'd enjoyed the give-and-take with fellow officers. But
he preferred freedom, even when it meant long hours and un-
paid accounts receivable.

When he'd decided to leave, another former officer had invited him to join his security firm. However, he'd decided to
strike out on his own, and he'd never regretted it.

Kevin unlocked the front door of the small office building

and, bypassing the elevator, mounted the stairs to the second floor. At this hour—nearly 7:00 p.m.—the accounting firm and escrow company that shared the premises had closed for the day.

He hoped his secretary had left as well. He'd informed Heloise in no uncertain terms that her day ended at five o'clock. He wasn't paying overtime and he didn't need her to babysit his phone messages.

But she sat at her desk, short blond hair revealing a hint of dark roots, acknowledging him with a smile as she adjusted her grip on her cell phone. "Betsy, it's up to your sister to decide whether she wants another baby," Heloise was saying. "I know it isn't your fault you had triplets, but if you can manage three, why can't she?"

"Mom!" Kevin said. "Would you please go home?"

"It's your dad's pizza and poker night, so nobody needs me," his mother replied calmly. Into the phone, she added, "Your brother just got back. Darling, whatever happens, I promise to keep watching your kids on Saturday mornings."

Kevin collected his mail and escaped into his private office. He'd had more than enough of his younger sisters' jockeying for their mother's attention. They were welcome to it. As the eldest child and only son, he received far too much.

Still, Mom made a great assistant. He knew before he even checked that his e-mail had been culled of spam, his clients billed and his phone messages screened so he could be notified of anything urgent.

During his first two years in business, he'd put up with a series of secretaries who ranged from inept to barely tolerable. Even the halfway-decent ones didn't stay long. He knew his sharp manner had something to do with this, but who could blame him for losing patience with repeated screwups?

When his mother offered to fill in short-term, he'd agreed out of desperation. Although Heloise's only previous paid experience had been decades ago as a preschool teacher, her experience as head of the PTA and other volunteer groups had made her a whiz at management.

They got along surprisingly well. She dismissed Kevin's bouts of grumpiness with aplomb, claiming he'd been much worse as a teenager. She matched his obsession with neatness, and she kept her motherly instincts in check during regular hours.

After five o'clock, however, all bets were off. So it didn't surprise him when she appeared in the doorway to ask, "Have you eaten?"

"I had a hamburger." He'd grabbed one an hour ago. "Thanks, Mom." Pointedly, Kevin turned on his computer and began downloading photographs.

"You haven't forgotten about this weekend, have you?"

"I'm working this weekend," he said automatically.

"Not tomorrow night. It's Betsy's tenth high-school reunion and you know I'm giving a party for her friends. Some of them are still single. And some of them are single again. You'll have your pick."

Although aware that he'd have to put in an appearance, Kevin shuddered at the prospect of being surrounded by his younger sister's husband-hungry buddies. He'd barely survived their fifth reunion, and by now their maternal instincts must be roaring into full gear. "I'll drop by."

"Don't make us come fetch you," his mother warned.

He should never, never have bought a house so close to the Vickers homestead, Kevin reflected for the umpteenth time. Why had he figured three blocks and one busy street would prove any kind of barrier to matchmaking? His two sisters, who also lived in the area, were almost as bad as Heloise.

"I'll be there," he muttered, wishing he had an excuse to leave town.

"You'll enjoy the party," his mother replied. "Don't work too late."

Realizing she was leaving at last, Kevin glanced up from the screen. "Love you, Mom."

"I love you, too." A smile brightened her face before she went out.

Kevin made a mental note not to shave tomorrow. While

he doubted a grubby appearance would deter his sister's pals, it might at least discourage cheek kissing.

Refocusing on the computer, he sorted through the photos, picking the most telling ones to forward to his clients. It had been a productive day in which he'd wrapped up a couple of small cases.

Unfortunately, he'd drawn a blank on Mary Conners's behalf. Dr. Abernathy hadn't returned phone calls and Dr. Graybar's office had informed him that the physician declined to meet with him.

Kevin finger combed his hair back from his forehead. He'd have to try another tack.

A rustling in the outer office caught his attention. "Forget something?" he called.

The woman who came into the doorway bore no resemblance to his mother. Alli Gardner was considerably taller and had a sensual shape emphasized by tight-fitting jeans and a clinging emerald top.

"It's me," she said. "Tough luck, huh? I guess you were expecting someone else." She strolled into the room.

"If you want some of my time, I charge by the hour," he replied.

"Are you always this warm and welcoming?"

"This is nothing. Sometimes I'm rude."

She slid onto the edge of his desk. Obviously, she wanted something. He folded his arms and waited for her to enlighten him.

"You aren't married, are you?" Alli asked.

"What?" Despite her naturally seductive manner, he hadn't gathered she was here for personal reasons.

Leaning across the desk, Alli caught his left hand. The touch wreaked havoc with his rebellious hormones. "No ring. I'm not surprised."

"How charming of you."

"I didn't mean it as an insult. It's just that if you were getting laid regularly, you wouldn't be so crabby." She grinned.

She might be right, but he'd rather shave his head than

admit that. Annoyed, he cleared his throat and said, "Do you have a point?"

Tilting her head, she took her time scrutinizing him. "I was wondering what you look like in the morning. I guess I'll find out, because I'm going to be staying at your place for a few days."

Yeah, sure. "Thanks. I needed a laugh."

"Seriously," Alli said. "I saw the gray van parked in front of my flat. I barely escaped with my life."

"They fired at you again?"

"No, but they would have if they'd seen me. I *could* call the cops, but it would mess up my story and I'm guessing your client doesn't want that, either. Right?"

"Don't assume we're on the same side."

"There's something in it for you, naturally," she proceeded. "You can listen to my interview with the doc and I'll give you a transcript, too. And together we'll have a much better chance of helping these families. At least, I assume there's more than one. You didn't by any chance talk to Rita Hernandez, did you?"

"My client information is confidential." All the same, she'd managed to pique Kevin's interest. He did need that interview.

Alli bent over him, so close her chestnut hair tickled his neck and her apple-cider scent clouded his mind.

"What're you working on right now?" she asked.

"Hey!" Before he could clear the screen, however, she glimpsed a photo of a cheating husband and his paramour doing the deed in front of a curtainless window.

"I can't believe they'd do *that* with the shades open! And one of them is probably married, right?"

"Both of them. Not for long, I suspect." Kevin closed the program.

"What else have you got? Never mind." Standing so close he could feel her heat, she said, "Listen, I've got a friend at the paper researching background for me, and I promise to share it. I just need a place to hole up and a computer, because mine has a virus."

"Tell me again why you're not at the *Outlook* anymore,"

he said, partly to gain control of the conversation and partly because he wanted to know.

"I never told you in the first place."

"Make it short," he advised.

"They fired me." She spread her hands in a helpless gesture. "Office politics."

There had to be more to it, but he knew it wasn't a matter of competence. Although he had no intention of admitting it, he read her articles frequently. Alli had a gift for digging up information and persuading people to talk.

Although her talents might prove useful, the idea of this woman moving into his house was preposterous. Even if he had a guest bedroom, which he didn't, she was the last person in the solar system he would choose as a roommate.

On the other hand, if the van really was trailing her, she might have no other recourse than to call the police. For his client's sake, he'd hate to see that happen.

"Do you have any idea who those guys are?" he asked. "The ones who're stalking you?"

"They're the mayor's bodyguards. I've been investigating LeMott, and I guess you've seen the stories in the paper."

Kevin disliked the mayor, both for his unsavory reputation and for his arrogance, but to authorize a drive-by shooting showed a truly brutal nature. It would serve the man right if his hair-trigger temper ruined everything he'd fought for. Unfortunately, it might cost Alli Gardner her life before he got caught.

Then the full meaning of her words sank in. "That wasn't your byline on the articles. When exactly were you fired?"

"Yesterday morning."

"Office politics, you said?"

"Something like that."

He'd seen police investigations snarled by competing jurisdictions and rival egos, so it made sense that this happened at newspapers, too. "Who are you writing for now?"

"Like I told you, myself," she said. "I'm working on speculation."

Kevin couldn't suppress a twinge of sympathy. "If I were to give you a place to sleep—and I haven't made up my mind about that—you'd have to promise not to publish anything until the case is completed. And you could never mention my name or my client's."

"I don't know your client's name."

"That isn't the point." Another angle bothered him. "The problem is, if these adoptions do turn out to be illegal, my client could still lose her child even if we nail the extortionist."

"I suppose so," Alli agreed. "But it seems to me the blackmail angle needs to be handled first, because that's the most pressing. Besides, we only have his say-so that there's a problem with the adoptions, right?"

Kevin saw no reason to withhold his data, since he'd confirmed what Mary had told him. "Unfortunately, it's true. The orphanage is under investigation in Costa Buena for buying and selling babies, although nothing's been proved."

"Are they going to try to take the babies back?" she asked.

"I don't believe they've gone that far yet."

"Don't you think you should find out for sure?"

"Are you telling me how to do my job?" he snapped.

She scooted away before replying. "Just pointing out the obvious."

Angrily, Kevin stood up. "Forget about moving in with me. If you're afraid to go home, stay with friends."

"You need me," she said.

"I think it's the other way around."

"Well, yeah. That, too. Look, I'm sorry I ruffled your feathers." On her expressive face, he saw a hint of desperation. "Isn't there *anything* I could do to persuade you? Clean your house? Wash your car? Walk your dog? I love animals, by the way, if you happen to have any."

"I don't." It would be cruel to keep a pet when he worked such long hours.

"I can answer the phone and cover for you if there's someone you don't want to talk to," she proposed. "Although I suppose your secretary does that."

"More or less." After hours, his mother was likely to quiz the caller to find out if he or she had an eligible daughter. Heloise also promoted his services shamelessly, even to people soliciting political donations or selling restaurant-coupon books.

His mother. The thought reminded Kevin that a bevy of single and divorced women had been given carte blanche to hound him a mere twenty-four hours in the future.

He had options, such as fleeing to Palm Springs or locking his doors and refusing to answer the phone. But either of those choices would interfere with his work. Also, he did need the interview with Dr. Abernathy.

"There is one thing," he added.

"You got it!" After a heartbeat, Alli added with a note of uncertainty, "What exactly?"

"Go to a party with me tomorrow night," Kevin said.

Chapter Three

The cottage, painted dove-gray with blue shutters, had a reserved air softened by flowering bushes along the edges of
the porch. "Cute house," Alli said as she followed Kevin up
the walk.

"Thanks." He'd slung her duffel bag over one shoulder but
hadn't made any macho noises about how she should leave
everything to him, so she was lugging her suitcase and computer.

He plucked a couple of envelopes from the mailbox before
opening the door and punching in the security code. The place
smelled nice, Alli thought in surprise, catching a whiff of cin-
namon instead of the aged sweat-sock odor she associated
with bachelor pads.

Inside, the house appeared bigger and brighter than she'd
expected. Off-white carpeting and pale yellow walls heightened the impression of spaciousness, aided by the scarcity of
furniture—no couch, just four comfy chairs that swiveled to
face either the entertainment center or the fireplace.

Alli, who'd grown in up in apartments, didn't understand
why a guy would want to rent an entire house, but she wasn't
foolish enough to look a gift horse in the mouth. Kevin had
agreed to let her stay for the weekend and hadn't demanded
sex, so how could she complain?

Not that she considered sex out of the question. The guy
looked hot from any angle. She liked his powerful build and
the fact that, at roughly five-eleven, he would make a perfect

dancing partner, neither towering over her nor bumping his head against her chin.

She hoped there'd be dancing at tomorrow's party. He'd refused to tell her anything about the party, however. She hadn't packed fancy clothes, but she'd brought a pantsuit that ought to do. Besides, his friends were probably cops who'd take way too much interest in ogling her legs if she displayed them.

"My office is this way." After tossing his mail on an end table, Kevin headed through a doorway. "The sofa doesn't open into a bed, but I never promised you the Ritz. I'll find you a blanket and a pillow, though."

Alli's idea of a home office featured a desk assembled from a discount-store kit, a dented file cabinet and piles of books and papers. By contrast, this room could grace a decorating magazine.

She admired the built-in oak shelves along one wall, not to mention the ultraneat computer-printer center and the sleek desk and chair. But where was the clutter? And how could he expect her to stretch out on that flimsy yellow-and-white striped love seat?

"This place must have come furnished." She turned slowly, taking in the cheery decor. "A guy would never buy stuff like this." Or else he'd get scuff marks all over it in about five minutes. "Your landlord certainly trusts you."

"I'm my landlord," Kevin returned levelly. "I bought the furniture at an estate sale. They sold me a whole houseful, except for the front room. Somebody else beat me to that."

"You own this place?" A private detective shouldn't reek of stability, Alli thought. She preferred the movie typecast of a grubby guy who lived in a hole in the wall and recycled his coffee grounds. Well, not too grubby; borderline shaggy would suit her fine.

"My grandparents left me a little money. I decided to do something sensible with it." Shrugging out of his suit jacket, Kevin draped it over the back of a chair.

"Blowing it on a trip to Europe would be sensible," Alli said. "You'd have memories to last a lifetime."

He positioned her laptop on a blotter, careful not to scratch the desk's gleaming surface. "You mentioned you've got a virus. I might have some software to clean it up."

"It's not exactly a virus." As Alli plopped her suitcase beside the love seat, she decided not to complain about the inadequate sleeping accommodations. For one thing, Kevin could still change his mind about letting her stay here. Also, after making several moves with her mother, she'd learned to be flexible.

"So what is it exactly?" He'd flipped the case open, switched on the power and begun scrolling through the computer's innards.

"Don't hook it up to the Internet!" Alli said.

"Okay, I won't. What's going on?"

She found another chair and stuck it beside the desk. For heaven's sake, she didn't see a coffee cup or an empty potato-chip bag anywhere. How could a person function among such neatness?

"A guy at work sneaked in a program to capture my key-strokes," she explained. "Anything I write shows up on his computer."

Kevin stopped poking around, although, since the device wasn't online, he had nothing to fear. "He stole your story?"

"You got it."

"That explains why some other guy's byline was on your story about the mayor?"

Alli nodded.

"Is he the reason you got fired?" he asked.

"Bingo." She filled him in about the assistant managing editor boosting his nephew's cause and the managing editor wanting to put his stamp on the news operation. "Basically, they didn't believe me because they didn't want to."

"How come you don't sound angrier?" Kevin inquired.

"Because it wouldn't do any good."

"I never thought of you as the passive type."

In Alli's experience, most guys would have leaped to her defense, maybe even tried to take over her problem, or gone the opposite route and assumed she was at fault. She liked the way this man waited for her response without trying to put words in her mouth.

"I'm not passive. I'm realistic," she told him. "My mom spent ages being bitter after Dad dumped us." That was a rather personal detail to reveal to someone she scarcely knew, but she'd learned that being open about the past helped take the sting out of it. "Finally she figured out that living well is the best revenge. She's been much happier since she let go of her anger."

Kevin eyed her suitcase. "You call this living well?"

"Hey, I landed in a nice place, didn't I?" Alli quipped. "Anyway, I plan to take the laptop in tomorrow to have it debugged."

He tapped one finger on the desktop. "I wouldn't be in such a hurry."

"Why not?"

"We might be able to make creative use of this situation."

"You have a devious mind." She grinned. "That raises all kinds of interesting possibilities."

"Let's save it in case we really need it," Kevin said. "In the meantime, I've got an old laptop I was keeping for spare parts. It's slow but it still works, and I cleaned all my files out of the hard drive."

"You're letting me stay in your house but you don't trust me with your files?" she said.

"I have a responsibility to protect my clients from unauthorized intrusions, even accidental ones." Kevin shut her laptop and set it aside. "By the way, you should put password protection on this thing. That will keep your colleague's paws off it in the future."

"He's not my colleague anymore. And thanks. I'd love to borrow your laptop."

"I'll drag it in from the garage later. Also, you should put your car in there in case our shooters decide to cruise around looking for it," he said. "Now, let's listen to Dr. Abernathy."

"Sure." From her bag, Alli produced the minicassette and recorder. "I made a transcript if you want a copy."

"I'll take one later. First I'd like to hear him for myself."
He turned on the tape.

As Kevin listened to the recording, he half closed his eyes
in concentration. At this angle, she noticed the sharpness of
his cheekbones and the strength in his jaw. He looked like the
kind of man a woman could depend on, or maybe the kind
she believed she could depend on until push came to shove.

Alli would never make that mistake. Not about any man.

KEVIN LIKED THE WAY Alli handled the interview on the tape.
Her supportive comments and well-thought-out questions en-
couraged the doctor to trust her.

His own police-style approach had its strengths, but warm-
ing up reluctant subjects wasn't one of them. Also, he conceded, an attractive young woman had to be more appealing
to a guy.

Alli got under way by saying she was writing a story about
local people who'd adopted children from Central America,
then proceeded to cite the doctor's good reputation in the
community and praise his desire to help infertile couples. Put
at ease, Abernathy related how he'd never considered becoming involved with adoptions until he took on a younger partner eight years previously.

"Dr. Graybar volunteers at the El Centro Orphanage. After
we'd been partners for a while, he suggested we find homes
for some of the children," the man informed her in a deep, reassuring tone.

The doctors had started slowly and informally. As demand
increased and they began serving referrals in addition to patients, they'd hired a full-time adoptions coordinator.

"That side of our practice just kept growing," he said.
"There's a lot of need in our community and among the children of Costa Buena. Of course, we try to help patients have
children of their own, if that's what they're seeking. Provid-
ing first-quality medical care has always been my primary
mission."

Doctors Abernathy and Graybar were obstetrician-gynecologists, not fertility specialists, he explained, but they conducted initial workups and offered low-tech treatments that sometimes took care of the problem. More difficult cases were referred to nearby Doctors Circle, a women's medical center whose staff included internationally known fertility experts.

However, some patients decided to go straight for adoption, fearing the fertility treatments would prove a costly and frustrating ordeal. Others returned a few years later, still childless and more desperate than ever to become parents.

"I was glad to offer them a range of options," he continued. "Frankly, I'm happy to leave the whole high-tech infertility business to others, but Randy's more aggressive. He felt we should keep up with the latest procedures so we wouldn't lose our most challenging cases and, in addition, he wanted to 'market' adoptions to a larger clientele. Those were his terms, not mine."

"Wouldn't that tax the resources of a two-man office?" asked Alli's taped voice.

"I thought so. He disagreed. That's part of the reason I decided to retire about six months ago," the physician conceded. "Randy and I didn't see eye to eye on a number of issues, although I certainly respect him. I enjoy playing golf and taking trips with my wife, and this way he can find a new partner or partners who think the way he does."

"Has he found someone?" she asked.

"He's interviewed a few, but I don't think any of them have worked out."

Listening between the lines, Kevin wondered why Dr. Graybar couldn't find a new associate. Did his setup make other doctors leery for some reason?

"Let's talk more about the adoptions," Alli said. "Did you run into any problem areas?"

"Quite the opposite." Her subject waxed lyrical about the outcomes. He took pride in the fact that they'd been able to place some special-needs youngsters as well as to find babies for what he half humorously referred to as special-needs parents.

"There's so much demand for adoptions that agencies often

rule out people who would make fine mothers and fathers," he explained. "Sometimes they're over forty or have a chronic health condition or perhaps a minor criminal record that's long in the past. We tried to look beyond that. Even so, all our parents had home studies, so you can be assured we weren't placing children in unsuitable situations."

Alli asked how much money the adoptions brought into the partnership. "It's quite lucrative," Dr. Abernathy admitted, "although there were additional expenses for us, like hiring a counselor. Most of the fees went to the orphanage and officials in Costa Buena."

Kevin wondered how big a part the money had played in Dr. Graybar's push to expand the clientele. He had no objection to anyone turning a profit, but he was receiving a questionable impression of the younger doctor.

Kevin made a note to examine the man's financial background and to check out the counselor, as well. Both of them had entrée to the adoption records, which meant either could be involved with the extortion.

As the tape continued to roll, Alli probed for more details about the orphanage. However, Abernathy claimed his partner had been the one who maintained contact. The prospective parents also saw the facilities, since they had to travel to Costa Buena and complete paperwork before bringing their children home.

"I never went there," he said. "Everyone reported the place to be clean and pleasant. A little disorganized, but the kids were well fed and the caretakers showed plenty of affection."

The interview ran for nearly forty-five minutes before Alli mentioned the investigation and the blackmail demand. The doctor, sounding astonished, asked twice whether she was sure the woman had adopted through his office, and then concluded, "She should go to the police. That's intolerable."

It was the kind of reply Kevin would expect from an innocent guy. In his experience, a guilty one was more likely to bluster, suggest that the informant must be lying or fly into a righteous rage.

"What about the blackmailer's allegation that the orphanage is involved in baby selling?" she asked.

"I don't believe it. And I'm receiving the impression you haven't been entirely honest with me, young lady." His tone became crusty. "Is that why you came here? To make accusations?"

"I'm just trying to understand the situation," Alli replied.

"How do I know you won't twist what I've said to make me look bad?"

Kevin sympathized, because he'd had exactly that experience with a couple of reporters in the past. That was why he'd been so hostile to Alli.

"I try to be fair and accurate," she explained.

"I have only your word for that," the doctor replied. "This interview is over."

After a few unsuccessful protests, the recording ended. Kevin wished she'd asked whether Dr. Abernathy still profited from the adoptions. But he probably wouldn't have answered.

If Kevin had the resources, he'd have liked to hire an investigator in Central America to probe the orphanage, but that seemed out of the question. His goal was to help Mary Conners keep both her son and her life savings, which meant he had to find the extortionist as simply and inexpensively as possible.

One suspect had already become evident. "Several things bother me about Dr. Graybar," he said.

"Like the fact that no one has jumped at the chance to join his practice?" Alli asked, stretching her long legs beneath the desk. When her knee bumped his, she shifted lazily away. "Or the fact that he's the one who initiated the adoption project?"

"Both."

"That reminds me, I've been meaning to find out whether he's related to our former lieutenant governor."

"He's his son." Kevin had done some preliminary sniffing into the man's background. Although the lieutenant governor was retired, he still wielded considerable political influence. "But I haven't heard of Dr. Graybar's having any ambitions to run for office."

"Neither have I," Alli replied.

It was nearly eight o'clock. "Time to knock off," Kevin said.

She uncoiled from her seat. "If you'll give me a tour of the house, I'll figure out where I'm going to sleep."

He thought he'd made that clear. "You're sleeping in here."

"On that?" She indicated the couch. "Sorry, but my legs don't detach at night."

It *was* small, Kevin conceded. Because he towered over his mother and sisters, he tended to think of women as short.

"There's no spare bedroom," he explained. "If I were a gentleman, I'd give up my bed for you—but guess what?— I'm not."

She pretended to sigh. "You wouldn't happen to have a mink-lined bathtub I could borrow?"

An image sprang to mind of Allie's deliciously nude body reclining on fur. Kevin stifled it. "No such luck."

"How about a hammock in the garage?"

It was a tempting notion to get her out from underfoot, but it wouldn't work. "No hammock and no space once you put your car inside."

"I'll figure out something. Why don't you show me around."

Since he could hardly refuse, Kevin escorted her through the one-story structure. She gave an appreciative nod to the open entertainment area that stretched from the living room to the kitchen, where she exclaimed over the large cooking and breakfast areas.

As for the master suite, she took in the art deco bed and dresser skeptically. "They're pretty but totally wrong."

"What makes you say that?" The estate-sale price had been right, the furniture had required a minimum of refinishing, and his mother and sisters had given their stamp of approval.

"Because you're a guy." Alli swung around so suddenly that Kevin found himself nearly nose to nose with her, give or take a few inches. "You need rough stuff that you can collapse onto when you're drunk."

"I don't drink to excess." After observing how obnoxious

some of his friends became, he never quaffed more than one or two beers per evening. "I hate to think what kind of man you usually associate with."

She peered at him mischievously. "I have wide experience. How about you?"

"I've been around."

"Then how come you need to barter a date for tomorrow night?"

He preferred not to admit he wanted protection from his matchmaking family. "I'm not seeing anyone currently."

"At the PD, someone told me you were engaged," she said.

"I had a serious relationship, but it didn't work out." He turned away. "Could we change the subject?"

"Did she pick the furniture?"

"The house came after her time," he told Alli.

He hadn't reached the point of buying furniture with Lisette Collins, the woman he'd nearly married. Oddly, when he tried to summon an image of her face, all he got was a vague impression of petite femininity marred by petulance.

Kevin had believed they suited each other fine until they'd started discussing their future. That was when she'd produced a list of requirements, including a big house and several kids right away, with her staying home full-time.

When he'd pointed out that he couldn't afford all that on a policeman's salary and that she'd need to keep working for at least a few more years, her mouth had formed a hard, stubborn line. Over the next weeks, he'd seen another side of Lisette, alternately pouting and pressuring him.

It had become clear that what she loved was the idea of a man who fit into her preconceived mold. In fairness, Kevin had to admit that he'd been drawn to Lisette because she seemed like the right type rather than because they loved each other.

He considered it unrealistic to expect a wildly passionate marriage, but whatever the two of them had felt didn't even come close. Once they started facing reality, matters had deteriorated fast, until they parted by mutual consent.

After inspecting the master bathroom, Alli gave a thumbs-up to the whirlpool spa. "Too bad I can't sleep there," she said. "It's big enough, but I'd come out looking like a prune."

"You could spread my sleeping bag in the living room," Kevin offered.

"Okay. In fact, an idea just hit me."

"What?" he demanded.

"If I tell you, it'll spoil the fun." Her athletic stride carried her out of the bedroom. "Why don't you go find your laptop for me," she called back.

"It's in the garage." The small detached building lay behind the house.

"My point exactly." She folded her arms. "I'd like a little time alone to get things organized. Go on, Kev. I'll be fine."

He hated bossy women. But she wasn't exactly pushing him around. She was just…maddeningly stubborn.

"You are not taking over my bedroom," he warned as he passed her.

"Definitely not." She widened her eyes in mock innocence. "I promise I won't make a pass, big boy."

He ignored the gibe. "The extra blankets and pillows are in the hall closet. You can store your clothes in there."

"Great."

Kevin exited through the kitchen and across the back patio. Since the house dated from the 1930s, the two-car garage faced a rear alley, following the style of old carriage houses.

Inside, he set to work moving boxes so he could reach his spare laptop. Once he found it, he realized he needed to dig out the sleeping bag as well. That required shifting yet another set of containers, and then using his Shop-Vac to suction out the accumulation of spiderwebs and grime that he uncovered.

By the time he finished restoring order, he'd been absent nearly twenty minutes. How much trouble could a woman create in that time? Kevin wondered as he hauled his gear indoors.

Emerging into the entertainment area, he broke stride. What had happened to his beautifully arranged home?

In the center of the living room his swivel chairs served as tent poles for a quilt and an assemblage of blankets and sheets that formed a complete, if ragged-looking, enclosure. The tall, multishelved entertainment center against the wall had almost disappeared beneath an assortment of female garments arranged like a shop-window display. Make that a *lingerie* shop-window display. Alli hadn't only hung her blouses and skirts in full view, she'd dangled frilly underthings, as well.

"Oh, good, you brought the sleeping bag!" His guest, who'd been lurking to one side observing his reaction, darted forward to lift the bedroll from his arms. "I needed this to finish it off." She hauled it into the impromptu yurt through a flap.

Kevin couldn't believe she'd transformed his well-ordered home into chaos. He hated to think how his mother and sisters would react. "Your clothes," he said.

"Excuse me?" Through the flap, her face popped into view, strands of hair drifting across her nose.

"Put the clothes in the hall closet," Kevin instructed.

Emerging, Alli plucked some lint from her sweater and dropped it on the carpet. "You have to admit, this place needed livening up."

He would admit no such thing. "I liked it the way it was."

"It's as if nobody really lives here," she protested. "It isn't civilized to be that tidy."

Kevin considered himself distinctly civilized. Well, maybe not at this moment, because he had a strong desire to rip down the mess in his living room and evict his guest, underwear and all. "You can't leave this—"

The doorbell rang. "I'll answer it!" Alli sang out.

"Stop right there!"

Alarm flashed across her face. "You think the bodyguards found us?"

"If they had, I doubt they'd be polite enough to ring the bell." It was far more likely that his mother, Betsy or Barbara had dropped by.

Kevin didn't require another look to know how his living room must appear, but he couldn't help it. The place exerted a kind of horrifying fascination, like the scene of a crime. Especially the crimson panties and bra trimmed with black lace that occupied the center of Alli's fashion monstrosity.

The doorbell rang again. He couldn't pretend he wasn't home, since he'd made the mistake of leaving his car in front.

"I'll handle it," he said.

He took the precaution of glancing through the window, but the figure on the porch remained out of view. His mother and sisters had perfected the art of avoiding surveillance.

There was no point in delaying. That could only make it appear that Alli had been detaining him—perhaps by doing a striptease to remove all that lingerie.

Gritting his teeth, Kevin opened the door.

Chapter Four

"Is, um, Alli here?" she heard a young man ask, and knew immediately who it was, mainly because she'd invited him.

"Larry! That was quick." Alli squeezed into the doorway next to Kevin, who showed no inclination to move.

The photographer glanced between the two of them. With his round, freckled face and Harry Potter glasses, he made an amusing contrast to the hard-bodied detective.

"I thought you were staying with a girlfriend."

"I said a friend," she corrected, and introduced the two men. They shook hands, which seemed to calm Larry somewhat. He apparently found Kevin intimidating, perhaps because he was scowling.

Okay, she should have asked his permission before inviting someone to his house, Alli mused as she escorted her visitor inside, but he'd been in the garage when Larry called.

"Let's see what you found." She slipped a file folder from the photographer's grasp. He'd offered on the phone to e-mail the document until she'd reminded him that Payne might have managed to access her account.

Inside lay several photocopied pages of a news story carrying Madge Leeky's byline. It was dated three years earlier.

"It's about the adoption counselor those two doctors hired," Larry explained. "It's all I could find."

Kevin's frown eased. "You're helping with her research?"

"Uh, yeah," he said.

"Did she explain what the story's about?" he asked.

"Not exactly," Larry said. "I don't care as long as she makes a splash. We all want her back at the paper, except for a few idiots. Like maybe two with the same last name."

Kevin nodded. "Care for a beer?"

The offer apparently indicated Larry had passed muster. "Say yes," Alli prompted.

"Okay."

"Alli?" Kevin asked.

"Sure." She liked being treated as one of the guys. Well, sometimes.

A pucker formed between the photographer's eyes as he stared past her at the entertainment center. "What hit your clothes, a hurricane?"

Alli gave a little cough, wishing he could have avoided the touchy subject. She hadn't missed Kevin's dismayed reaction earlier to her attempt at livening up his decor.

Her true motive had been more self-defense than aesthetics. Despite the spotlessness of the house, the man's essence infused the place with he-man hormones. As she'd started to hang her things in the hall closet next to a leather jacket, she'd realized that his pheromones were likely to pervade her clothes forever.

That was all she needed: to carry Kevin's scent around with her, arousing images of the two of them dancing cheek to cheek and thigh to thigh. Mr. Law-and-Way-Too-Much-Order was not even remotely the kind of guy she wanted imprinted on her psyche.

"I threw them up in the air and that's where they stuck," she improvised for Larry's benefit.

"Unfortunately, I wasn't around when it happened," Kevin said. "Do you think it looks too revealing?"

Larry cleared his throat. "I guess you'd know more about that than I would. Right?"

He was trying to figure out the relationship between the two of them, Alli thought, and tried to figure out how to describe it. Reluctant colleagues? Victims of circumstance? People who bucked a trend by moving in together *before* their first date?

"I think we should have it shellacked and preserved for posterity," Kevin replied, and headed for the kitchen.

Alli rattled the article in her hand. "I appreciate this. Did you have any trouble checking it out of the library?"

"I didn't take it from the library. They make you fill out a form to say what you're working on," Larry said. "I got paranoid that the editors might start asking questions, since photographers don't usually research stories. So I tried another route."

"What route is that?"

Kevin returned with three beers. "I could pour these into glasses if you prefer, but that takes half the fizz out."

"I like my beer out of the can," Alli said.

Larry accepted his with thanks. There was nowhere to sit without knocking down her tent, so they stood there sipping while he continued.

"I asked Madge if she remembered any stories about those doctors. She mentioned she'd written one, and she photocopied it from her files without asking who it was for. I think she knew it must be you."

"Please thank her for me," Alli said. "I'll tell her in person the first chance I have."

They stood there in increasingly awkward silence. At last Kevin turned to Larry. "Want to go to a party tomorrow night?"

That was the last thing Alli had expected him to say. Why would he invite her friend to join a bunch of cops? "What kind of party is this?"

"A casual gathering." Kevin swallowed more beer before adding, "With plenty of women."

"Then why did you invite me?" she asked.

"They're the wrong kind of women. For me," he added quickly. "But Larry might hit it off with someone. Unless you're busy?"

The photographer managed a weak smile. "No, I'd like to come." Alli was surprised, since at social gatherings with staff members, he always stood around looking uncomfortable. "Uh, where and when?"

Kevin wrote the details on a pad and handed them over. "There'll be plenty of food. When you arrive, just tell whoever's at the door that I invited you."

"You're sure they won't mind?" he inquired.

"They'll be thrilled."

Something was wrong with this picture. Alli began to have an unpleasant suspicion about the whole party scenario, at least as far as it concerned Kevin. However, she didn't want to air her concern in front of Larry.

She made polite conversation until they finished their beers. Then she escorted her friend outside and thanked him again for the article.

"I'll keep my eyes open for anything else about those doctors," he told her.

Alli wanted to hug him. "You're my lifeline. I miss you and everybody else, with a few exceptions."

"About this Kevin guy," Larry said. "Is he...I mean, are you two...?"

"Dating?" She shook her head. "I had to get out of my apartment. Don't tell anyone, but I think Mayor LeMott was having me followed." She decided not to mention the shooting. That would be too big a deal to expect him to keep hush-hush. "So here I am."

"You and Kevin are old friends?"

"Sort of." Seeing his confusion, she clarified, "He's a private detective. We're helping each other on a case."

"I think he likes you," Larry warned.

"He probably likes a lot of women," Alli said. "But not particularly me."

"Oh, yeah? I'll bet he doesn't let them hang their underwear in his living room."

"I didn't exactly obtain his permission to do that." She resisted the urge to pat Larry's freckled cheek. "Trust me, there's nothing going on."

"It's none of my business, anyway," he replied. "And it was nice of him to invite me for tomorrow. I *would* like to meet a girl."

She hoped Kevin was right about Larry's chances. "See you at the party."

"You bet!"

After he drove away through the tree-lined neighborhood, Alli remembered Kevin's advice, so she borrowed his garage opener and put her car away. When she returned, she found him standing by the fireplace reading Madge Leeky's article.

"Anything useful?" she asked.

"It's mostly puffery," he said without looking up. "But there's some interesting background."

Alli strolled to the master bedroom. She kept expecting Kevin to ask what she was doing, but he seemed to be absorbed in the article.

It was time to check out her suspicions about what he had up his sleeve. She intended to be prepared for whatever might happen tomorrow night.

Out of his sight, she opened the master closet, where a row of dry-cleaner–bagged suits and shirts met her gaze. Pairs of perfectly creased jeans lay folded over hangers. Even his sweatshirts appeared ironed.

But there was nothing here to confirm her theory. She didn't see so much as a forgotten skirt tucked in one corner or a high-heeled shoe left on the carpeted floor.

Quietly, she moved into the kitchen. A peek into a few cabinets and drawers revealed only that Kevin's passion for order extended to hanging pot lids in place and organizing utensils in plastic trays. The man was seriously in need of some craziness.

The refrigerator offered Alli's last hope. Opening it, she nearly uttered a whoop of triumph.

On the shelves sat no fewer than three casseroles, which, upon inspection, turned out to be filled with a tuna-noodle dish, a bean mixture and potatoes au gratin. No bachelor since the dawn of time had ever made three casseroles simultaneously.

She found further evidence in the freezer. Foil-wrapped packages fixed with "From the kitchen of" labels had been marked "meat loaf," "chocolate cake" and "beef stew."

The scary part was that the labels had three different names on them. These goodies had come from the kitchens of Heloise, Barbara and Betsy.

Kevin didn't want a date to keep his ex-girlfriend at bay as she'd surmised. He was juggling three women, and he expected to show up with a fourth!

"Having a good time?" his voice asked close to her ear.

Alli gave a guilty start. Although her instincts urged her to brazen it out by claiming she was hungry, she decided not to lie.

Closing the freezer, she pivoted to face Kevin. He stood inches away, a mocking twist to his mouth.

"You haven't told me the whole truth about tomorrow night," she challenged.

Was that guilt fleeting across his face? "Certainly not. I haven't told you *anything* about tomorrow night."

Alli decided to force the issue into the open. "Which of them is going to be there, or is it all three?"

"All three what?"

"Your fan club," she said. "The ladies who bring lunch. The adoring trio of Heloise, Barbara and Betsy. Do they know about one another? Is this some kind of competition? Where does your date for the party fit in, lover boy?"

Instead of reddening with well-deserved shame, the man got a gleam in his eye. "They're acquainted with one another."

"What's the plan?" Alli pressed. "Are you trying to make them jealous or what?"

"I doubt they'll be jealous," he said smoothly. Of all the untrustworthy men Alli had ever met, this one had the most nerve! "You'd be surprised how well we rub along."

"Do you date them on alternate nights? What are they, your personal harem?" She didn't really suspect him of promiscuity. However, there was the evidence, right in his refrigerator. "You may think this is funny, but I doubt that they do."

"I don't consider the situation funny," Kevin responded levelly. "You want the truth? Those women are hounding me to death."

"And you never gave them any reason to think they had some claim on you, right?" she countered.

"We used to be close," he conceded. "But, you know, people change."

"So you're not currently dating any of them?"

"Not a one."

"And they drop off casseroles purely out of habit?"

"Can I help it if hope springs eternal?" he asked.

Alli was tempted to bop him with a utensil. "I know we made a deal, but I don't want to get involved in whatever game you're playing."

"Tell me something." Stretching out one arm, he leaned against the fridge and enclosed her in a private space. "Which is crueler, to let them keep showering me with food in hopes of winning my heart, or to show up with a tasty dish like you and put a stop to it?"

Being referred to as a "tasty dish" pushed Alli over the edge. She raised one knee to the exact location of his masculine portions. "You want to hear what I think of Don Juans? I think they deserve what they get."

The next thing she knew, he'd tossed her over one shoulder, fireman style. "Never threaten an ex-cop," Kevin advised, and hauled her through the house into the master suite.

Alli waited until he'd almost reached the bed before she kicked out, made contact with the bed frame and shoved in the opposite direction. Releasing a string of swearwords, Kevin staggered backward.

As he stumbled, Alli felt herself begin to slide. It occurred to her that she should have given more thought to the fact that, if he fell, she was going down with him.

Or maybe underneath him.

At the last moment, Kevin managed to avoid dropping her entirely. Instead, he ricocheted across the room and flopped her onto the mattress before toppling across her.

He did more than knock the air out of her lungs. He landed in such a position that, had they not both been wearing slacks, they'd have become lovers by default.

Alli could trace every thoroughly male detail of his anatomy. The process was heightened by the fact that he'd become inexplicably but impressively aroused.

If Kevin Vickers expected to add *her* to his harem, he was the least perceptive man in history. And she intended to leave him in no doubt of that.

KEVIN WISHED he did have a string of adoring mistresses. They might have taken the edge off his desire, in which case he wouldn't be responding to Alli Gardner like an overgrown adolescent.

He'd only been joking when he tossed her over his shoulder. He hadn't intended to do anything except set her on her feet once they got in here.

Still, he understood Alli well enough not to let on what he was thinking. He pitied the man who ever became vulnerable to her, even by so much as an apology.

"Is this what you had in mind when you decided to drag me down on top of you?" he asked.

She sputtered. "I was trying to discourage you, in case you hadn't noticed."

"I judge people's intentions by their actions, and here we are," he replied. "So if you're curious about what those other ladies find so irresistible…"

"Kevin," Alli said.

"Hmm?"

"I can't breathe."

"Sorry." He rolled off. "Normally, I approach a lady with more finesse."

She sat up, hair tangling around her face and her emerald top revealing a tantalizing strip of lean waistline. The sight of her made Kevin's groin tighten harder, entirely against his will.

He wasn't normally attracted to shoot-from-the-hip women. His type was more like Lisette, who, when it came to intimacies, had waited for him to make the first move, and the second and the third. He'd found her tantalizing at first, until he began to wonder if she ever experienced true passion.

Alli's boldness tantalized him with possibilities. He'd be willing to bet she could match him every step of the way.

What he needed, he thought firmly, was a woman somewhere between Lisette and Alli. But definitely not this tigress, all fangs and claws. He might survive the battle, but she'd leave scars.

"Since we're not going to make use of this bed, I suggest we remove ourselves." Kevin suited actions to words. "So are you reneging on your promise to be my date?"

"I can't afford to. I still need a roof over my head," she conceded. "Just promise you aren't going to use me to break off a relationship with some woman."

"I promise," he said.

Although she didn't look convinced, she let it go. Briefly, Kevin considered telling her the truth, but his instincts weighed against it.

The most effective way to handle his mother and sisters was to keep them off balance, and he had the strong sense that this would work with Alli, too.

A scary thought occurred to him. He'd let a woman move into his house who was way too much like his own family.

It was only for the weekend, though. On Monday, Alli Gardner could go storm somebody else's castle.

ALLI SLEPT SOUNDLY inside her makeshift tent. The sense of camping out comforted her because as long as she kept on the move nothing could tie her down and no one could leave her behind.

Fragments of dreams survived when she awoke. They involved a dark-eyed man, a mattress and a wonderful sense of longing.

If I ever start bringing him casseroles, I hope somebody shoots me, she thought as she stretched in the filtered morning light.

The smell of coffee drew her out of her shelter. After finger combing her shaggy hair—the bangs, which were growing out, fell to an awkward length—Alli smoothed her crumpled nightgown and decamped to the kitchen.

At the table sat Kevin, bandbox perfect in a sport jacket, slacks and a wrinkle-free shirt. He must have already removed his breakfast plate, because the only thing in front of him was a mug.

The clock read 8:33 a.m. Who got this dressed up on a Saturday?

"I'll be gone most of the day," he informed her without wasting so much as a "good morning." "There's a spare key in the silverware drawer and I've written down the security code. Please activate the alarm if you go out. Don't forget there may be people gunning for you."

Alli poured coffee from the pot and sank blearily into a chair. "You trust me with your security code?"

"I change it every Wednesday," he said. "You won't be able to access the house after that."

"Why Wednesday?"

"I installed the system on a Wednesday. That makes it easy to keep track of when to switch."

Easy? To Alli, it sounded like a pain in the neck. She never changed a password on the computer or her ATM unless the system required it, and then half the time she forgot what it was and had to go through a ton of trouble to have it reset. She felt certain Kevin never encountered that problem.

He seemed all business this morning, unlike the playful scamp who'd thrown her over his shoulder last night. She missed that scruffier, almost human version of him, although she was pleased that he'd left an appealing hint of dark fuzz around his jaw and cheeks. "I take it your work doesn't concern our doctor friends?"

"I do have other cases." He carried his cup to the sink. "Help yourself to the casseroles for lunch. I'll catch something while I'm out."

"I'll bet your girlfriends would be hurt if they knew another woman was eating their stuff," she said.

"Food is food. If it isn't eaten, it has to be thrown out." After rinsing the mug, he put it in the dishwasher.

Alli supposed she ought to be repulsed by Kevin's compulsive neatness, but instead, she was thinking how perfectly even and white his teeth looked, without even a hint of coffee brown. He probably used an electric brush on a timer.

One of last night's dreams rushed back, inspired by that tempting mouth or perhaps by the small dent in his left cheek. The dream involved tangled, bare limbs, soft hair ruffling beneath her hands, and his lips parting as her tongue explored his mouth.

"Are you okay?" Kevin asked.

"Sleepy," she answered. "Did you set up the laptop?"

"It's in my office. Hooked up to high-speed access and the printer."

"Thank you."

"See you around five-thirty," he said. "The party starts at six." With a nod, he went out.

It annoyed Alli that she immediately missed him. Usually, she liked being alone.

Determined to put him out of her mind, she read the paper. She didn't see any stories with Payne's byline, which meant he must not have found anyone's notes to steal.

The editors probably wanted him to stay on the LeMott story. Alli had only scratched the surface of the mayor's corrupt activities in her initial foray, detailing how he had arranged for his company to bypass city procedures to obtain speedy zoning variances and conditional-use permits.

Friday's piece under Payne's byline, also based on her unpublished notes, had hinted at more explosive topics to come. She'd been trying to uncover information about the mayor's old loan-sharking operation but so far had found only unproven allegations.

Ideally, she'd have delayed the entire article until she'd completed her investigation. However, she'd been afraid Payne might steal her work again. Unfortunately, she'd been right.

The readers would expect him to follow through. Where was he going to find evidence that, if it even existed, had undoubtedly been camouflaged?

Well, that wasn't her problem. It belonged to Payne and, when he botched the job as no doubt he would, to the *Outlook*.

Alli found little comfort in that prospect as she spent the next few hours searching job sites online. Nobody advertised newspaper positions; they had too many résumés on file. The ads sought technical writers and advertising/public relations copywriters.

Leaning back in Kevin's chair, she allowed a flash of self-pity. She loathed the prospect of issuing press releases as she'd done years ago. It was so *boring*. Hadn't she earned the right to follow her dream?

Giving up the job search, she reread Madge's article, making notes about its main subject, adoption counselor Binnie Reed. A forty-two-year-old social worker, she'd previously served at an adoption agency in Los Angeles.

Her photograph showed a businesslike woman who exuded professional concern. In her quotes, she said the kind of reassuring things that adoptive parents might want to hear.

When Alli researched Ms. Reed on the Web, she found a few references to speaking engagements and organizational memberships. Nothing pointed to a motive or an aptitude for extorting money from desperate parents.

As she reexamined the newspaper shot of Binnie, Alli's thoughts drifted. She wondered what Heloise, Betsy and Barbara looked like. Did Kevin go for some particular physical type, or did he prefer variety? She doubted it; based on the fact that they'd all bought kitchen labels printed with their names, his three girlfriends must be as regimented as he was.

She imagined them showing up for breakfast fully dressed, perhaps polishing the bathroom mirrors before they departed after a night of less-than-wild lovemaking. Oh, come on, she thought, Kevin *had* to possess some fiery instincts beneath that stuffy exterior. How could he be satisfied with lovers who wrapped and labeled packages of beef stew as romantic keepsakes?

Alli hoped they weren't all going to attend the party, but

at least one of them was sure to be there, or why would Kevin have invited her? How annoying that she had nothing to wear but a pants outfit. If she'd been cast in the role of the sexy other woman, then for goodness' sake, she ought to look like one.

To fetch an appropriate outfit, she'd have to sneak back into her apartment. Competing for a man she didn't like seemed a stupid reason to put herself in danger.

Undecided, Alli went into the kitchen for lunch. Although she suspected these too-perfect ladies must be bland cooks, she took out the three casseroles and spooned a selection of each onto a plate, covering it with a paper towel before microwaving so Mr. Clean wouldn't have a fit.

The results tasted dismayingly good. The tuna-noodle casserole had been made with real cream instead of canned soup. The beans had been cooked fresh and doctored with slivered almonds and real butter. As for the au gratin potatoes, she could tell that the cook had grated the cheese fresh.

What did Kevin do, select his female companions based on their cooking skills? Alli wouldn't put it past him. She also wondered if the three women knew how much they had in common, aside from lusting after the same guy.

And they have practically nothing in common with me.

She didn't care what Kevin thought of her, but she hated to come across as a frump in front of the cook-off champions. She'd already gone by her apartment once without getting caught. What was the big deal about slipping inside one more time?

Having remembered to take the spare key and activate the alarm, Alli pointed her car across town. A June haze kept the temperature cool, and through her open windows floated the moist scent of brine and the mewing of seagulls.

Too bad the sun hadn't come out, or she might be tempted to grab her bikini and head for the beach. If she got enough of a tan, she could wear her swimsuit to the party and forget the dress. Alli smiled, imagining what an entrance she'd make in nothing but two strips of cloth. Watching Kevin's reaction would almost be worth the awkwardness.

At her apartment complex, she parked one building over and scurried along a walkway. She saw nothing suspicious, only children frolicking, a young woman emerging from the laundry room and a couple lost in conversation as they strolled side by side.

There was no sign of the gray van. By now, the guys must have figured out she wasn't hanging around.

Alli skimmed up the back stairs and down the hall. As she turned the key in the lock she found the bolt already retracted, which meant the door hadn't been secured.

She ought to slam it and sprint for cover. But she'd been so rattled yesterday that she might have left it this way.

Determined not to scare too easily, Alli opened the door in time to spot a sudden flurry of movement behind her desk. Someone really had invaded her premises.

And she'd walked right in on him.

Chapter Five

Alli made a split-second decision based entirely on the fact that she was boiling mad. She burst halfway across the room before it occurred to her that the intruder might have a gun, and by then, sheer momentum propelled her.

At the last minute, she registered the familiar thin frame and full head of blond hair. It gave her tremendous pleasure to body-slam Payne Jacobson against her desk and punch him in the eye.

He staggered backward, gasping and waving one hand in front of him to ward off further blows. Alli cried out—for benefit of any future legal depositions he might make—"Payne? Is that you? Oh my gosh! I thought you were a burglar!"

Whimpering, he banged into the wall and stuck there, too stunned to move. Yet she thought she noticed a furtive movement with his left hand.

"What are you doing?" she demanded. "Actually, you *are* a burglar."

"It's not what you think!" Payne protested as she picked up the phone. "I tried to call you a couple of times to, uh, see how you were doing. When nobody answered, I got worried."

"Aw, Payne, I didn't know you cared." Since this wasn't a 911-level emergency, Alli groped for a phone book to look up the regular police number. "You could have left a message."

"Your machine didn't answer." He pointed to the device. The on light had gone dark.

Alli was almost certain she'd left it switched on. "That's because you've been listening to my messages, haven't you?" She punched the play button, but either there weren't any messages or he'd erased them. "What did you find out, you little sneak?"

"Honest, I just stopped by to make sure you were all right." Payne was gaining confidence. He must have worked out his excuse before he came, because he didn't usually think this fast. "The assistant manager let me in."

"And left you alone?" As she spoke, Alli recalled that the last time she'd paid rent she'd dealt with a new employee in the office. The young woman, who'd been yakking on the phone, had acted annoyed about having to write a receipt.

"She had to run out for a minute. I needed to search your desk to see if you'd indicated where you'd gone." Despite a wince of pain, Payne managed a glib smile.

He'd either bribed the woman or played on her irresponsibility. In any case, Alli noted unhappily that she had little chance of persuading the police to lock him up.

However, his eye was reddening nicely. With any luck, it would turn black by tomorrow.

"What did you think you would find?" she snapped. "You've already stolen everything I had, and besides, you can't keep ripping off your career from other people. Sooner or later, J.J.'s going to find out you're incompetent."

"You don't get it." His lip curled in a sneer, although he took a precautionary step sideways when she made a slight movement. "I've got more talent than you'll ever dream of."

"If you're so gifted, why don't you show the rest of us how it's done instead of plagiarizing?" she taunted.

"I'm saving my best efforts for something worthy of a Pulitzer, not for this small-town garbage," Payne said.

"You must have the world's largest ego!"

The weird part was that he evidently believed his hogwash. This kid who couldn't write a decent lead paragraph or interview a subject without misquoting had convinced himself he was a genius.

Apparently he'd convinced his uncle, too. And as long as Payne kept swiping other people's stuff, neither of them had to face the truth.

"Now that I know you're all right, I'll leave." He shifted toward the door. "I really was concerned about you, Alli."

"Wait!" From a bureau drawer, she retrieved a disposable camera she kept on hand for emergencies. Taking a shot of her trespasser would at least document the visit.

One look at the camera and he took to his heels. All Alli captured was his skinny butt going out the door, and there wasn't even anything in the frame to prove she'd taken the shot in her apartment.

"Creep!" she yelled. Picking up the phone, she called the front office. At least she could register a complaint about the assistant manager that might prevent Payne from sneaking in again.

The manager apologized. The young woman's actions had violated policy, he said, and promised there'd be consequences.

Alli felt a bit better as she hung up. Disturbing as the incident had been, it didn't appear to have caused any real damage.

Then she remembered the furtive movement Payne had made. Could he have been stuffing something in his pocket? If only she hadn't gotten distracted in the heat of the moment and had followed it up!

For one heart-stopping moment, she feared he'd found a clue about the adoption blackmail. Terrific stories didn't fall in one's lap every day, and if he undercut this one, she'd lose her best chance of proving what she could do. Also, he'd probably write a story prematurely, alerting the blackmailer he was being investigated.

Going to the desk, she riffled through the disordered papers. For once, Alli wished she had Kevin's organizational skills, because then she might have been able to figure out what was missing.

Old receipts, letters, tax records, computer discs and clippings stuffed the drawers, along with items she'd removed from work. Still, she felt certain she'd taken her notes about Rita Hernandez and all trace of the Abernathy interview to Kevin's.

Whatever Payne had pilfered must have fit inside his pocket, which suggested one of Alli's spiral-bound pads. After flipping through several of those that remained, she finally deduced which one must be missing.

It contained brainstorming notes on possibilities for follow-up articles about Klaus LeMott. She'd jotted down some of her speculations as to what else he might be involved with, plus a lot of what-if questions. None of this was usable because it hadn't been confirmed or even researched.

Payne must not have had time to read her notes carefully. When he did, he'd discover that what he'd taken was useless except as a guide to future legwork that he had neither the skill nor the patience to handle.

Alli let out a long breath. She hadn't lost anything vital. And she was glad she'd given the jerk a shiner.

Her spirits lifting, she turned her energies to the main challenge: deciding what to wear tonight. One by one, she lifted outfits from her closet, discarding some and setting aside others to try on, the shorter, tighter and flashier the better.

She intended to stand out at the party. Her heart might not be engaged, but her pride was.

Just because she'd promised to go on Kevin's arm didn't mean she had to resemble one of his domesticated groupies. She was going to make sure nobody confused Alli Gardner with Bipsy, Bopsy and Boopsy.

KEVIN SPENT most of the day trailing a man named Wilmer Lee, who claimed to have suffered long-term disability since breaking a leg at a construction job. The insurance company suspected him of malingering and wanted proof.

Some subjects didn't bother to hide their healthy state, making it a cinch to collect photographic evidence, but either this guy was the real deal or he'd learned caution. Hour after tedious hour, Kevin tailed him to an auto-parts store, a plant nursery and a hardware outlet, while Wilmer religiously used his crutches and arranged for store personnel to carry purchases to his car.

Finding a parking place near the man's house that wouldn't attract attention wasn't easy, and once Kevin wedged his car partially out of sight behind an RV, he didn't dare leave. So he hunkered down with binoculars, eating a stale candy bar from the glove compartment while his stomach grumbled.

He would have given a great deal right now to dig into one of the casseroles his mother and sisters had left. Barb's green beans had been especially tasty, even though they were getting old by now.

He grinned as he pictured Alli's indignation when she'd concluded that the dishes came from a trio of girlfriends. Watching her expression tonight ought to prove royally entertaining, although the last thing Kevin had expected was to look forward to the party. Even if Alli tried to kill him later, it would be worth it.

He peered into his side mirror at the postage-stamp view of Wilmer Lee's front lawn. The man knelt on a pad while planting pansies and marigolds around his yard. Once or twice, when he stood up to fetch an item, he took a rather healthy stride, but he sank down again before Kevin could snap a picture. Besides, one step didn't prove anything.

A rumbling made him turn as two boys on skateboards clattered by, speeding down the sloped street. One of them hopped over a curb, nearly lost his balance but stayed upright and zipped away on the sidewalk.

Wilmer frowned at them. For one alarming moment, Kevin thought the man's eyes fixed on him, but then his subject squinted painfully and averted his face. He must have caught a shiny reflection from the car window.

Minutes ticked by. Into Kevin's otherwise unoccupied mind flashed the image of Alli lying on his bed with her top in disarray. He saw her again parading into his kitchen in her nightgown the way she'd done this morning, and, best of all, he imagined her stark naked, winking at him…no, forget that.

Maybe his family was right when they claimed he'd been alone too long. A man needed certain things that only a woman could provide. The hard part was finding the right one.

No matter how strongly his body reacted to Alli, he knew that following his instincts would lead to messy quarrels and a breakdown of their working relationship.

Another rumble announced the return of the skateboarders, who must have circled the block. They flashed by even faster than before. Again, the daredevil made a run at the curb and, this time, hit it at a disastrous angle that pitched him onto the sidewalk, no doubt scraping the heck out of his palms.

His skateboard kept going. Up, up, up and then down in a curving arc until it landed *splat!* in the middle of Wilmer Lee's freshly planted flower bed. Soil and flower parts flew into the air.

With a roar, the home owner wrenched the offending board from the dirt and sprang to his feet. Face red as a carnation, he stalked across the yard yelling curses at the fallen offender.

Kevin barely watched for traffic before springing from his car and snapping away. A series of shots captured Wilmer storming toward the boy and brandishing the skateboard.

It took several seconds for the enraged gardener to notice the man standing in the street. When he did, his fury refocused.

As Wilmer lumbered into the road, Kevin pressed the button for one more burst of photos. Then he dived into his car, rolled up the window and keyed the engine as the man stomped up.

They faced each other in a suspended tableau, their roles of hunter and hunted suddenly reversed. Kevin wondered if Wilmer would smash the skateboard through the glass.

However, the fraud simply stood there with his expression shifting from rage to ruefulness as he realized the game was up. Giving him an apologetic shrug, Kevin pulled out of the space. He never deliberately provoked a subject or hung around any longer than necessary once he'd obtained his proof.

Catching petty connivers wasn't exactly what he'd planned to do with his life, he reflected as the disgruntled home owner shrank in the rearview mirror. On the other hand, he'd never been a raving idealist, either.

In college, Kevin had taken a look at the job opportunities

available to a young man who disliked sitting behind a desk and demanded order in a chaotic world. He'd weighed the fact that he also wanted to help make Serene Beach a better place for his future children.

Serving on the police force had fulfilled his requirements. It had also contributed to his personal growth. During his years on the force, he'd become less impatient and more tolerant of those who hadn't been fortunate enough to grow up in a supportive, stable family.

He'd also become frustrated with a legal system that expected perfection from its protectors and let evildoers off easy if their attorneys could manufacture enough clever excuses. Kevin had briefly considered going to law school so he could join the ranks of prosecutors, but that cost too much and, besides, he didn't want to spend more years plowing through books.

He'd decided to strike out on his own. So here he was, booting cheaters like Wilmer off the gravy train and helping brokenhearted spouses run damage control. Once in a while he got a chance to assist someone like Mary Conners, and that made up for the tedium.

Thinking of Mary reminded Kevin how useful he'd found Allie's interview with Dr. Abernathy. The problem now was determining how to obtain more information when Dr. Graybar had already turned down his request for a meeting.

He stopped at his office to write a report on Mr. Lee, download the photos and e-mail them to the client. It was after five o'clock by then. He was right on schedule to collect Alli before heading for his parents' house.

It pleased Kevin when his schedule proceeded like clockwork. He hated wasting time and, besides, he was hungry. There'd be plenty of food at his mother's house.

He cruised home through quiet streets redolent of newmown grass. To his surprise, Kevin discovered that he was looking forward to seeing Alli, despite the likelihood that she'd go after him with a pickax when she learned he'd been teasing about his girlfriends.

He pictured her tossing back her chestnut hair, looking stern in one of those pantsuits she usually wore. She'd be perfect for keeping the other ladies at bay, and surely his family would quickly discern the lack of any real connection between them.

Everything seemed under control, he reflected contentedly as he entered. "Ready to go?" he called.

"I'll be right out," her voice responded from the office.

Ducking into the bathroom, Kevin ran a brush through his hair. He'd skipped shaving this morning, but instead of turning him into a human porcupine, the bristly growth added a rugged touch. He decided to leave it for now.

Humming, Kevin strolled out. A short distance later, he halted so sharply he nearly lost his balance.

The woman in his living room bore a passing resemblance to Alli Gardner, but she looked even more like a Greek goddess—a sultry Greek goddess. From the hair piled atop her head, a tendril curled along her neck and down to the tantalizing cleavage displayed by a low neckline.

That wasn't all her dress displayed, if you could call it a dress. Spun of black silk woven with glittery threads, the chemise clung to her figure, starting with spaghetti straps and ending at the tops of her thighs.

"Nice underwear," he said. "What are you wearing over it?"

Laughter rang out. "Maybe a light jacket. Is it cold?"

"I meant, indoors."

She pivoted, model-fashion. Those long legs and slim ankles made the desired impact, and then some. "How do you like the shoes?"

Shoes? On her feet, he noted a pair of spike-heeled black sandals. Stones glittered on the thong between her toes. "Fascinating."

"Hey, with these on, I bet I'm taller than you." She eased over, grazing his hip as she measured her stature against his. "About the same height."

That low neckline and alluring dress called out to be touched. However, Kevin had no intention of handling Alli other than to grab her arm when she tripped and fell, as she inevitably would in her daredevil shoes.

"It's a casual party. I suspect most of the guests are going casual." For example, his dad, Frank, an auto mechanic, considered a clean pair of overalls the height of formality. "You'll stick out."

"Good," Alli said. "Bipsy, Bopsy and Boopsy can gossip about me all night."

"Who?" He shook his head. "Never mind. I get it." The prospect of being scrutinized by rivals had obviously affected Alli's mental state.

"I was tempted to wear my bikini," she added, "and pretend I thought it was a pool party. Is there a pool, by the way?"

Kevin shook his head. "Seriously, you might want to re-think the outfit."

She grinned. "You're embarrassed."

"Only because you're half-naked."

"Want to see the other half?" She waited long enough for the heat to begin climbing his neck before she said, "I love when you turn red like that."

Further objections would be futile. And likely lead to more embarrassment. "Grab a jacket and let's go."

Alli ignored the command. Instead, she smoothed her palm over his cheek. "I like the stubble."

Then she did something totally unexpected. She cupped Kevin's chin and kissed him.

The heat inside him rippled with liquid pleasure. Acting on pure instinct, he pulled her close and felt her curves melt into him.

As the kiss deepened, her breasts swelled against his chest and her breath speeded. When she raised her head, intense slate eyes bored into him.

"We could take this in the other room," she murmured. "Or stay right here. You're the perfect size for me, Detective." Catching his tie and drawing him harder against her, she added, "And I do love the primitive look."

His hormones demanded he find out just how perfect a fit

he was. His brain shouted at him to wake up. Did he really want to deal with the consequences of making love to Alli?

Furthermore, if they lingered, a knot of women was likely to descend on this house to find him. Then she'd discover exactly how much Bipsy, Bopsy and Boopsy could gossip.

"Thanks," he said dryly. "But we have to go."

Reluctantly, she released him. "Can I have a rain check?"

"It hardly ever rains around here in June." He straightened his tie.

"You're cute when you're grumpy. Did I ever tell you that at the police department?"

"You didn't dare," he replied, and held the door.

She sauntered outside. "I'd have gotten around to it if you'd given me a chance. I always loved starting the morning at your office, you know, just to annoy the heck out of you. It gave me more of a buzz than coffee."

Looking back, he had to admit that a part of him had enjoyed the sight of her appearing in front of his desk to bug him about some case or other. But there'd been too many other officers tripping over their tongues at the sight of her. Kevin had had no desire to join the crowd.

On the three-block drive, he reflected that even though he found Alli's audacity exciting, making love to her would mean relinquishing control over their mutual project. Even now, she invaded his carefully guarded spaces and showed no respect for boundaries. Either they'd end up fighting or he'd have to freeze her out.

He didn't want bad feelings between the two of them. Better to keep her as a sometimes exasperating but very entertaining friend.

Although cars already claimed several spots near the Vickers' house, Kevin managed to maneuver into a compact space at the curb. Alli gave a low whistle as she examined the two-story pillared house with its upstairs balcony.

"Welcome to Tara," she murmured. "Who owns this place, the police chief?"

"Heloise, as a matter of fact," he said.

Her eyebrows formed a slash of protest. "You're kidding. Heloise of casserole fame lives here?"

He cleared his throat. "With her husband."

Alli folded her arms, which had the effect of pushing up her cleavage. To Kevin's chagrin, his gaze flicked over her chest before he could stop it.

"Let me get this straight," she said. "You're carrying on with a married woman under her husband's nose?"

"We're not carrying on." The time had come to clue her in. "I know I let you believe—"

A tap on the passenger window interrupted him. In peered a female face framed by riotous red hair. "Hi!"

"Hello." The glass rolled down. "I'm Alli." She extended her hand.

His sister shook it. "I'm Barbara."

Alli seemed, for once, at a loss for words.

An eight-year-old girl and five-year-old boy appeared beside their mother, followed by a slightly frazzled man. "This is my husband, Ernie, and our daughter, Rebecca. That's our son, Monster. His real name is Ernie Jr., but he prefers his nickname."

"Grrr. I'm Shrek." Monster illustrated by grimacing.

Barbara spotted someone else and waved. "Betsy! Come over here!"

As Alli stared, Kevin wished he could read her thoughts. She must have figured out something was amiss with the scenario she'd painted. Was she amused, annoyed or ticked off?

His younger sister arrived, her dark hair pulled back in the knot she'd worn since giving birth to triplets four years earlier. "Who's this?"

"Kevin's got a date!" Barbara crowed. "Your classmates are going to have to fend for themselves." To Alli, she explained, "It's her high-school reunion. Mom was all set to matchmake, but don't worry. I'm sure she'll love you."

"Maybe we should go in," Kevin said.

Alli didn't move.

"Are you all right?" he asked.

"She's probably in shock." Betsy hoisted her daughter, Fleur, onto her hip, although the girl was large compared to her mother's petite frame. All the Vickers women were on the short side. "Our family can be overwhelming."

"I have to tell you guys something," Alli said.

"What?" Barbara and Betsy studied her expectantly. Kevin held his breath and hoped he was paid up on his life insurance.

"You are both terrific cooks," she told them. "And Heloise. That's your mom, right?"

They nodded in unison.

"She's amazing," Alli said, and slowly opened the door. Everyone moved back as she unfurled from the seat. "I can't wait to meet her."

By the time Kevin emerged and followed her up the walkway, Alli was floating toward the house in the middle of a bunch of chattering people. That went well, he thought, and wished he believed it.

Chapter Six

As Alli circulated at the party, she had a hard time keeping from laughing aloud. Kevin had certainly put one over on her—or, rather, he'd allowed her to put one over on herself.

She could see that she'd invented the entire story about dueling girlfriends and he'd simply gone along with it. Certain he had an ulterior motive for inviting her to the party, she'd been so proud of figuring it out that she'd never imagined she might be wrong.

He'd invited her for protection. This whole weekend had been designed to keep his sisters' friends from cornering him, and what had she done? Practically dragged him into the bedroom.

It struck her as hilarious. But she had no intention of letting Kevin know that.

She wished he didn't look so darn cute with that hint of a beard on his face. The impulse to kiss him had been too strong to resist, and then—for an all-too-brief moment—he'd reacted like a man who hadn't had sex in years. Of course, she supposed most men reacted that way to almost any stimulation, but she hadn't expected this from Mr. Self-Control.

Why on earth had she challenged him to an unplanned sex act? She wondered what it would have been like if he'd accepted, and whether she'd ever find out what she'd missed.

Across the room, the man gave out incredibly sexy vibes. But she didn't intend to hang on his arm, not when there was world-class cuisine to sample, including a hot buffet and a death-defying selection of desserts.

As for the people, one individual dominated the bevy of young women and a few young men: Heloise. Although Alli guessed she barely cleared five foot two, her energetic manner made her seem larger than life.

Mrs. Vickers bustled about making introductions and carrying trays of food. She took Alli's measure in a couple of bats of the eye, gave her a knowing smile and asked just enough questions to determine that her association with Kevin focused on work.

"Don't let him take advantage of you," Mrs. Vickers said, offering Alli a plate of stuffed mushrooms. "I know my son. Women are always doing favors for him, and he never appreciates it."

"I can understand it," Alli replied. "He really is cute." She enjoyed her first mushroom so much she took a couple more.

"Women bounce off him like Teflon," his mother said. "At this rate, he'll never settle down."

"He seems pretty settled to me." To Alli, ownership of a house and a complete set of furniture qualified a man for major stick-in-the-mud status.

"He loves kids," Heloise told her. "I'm afraid he'll put off finding a wife until he's in his forties, and then he'll meet someone who doesn't want children or already has grown ones. That would be a shame."

Alli decided not to mention that she loved reporting too much to put her career on a back burner. Besides, a role as supermom was inconceivable for a woman who couldn't microwave popcorn without burning it.

"Kevin strikes me as the kind of guy who sets his own priorities," she said. "If he wants kids, I'm sure he'll find the right woman to have them."

"How can he find her when he works such long hours?" Heloise grumbled. "And his clients! Married people with cheating spouses, insurance companies—you think there's a pretty girl among them? Hah!"

She seemed to know a surprising amount about her son's work. "He tells you about his cases?"

"Didn't he mention that I'm his secretary?" Heloise asked. "I filled in a couple of years ago and it turned into a regular job."

Kevin employed his mother? That was unusual. "Isn't it hard to switch gears and take orders from him?" Alli inquired.

"I can see why those other women quit." Heloise softened her words with a grin. "He's a tough boss, but he's fair and he pays on time. Fleur!" she cried as the little girl lifted a vase to examine it. "Be careful with that!"

After Heloise rushed off to rescue the pottery from her granddaughter, Alli went into the family room. Kevin's father, Frank, a weathered fellow in denim overalls, had retreated to a recliner with a can of beer in one hand and a full paper plate beside him on a tray. He kept staring at the TV set, although his wife had turned it off.

A small dog lay on the floor beneath the recliner's upraised foot. While Alli was introducing herself, it growled.

"What's the dog's name?" she asked.

Frank shot her a baleful stare, as if she were interrupting the climax of the Super Bowl. "It's Mindy."

"Is that short for Mind Your Own Business?"

He gave a snort of laughter. "That's good. She's a mind-your-own-business dog, that's for sure." He considered for a minute before saying, "So you're Kevin's girl."

"We're friends, in a manner of speaking. The truth is, I'm really good at provoking him."

"He's tough on women," Frank said. "I think it comes from growing up in a houseful of them."

"I grew up in a house with no men," Alli admitted, taking a seat. The dog had dropped its head and appeared to be snoozing.

"That's not good, either. No father in the picture?" he queried.

"You couldn't have spotted him with a telescope."

"Kev will make a great father when he's ready," Frank told her. "He's steady as an anchor."

"Your son's a great guy," Alli conceded, "but I don't need an anchor. I want to spread my sails and fly."

He regarded her thoughtfully. "You know what they say about opposites attracting."

"Are you matchmaking?" she asked.

Frank gave a dry chuckle. "I'm not the matchmaker in the family. But there's something about you. You're not like the other girls he's brought home."

"What do you mean?" she asked.

"They hang on his every word," said his father. "You say you're good at provoking him, but what he really hates is being fussed over."

"I'd hate it, too," Alli replied.

One of the children came to climb on Grandpa's lap, and she made her getaway. All the same, she'd been intrigued by Mr. Vickers's remarks and buoyed by his approval. Kevin was lucky to have a father like that.

In a large living room filled with traditional furniture and a few too many pictures, lamps and doilies for her taste, Alli caught sight of him tussling with a pair of four-year-old boys. The youngsters shrieked with glee as Uncle Kev rolled and play-wrestled, heedless of the damage to his suit.

Through the chatter of voices, his chuckle rang out. He seemed to glow brighter than anyone else in the room.

Tenderness lit his face as he allowed his nephews to gang up and knock him over. He really did love kids, Alli noted.

The insight troubled her, although it shouldn't have. It was perfectly okay with her if Kevin turned out to be a family man. In fact, since he already had a home, furnishing it with little ruffians seemed like the logical next step. Why should she care if he craved a lifestyle that couldn't possibly include her?

A young woman crouched on the carpet near him. Red-gold hair tucked into a French braid gave her a cozy look accented by the embroidery on her bodice and the full, flouncy spread of her skirt.

She blinked adoringly at the children but did nothing to stop them from climbing atop their fallen uncle and sitting on his face. As he disappeared beneath them, Alli wondered if he needed help.

Heloise stopped by with a tray of brownies. "What do you think?"

"They smell fantastic." Feeling in dire need of chocolate, Alli had several.

"No, I mean, do you think she might be his type? You seem to know him pretty well." She indicated the woman on her knees beside a whirling mass of arms and legs. "I've known Nora Kingston since she and Betsy were in high school. She moved to San Francisco for a while to work in fashion merchandising, but now she's back, and I'd say she's interested."

The two kids combined must weigh at least a hundred pounds. It looked to Alli as if their uncle was trying to gently dislodge them, and getting the worst of it.

"Can he breathe under there?"

"Children don't weigh anything," Heloise responded.

Nora made a shooing motion at the boys, to no effect. Helplessly, she stared around as if hoping a firefighter would materialize and save the day.

"Excuse me." Making short work of the brownies, Alli marched across the room and scooped one of the boys off the fallen warrior. Freed of his burden, Kevin lay blinking at the ceiling and taking deep breaths. "Hey, kid, even grown-ups need to come up for air once in a while," she said.

Nora blinked at her. "How did you do that in those heels?"

"Adrenaline," Alli replied. "I think he was going down for the count."

"Who're you?" the boy demanded.

"Lois Lane." When his brother scooted forward to take over the task of face-sitting, she hauled him off, as well. Kevin sat up before the first kid could smother him again.

"Are you all right?" chirped the ginger-haired woman at his side.

"Never better," Kevin answered, but looked relieved when the children scampered off to join their cousins.

"Oh, dear, they've made a mess of your clothes." Nora plucked at his wrinkled collar. She didn't seem to notice how he shrank from her touch.

"Just whack him between the shoulder blades," Alli said. "That'll invigorate his lungs."

"No, thanks." Withdrawing from Nora's ministrations, Kevin straightened his clothes.

It struck Alli that they made a revolting tableau: both women kneeling on the floor as if Kevin were lord of the manor and they his fawning devotees. People were glancing their way with far too much interest.

Disgusted, she wobbled to her feet. Just then, she spotted Barbara admitting a newcomer at the front door and recognized Larry's freckled face.

Alli hurried to extend a welcome. She stayed at her friend's side as she introduced him around.

"Shooting photos for the paper sounds exciting," said a chubby young woman named Adrienne. To Alli, she said, "Are you a photographer, too?"

"She's a reporter. We work together at the *Outlook*," he explained. "At least, we used to."

"You aren't Allison Gardner, are you?" Adrienne asked excitedly. "Oh my gosh! I read your stories all the time! I love the way you write!"

After thanking her, Alli explained that she'd been fired.

"What on earth were they thinking?"

Although she hadn't intended to go into detail, her listener's sympathetic manner drew her out until she'd spilled the whole story of dishonest Payne and the politics of the newsroom.

Others who'd stopped to listen expressed sympathy and a gratifying amount of outrage. When Heloise heard the tale, she became so incensed Alli thought she might personally stomp over to the *Outlook* and ream out the senior staff.

"Payne's going to land in trouble sooner or later," she told the group. Kevin stood at the mantel, consuming an hors d'oeuvre while Nora hovered nearby, her fingers waggling as if she could barely keep from feeding him by hand.

In her own way, his admirer was more smothering than his nephews, Alli thought. How could Heloise believe the woman was his type? And why didn't he march off to get some fresh air?

"I'm not so sure," Larry said glumly. "I went by the paper this afternoon and Payne was grinning so hard I could see his fillings."

"I hope he's not doing what I think he's doing," Alli said.

Heloise, who'd perched on the arm of a chair, leaned forward intently. "What do you think he's up to?"

"It's kind of a long story." She hadn't meant to take over the party with her personal situation. "I don't want to bore anyone."

"Are you kidding?" asked another woman, who'd been introduced as Tara Durban. "I've been following those articles about the mayor. I had no idea there was all this skulduggery behind the scenes!"

"She loves soap operas," explained her husband, Ralph. A large man about ten years her senior, he had a short haircut and a watchful air. Alli hadn't been surprised when Mrs. Vickers mentioned he was a security consultant who used to work at the PD with Kevin, although it must have been before she joined the police beat.

"This is more like a comedy routine than a soap opera," she replied. "Payne broke into my apartment this morning." At the mantel, Kevin's eyes darkened. Hurriedly, she explained, "He conned the assistant manager into letting him in and then he went through my desk."

"Whoa!" Larry said. "That's unbelievable."

"I hope you called the cops!" Adrienne put in.

"I did better than that. I punched him in the eye," Alli crowed. "And body-slammed him into my desk. Boy, did that feel good."

Everybody cheered. Kevin smiled but looked concerned as she described the stolen notebook and what it contained.

"I hope he won't try to use it as the basis for an article," she said. "That would be totally irresponsible."

"Maybe it'll be the final straw," Larry responded without much conviction.

Their listeners gleefully expressed the hope that the duplicitous Payne would be fired. Grateful as she felt for the support, Alli didn't believe he'd be that stupid. Or, if he were, that his uncle would let him get away with it.

However, she was beginning to wonder just how far Ned's blind faith in his nephew would carry him.

THE LAST THING KEVIN had expected was to enjoy his sister's reunion party. But Alli was putting on quite a show and he had the best seat in the house.

He rooted for her when she described punching out Payne, and joined the others in hoping the fellow would screw up. Mostly, he enjoyed the way her eyes sparkled as she told her tale.

"Can I fetch you something else?" asked a voice near his shoulder.

He nearly declined without even glancing down until he remembered that would be rude. "No, thank you." He barely kept his tone polite. Couldn't the woman see he didn't want to miss any of Alli's account?

"You must be thirsty," Nora went on. "I'll go for some punch. Or would you prefer a beer?"

"Neither, thanks." Kevin used to find his sister's friend attractive, but she'd changed for the worse. Or else his taste had improved.

He glanced up, eager to hear more of Alli's adventures. To his disappointment, she'd finished regaling the crowd and moved to the refreshment table.

"You know what?" he said. "I'm going to go check out the food. Thanks, Nora. Enjoy yourself!"

Without waiting for a response, he angled away toward the dining room. When he glanced over his shoulder, the young woman stood staring forlornly into space. Guilt nearly drove him back until he saw Betsy stop by with one of her husband's friends in tow.

Another match in the making. He hoped for everyone's sake that it worked out.

"These are great!" Alli enthused when he reached the table. She was pillaging the last of the deviled eggs, as if he hadn't already noticed her consuming several desserts. "What does your mom put in them?"

"She swears it's a secret recipe," he said. "I think she got it out of the *Better Homes and Gardens Cookbook*, but don't tell her I said so."

"Well, there must be a love potion in the punch. Look at that." She nodded to indicate the photographer, who'd retreated to a private conversation with Adrienne. "I think Larry found a kindred spirit."

"Good for him." Kevin felt unexpected relief at confirming that she had no romantic interest in her friend.

"Did you find out anything today about Dr. Graybar?"

The abrupt change in subject gave him pause. "Nothing," he replied after yanking his mind onto the correct track. "I was conducting surveillance for a different client. Why are you bringing this up?"

"It's the first chance we've had all day to talk about the case," she pointed out. "I've been thinking about Binnie Reed. After reading her profile, I don't think she's going to give us the time of day. Maybe—"

"Did I hear you mention Binnie Reed?" asked Tara Durban. "Isn't she great?"

Alli leveled Kevin a completely unnecessary warning glance. Apparently, they'd run into a satisfied customer, and the last thing either of them needed was to tip her off to their real mission.

"I haven't actually met her," Alli answered. "I was reading an article about her."

"I can vouch for how wonderful she is," Tara said. "Ralph and I were going crazy trying to find a way to adopt that wouldn't take forever or break our hearts."

"Break your hearts?"

"Private adoptions are crazy—they expect you to pay all the birth mother's expenses and then she can change her mind and keep the baby anyway. We can't afford to take that risk," Tara explained. "We were thrilled when we found out about the El Centro Orphanage."

Kevin wished he dared warn her about the pitfalls, but that involved too great a risk of word getting back to Ms. Reed. Obviously, Ralph hadn't heard about the problems yet.

He'd go ballistic if anyone threatened his family. He'd been a hard-driving cop before leaving to start a security business half a dozen years ago.

Later, he'd invited Kevin to join him as a partner. However, a preliminary assessment had indicated his company was expanding too fast and had become overextended financially. Kevin preferred to work alone, although by now he presumed Ralph must be on a firm footing.

"How did you hear about El Centro?" Alli asked.

"From Reverend Weatherby," the blond woman replied. "He's our pastor at the Serenity Fellowship Church. He referred us to Dr. Graybar."

Mentally, Kevin congratulated Alli on turning up another potential source of background. The minister ought to have an objective view of the adoption service.

"Have you already completed the process?" Alli inquired.

"Not yet." Tara beamed. "We're flying down to Costa Buena in a couple of weeks. They've found our little girl! Would you like to see her picture?"

"Sure." The other woman produced a small photo, over which Alli made complimentary remarks.

Kevin didn't detect any signs of baby-hunger in her manner. He knew the symptoms from his sisters in bygone years: the wistful longing that revealed they were dreaming of holding a small bundle in their arms. Not Alli, as far as he could tell. He wondered if she even wanted kids.

He did, although not right away. Kevin considered it imperative to be prepared emotionally and financially before making such a major life change.

He tuned back in to hear Alli say, "You must be thrilled," as she returned the picture.

Ralph Durban wrapped one arm around his wife. "We can't wait," he said. "We feel like Rosita was meant to be our daughter."

"I can't resist buying adorable baby clothes and furniture," Tara mentioned. "My husband's been really understanding."

The authorities in Central America might cut off the adoptions at any time, Kevin thought. He hated to consider how devastating the blow would be to this eager couple.

"Best of luck!" Alli announced as she caught Kevin's arm and practically spun him away from the Durbans. In a low voice, she muttered, "Do you have to glare like that?"

He hadn't realized his emotions showed. "I was thinking about whoever's preying on these parents. I'd like to wring his neck."

"Have a lemon bar." She indicated the buffet. "That ought to sweeten your mood. But don't expect me to feed it to you."

"What's that supposed to mean?"

"Do you want me to straighten your collar?" she teased in a wispy voice. "Ooh, Kevin, those little darlings wrinkled it."

He chuckled at her imitation of Nora. "Jealous?"

"Do I still have any lipstick on?"

She'd made another conversational leap. "A little. Why…"

Leaning forward, she smooched him on the cheek. "There." Alli stood back to admire her handiwork. "The mark of the possessive female." She winked. "You can go wash it off now if you want."

"One of these days, I'm going to have a clue what you're all about," he said ruefully, but resisted the urge to dig out a tissue and wipe his cheek. He wasn't about to give her the satisfaction of making him squirm.

As Alli wandered off, Kevin spotted his mother across the room, watching with a puzzled expression. Apparently, she didn't know what to make of the audacious Ms. Gardner, either.

The discovery that Alli had flummoxed his mother made him like her a little. At least she'd earned her keep for the weekend.

Chapter Seven

Alli slept well that night in her makeshift tent, except for waking up two or three times in the middle of fiercely unsatisfying dreams involving Kevin, rumpled clothing and a great deal of lustful panting.

The astonishment on his face when she'd kissed him last night had been priceless. The man had no idea how charming his natural reserve made him. If only he were the type of man to indulge in a casual relationship, they could have a great time and then go their merry ways, but he'd rejected that.

She certainly didn't want anything serious. Not with Kevin arousing turbulent emotions best left unexamined. Not with his huge baby-loving family hovering around, either.

When she finally crawled out of her shelter, Sunday-morning light filled the living room and the scent of pancakes and maple syrup floated irresistibly from the kitchen. After straightening her nightgown, which covered her decently even if it did cling in a few places, she followed her nose.

Kevin sat at the table, reading the paper over a plate bearing the remains of toaster waffles. His dark plaid bathrobe fell open at the throat, revealing no sign of pajama tops underneath, and the dark stubble on his cheeks gave him the rakish air of a buccaneer.

For one fleeting but tempting moment, Alli considered slipping onto his lap and discovering exactly what he had or had not worn to bed. However, Kevin hadn't given any indication of welcoming such intimacies.

"Leave anything for me?" she asked.

"There's more in the freezer," he said without looking up. He was reading the sports section.

She found the waffles, wedged four of them into the toaster oven and rustled up a plate. From a neat stack of newspaper piled on a chair, she retrieved the front section.

On page one above the banner ran a story carrying not only Payne's byline but also a thumbnail photo of him. The headline read: Mayor Raises More Questions Than Answers.

She immediately grasped the tack the article was taking. "I don't believe it. He used the stuff he stole! Did you read this?"

"Did I ever tell you my theory about why they bury sports inside the paper?" Kevin turned a page, careful to keep it smooth. "They put it in the middle in case the rest of the paper suffers damage."

"Because it's the most important section," she finished for him. "That must be your way of telling me you read it first."

"Precisely."

"Since my finely honed sixth sense tells me you don't want to be interrupted, I'll keep Payne's story to myself," Alli said, and returned her attention to the article.

Kevin's nose twitched slightly, an indication that he'd expected her to fill him in. However, after the way he'd blown her off, he could hardly admit to being curious, and Alli wasn't about to indulge him.

Leaving him to stew, she read on. Couched in the casual style of a column rather than a news story, the article took a folksy approach to recapping allegations that the mayor had claimed special privileges for his business, and speculated even further:

Has LeMott really left his questionable past behind him, or are the inmates now running the asylum? Don't the people of Serene Beach have a right to see the mayor's complete financial records, even though the law doesn't require him to fess up?

Payne hadn't written this, she thought, but it wasn't Ned's style, either. She remembered that J.J. sometimes ran the desk on Saturday nights. He contended it paid to take a hands-on approach, since not only did more people read the Sunday paper than the daily editions, they often read it more thoroughly.

So it was the managing editor who'd risked running the story. Either he'd thrown caution to the winds or he believed Payne had evidence to support the speculation. She guessed that the reporter had lied about that. Why not, since he lied about everything else?

Following the stolen outline, the article alluded to earlier attempts by authorities to link LeMott to loan-sharking and racketeering.

How hard are the police working to find out what happened to the witnesses who disappeared? How motivated are they to locate them now that LeMott plays a key role in setting the department's budget?

It ran on in that vein. Alli had dreamed up those questions in an idle mood. Later, she'd learned that loan-sharking and racketeering fell under the aegis of the FBI, not local authorities, but hadn't bothered to change her notes because she'd never expected to see them in print.

"It's irresponsible," she said when she was done. "Just plain wrong, and probably libelous, too."

"Hmm."

"As if you cared!"

"The mayor isn't my problem." Having finished with sports, Kevin cast a disgruntled glance at the still-unavailable front section and reached for the business pages.

While Alli ate her waffles, she tried to focus on other news stories, but her thoughts returned to LeMott. Although he might seem just a colorful local figure to a relative newcomer like J.J., she considered him a force to be reckoned with.

In his late forties, the man had first surfaced as the owner of several pawnshops in Las Vegas. Later, he'd moved to L.A., where he'd taken over a small chain of small liquor stores. Soon, he'd bought a mansion in Serene Beach, and rumors began to fly that he dabbled in laundering money for the mob and loaning his profits at excessive rates.

Always one step ahead of the law, he'd sold the liquor outlets, hired a public relations agency to whitewash his image and taken over a struggling chain of computer stores. Gossip swirled that he was staging backroom gambling tournaments for high-stakes bettors, and rumor had it that federal, state and local authorities had all taken their turns at trying to nail him. Witnesses, however, had a way of refusing to testify or vanishing.

As the High Tech Emporiums forced one competitor after another out of the field, the stores had expanded from computers, software and peripherals to include games and sponsored online competitions. A year earlier, LeMott had won election to the city council and, a few months ago, his fellow council members chose him as mayor after Vice-Mayor Cathy Rodale, who'd been in line for the job, abruptly turned it down.

It was at that point that Alli had begun her investigation, trying to find out if LeMott was bribing or threatening people in city government who got in his way. She'd made discreet inquiries among the planning commission and in the public works department, always sensitive to how touchy this probing would be if anyone learned of it before she was ready to go to print. All of her sources had understandably insisted on remaining anonymous to the public, and Ms. Rodale had refused to discuss the subject at all.

Alli had persuaded the mayor to grant an interview about his plans for the city. A thin man with small eyes and a pencil mustache, LeMott had wreathed the city hall office in cigar smoke.

After giving short shrift to his duties as mayor, he'd expanded on his political ambitions. Soon, he'd declared, Serene Beach would have a new congressman, and since he had the wherewithal to finance his own campaign, he wouldn't be beholden to anyone.

If you're a thug, who cares that you're not beholden to anyone? she'd wondered, but carefully stuck to straightforward questions. Why was he declaring his intentions with the next congressional election almost a year away?

"I want to make sure any potential rivals understand what they're up against," he'd answered.

To Alli, this had sounded like a threat. The humorless cast to his face and the way he'd alternately avoided her gaze and stared for too long gave her the creeps. It also infuriated her that J.J. and Ned had ignored the obvious fact that she and not Payne had conducted that interview, which last Thursday's exposé had quoted liberally.

She considered it unlikely that Klaus would sue the *Outlook*, despite the carelessness of today's story. He undoubtedly knew that libel suits took years to wend their way through the courts, cost a fortune and were difficult to prove, especially for a public figure like him. Plus, a lawsuit would require public disclosure of business dealings that he'd probably prefer to keep quiet.

In any case, with the blackmailer threatening to clamp down by Friday, Alli had a more urgent story to pursue. After finishing her meal, she went to shower, and dressed with care. This time, a business suit seemed appropriate for the day's planned activities.

She emerged to find Kevin absorbed in the LeMott story. "What are you doing?" she demanded.

He glanced up, startled. "Trying to figure out why the newspaper thinks racketeering is a matter for the police department."

"Because they're stupid," Alli said. "You'd better hurry. I checked the schedule in the paper and it starts in half an hour."

"What does?" he asked blankly.

"Church. We're going to talk to the Reverend Alistair Weatherby."

"He can't talk to us during the service," Kevin pointed out.

"He might not talk to us at all," Alli said. "I've probably got 'lapsed churchgoer' stamped on my forehead. Besides, if he thinks we're investigating a crime, he might not be very frank."

"Are you suggesting we lie to a minister?" Kevin raised one eyebrow.

"No, just that we ask a few questions about the orphanage without telling him any more than we need to. We're only gathering background, remember."

He set down the paper. "Did you say half an hour?"

"Yes, and we've got to allow fifteen minutes to get there. What are you waiting for?"

He opened his mouth as if to argue, then shut it again. Score one round for her, Alli thought.

KEVIN HADN'T FIGURED OUT what it was about Alli that made him dig in his heels. He'd been eager to learn what was in the paper not so much because he cared about the investigation as because he wanted to hear the latest installment in the ongoing soap opera that was Alli's life. But he'd made the mistake of mouthing off, with the result that she'd shut him out.

He felt as if his mental well-being required him to keep her at arm's length. Yet she formed a natural center of attention wherever she went—at last night's party, and even here in the Serenity Fellowship Church, where her eyes glowed with pleasure as she listened to the choir.

The group had won well-deserved fame for its harmonies. Kevin, relaxing as best he could in a pew, found that the soaring hymns combined with the airy, sunlit sanctuary to give him a feeling that might almost be described as spiritual.

Amid a swell of music, the Reverend Weatherby arrived at the pulpit like a mellow bass note anchoring a chord. Despite having a face that reminded Kevin of a basset hound's, he possessed a sonorous speaking voice and a heartfelt, unpretentious manner.

Later, Kevin couldn't remember what the pastor said, but he would never forget when they all joined in song. The minister's resonance, the choir's inspiration and Alli's pleasant alto lulled him into contributing his own tenor line, which might not win any prizes but managed to stay on pitch.

"You're a good sport," she told him afterward, amid the chatter of the dispersing congregation. "I figured you'd glower through the whole thing."

"Just call me the singing detective." Kevin tracked Weatherby's progress as he crossed the sanctuary. "I wonder if he teaches a Sunday-school class afterward."

"Let's go head him off." It seemed an impossible task, but Alli had a talent for navigating crowds, Kevin discovered. Her cheerful "Excuse me!" coupled with high-voltage forward propulsion, persuaded all but the most obstinate or distracted congregant to clear a path.

They caught up with the reverend in a hallway that appeared to lead to the classroom wing. "Could you spare us a moment?" Kevin asked. Remembering Alli's warning not to be too forthright about their mission, he added, "We're trying to find out about adoptions."

The minister regarded them sympathetically. "You should contact Dr. Graybar's office, near the community hospital. He's placed a number of youngsters from an orphanage in Costa Buena."

"Do you know him very well?" Alli asked. "Is he reliable? We're afraid a foreign adoption might be difficult."

A woman down the hall waved at Weatherby. "Everyone's seated," she called. "Will you be long?"

"Only a minute." To Alli and Kevin, he said, "I'm leading a Bible-study group. But I can always spare a moment for a nice young couple like you."

Surely anyone could see that they were neither a couple nor particularly nice, given their duplicity, Kevin thought, but he dismissed his reservations. "Have you seen the orphanage personally?"

"Yes. I went down there last year to donate clothes and toys," Weatherby told them. "It seems very well organized, and the church members who've adopted from there consider themselves blessed. Dr. Graybar's office can help you with the home study and paperwork."

"Nobody's run into any problems?" Alli persisted with wide-eyed innocence. "I read something about an investigation. Maybe it was a different orphanage."

"No, El Centro has had a bureaucratic snafu in the past month or so," the minister agreed. "I talked to my contacts down there and they assure me it's just a mix-up."

A mix-up? That made a convenient excuse, Kevin thought.

"We're a little anxious," Alli added, as if confiding her deepest secret.

Weatherby glanced toward the woman who was watching him from the end of the hall. "I understand how vulnerable you feel. If you'd like to make an appointment for counseling, please call me in the morning. Right now, I'm afraid I must go."

"Thanks!" she said. "You've helped already."

"We appreciate it," Kevin seconded.

They didn't speak again until they reached the parking lot. "We're such a nice young couple," she quipped. "It would be a shame if we broke up."

"If that's your way of asking permission to stay at my place longer, no chance." He spoke without a moment's consideration. That was a good thing, because otherwise he might have been tempted to give in, for the entertainment value if nothing more.

"Wrong!" Alli didn't break stride. "What I meant was, we've got this couple thing down pat, so why stop now? It must have occurred to you that Dr. Graybar and Ms. Reed aren't likely to welcome a pair of snoops with open arms."

She had a point, since Kevin's request for a meeting had already been rejected, but it went against the grain to get even further enmeshed with her. "The Reverend Weatherby appears to be a trusting soul. I suspect the doctor's office requires considerably more in the way of ID."

"Maybe not for an initial visit," she countered. "Besides, the pastor referred us. Why should they be suspicious?"

As he slid behind the wheel, Kevin searched for arguments. The fundamental point was that he worked alone, and that if he had to choose an assistant, that person wouldn't be a freelance writer with her own agenda. "I don't like it. Too sneaky, and there could be problems if we're caught."

"We could say we're afraid to have kids because one of us might have a hereditary illness," Alli went on as if she hadn't heard. Stretching her long legs, she said, "There's a history of allergies on my mother's side, but I don't suppose that counts."

"What about your father's side?" he asked ironically. "Surely you could dredge up something."

"Wanderlust. That was his disease."

As they drove along Bordeaux Way toward home, Kevin thought Alli had finished talking, until she added, "My father radiated charisma. He was charming and energetic and my mom says he swept her off her feet. When I was little, I thought he was the greatest dad in the world. And he was— until he got bored and left."

Although this was obviously a painful subject, she seemed to want to talk about it, so he decided to indulge his curiosity. "How did your parents meet?"

"Mom's a graphic artist. She was working in Denver," she said. "He was promoting a rodeo and hired her company to do the ads."

"Promoting a rodeo? He didn't ride bucking broncos or anything, did he?"

"No more than he made touchdowns when he represented football teams," Alli said. "He's a promoter, not a cowboy. At least, I assume he still is." Her husky voice caught.

"When did he leave?" Kevin prompted as he turned a corner.

"When I was eight, he ran off with a woman ten years younger than Mom. Six months later, he came back. He stayed for two years and left again when I was eleven. I never gave up hope, although I think my mom had. Then he showed up again. I begged Mom to give him one more chance."

They'd almost reached home. "But he blew it."

"This time it was me he let down," Alli said shakily. "He promised to take me to New York for my twelfth birthday, but he disappeared a few days before. I'd packed my bag with my favorite clothes and put on my new birthday dress, and I'd bragged to all my friends at school. I kept expecting him to return. I couldn't believe he'd abandoned me."

"That was cruel."

"It was necessary, not from his point of view but from mine," Alli said. "I was this horrid adolescent girl who wanted to believe it was Mom's fault he'd left, that he'd never have treated me that way if she hadn't driven him to it, but I finally had to face the truth that he didn't care about anyone but himself."

"You never saw him again?"

She shook her head. "He signed the divorce papers by mail. When we left California, where we'd been living, and moved to Texas, my mother gave our new address to her lawyer, but he never contacted us. I heard later that he'd remarried and had more kids. I hope he treated them better than he treated me."

Suddenly, Kevin understood something even though she hadn't said it. "Sometimes you can't help hoping he'll see your byline and call you."

She stared through the windshield. Kevin turned into an alley. After activating the garage opener, he swung inside next to her red sports car.

Finally, Alli spoke, "I'm an idiot to think that if he contacted me it would change anything. The truth is, he'd only hurt me again if I gave him half a chance."

"You're not an idiot," Kevin said. "In spite of everything, you haven't lost your faith in people. You even trusted the editors at the newspaper to do the right thing. That's a quality I admire. Your father's the idiot and so are they."

She leaned across the front seat and threw her arms around him. Her cheek came to rest on his shoulder, and he held her, wishing he knew how to give comfort. Then he realized he already had.

He didn't dare speak, considering that right now he cared

more about her than he had about anyone in a long time. And it scared the heck out of him.

"That's one good thing about you," she murmured.

"What's that?"

"You never give a person false hope. And you're smart enough not to talk too much." With a teary smile, she released him and scooted out of the car.

Kevin was opening his door when his cell phone rang. He flipped it open. "Vickers."

"Kevin?" said a panic-stricken voice. "It's Mary Conners. You've got to help me. I don't know what to do!"

Chapter Eight

Alli hurried into the bathroom and washed her face before any tears dared break loose. She hated to cry, and she'd come close a few minutes ago.

Over the years, she'd stopped sharing her past with friends because their well-meaning advice proved more painful than helpful. One girlfriend had urged Alli to try to locate her dad and had harped on the subject with such tenacity that she'd become an ex-girlfriend. Obviously, she'd had issues of her own.

Kevin hadn't advised Alli to do anything. He'd simply listened, so steadily and calmly that she'd opened up. His quiet encouragement had enabled her to face the long-suppressed pain.

Yesterday, when she first saw this house, it had seemed like a haven. It had become even more so today, thanks to Kevin.

What if she and Kevin could actually mean something to each other? What if she lived here for real…awakened every morning beside him…could count on his support, whatever might come…

Longing swept through Alli, so powerful that she stared at her mirrored reflection in horror. He didn't want her to stay. And she didn't want to. It was dangerous even to think such things.

She was just feeling vulnerable because she'd dredged up old memories, Alli thought sternly. After she dug out her cosmetics bag, she set to work repairing the damage to her mascara.

When she finished, she emerged and tracked Kevin to his desk. He sat frowning at his computer.

"I think I'll wait until morning to pack, if you don't mind," she said.

"Sure." He didn't take his eyes from the screen. "Things have changed. We're going to have to speed our timetable."

"Care to clue me in?" When Alli came around, she discovered he was exploring a financial site, the kind available by paid subscription.

He flexed his shoulders. "My client called to say the blackmailer is demanding she pay by Wednesday instead of Friday. He cussed at her and made threats about what would happen if she didn't comply. Scared the heck out of her."

"This guy's a monster," Alli muttered. "I wonder why he's in a hurry."

"She's afraid he's figured out that she's having him investigated," Kevin replied. "Dr. Abernathy must have told someone about my visit. Yours, too."

"You think Dr. Abernathy ratted us out to the blackmailer? I had the impression he didn't know what was going on."

"I think the shots scared him badly enough he called someone in a panic," Kevin told her. "My best guess would be his old partner. In turn, either Dr. Graybar stepped up the pressure on the victims or, if he isn't the blackmailer, he passed on the information to someone else."

"That doesn't seem to leave much doubt that the doctor's involved," she noted.

"It's suspicious but circumstantial," Kevin said. "If we jump to conclusions, we could miss important clues."

"Agreed."

Alli felt tempted to renew her suggestion about posing as a couple in order to penetrate Graybar's office, but Kevin had already turned it down. Pressuring him, she'd noticed, had a tendency to bring out his defenses. Although patience had never been her strong suit, she decided to try it in the hope that he'd come around on his own.

She took out her personal organizer. "This creep might have made the same threats to my contact. I'm going to call her."

"Good idea." Kevin brought up another screenful of data. "I'm searching Dr. Graybar's credit report for a motive."

"It does seem odd for a physician to risk his reputation by stooping so low," she admitted. "He might even endanger his medical license."

"You'd be surprised what chances people will take when they need money." Kevin didn't remove his eyes from the computer.

Alli moved into the living room so as not to disturb him. Rita Hernandez's phone rang only twice before someone answered. "Hi," said a little girl's voice. "Is this Grandma?"

"Maria! For heaven's sake!" Rita sounded almost frantic as she grabbed the phone. "Hello?"

Alli had a good idea what had alarmed her. After Alli explained who she was, she heard the woman's sigh. "Has the blackmailer contacted you again?"

"About an hour ago," she replied grimly.

"He moved up your deadline?"

"Yes! How did you know?"

"You're not the only one," Alli said.

"That scumbag! How many people is he squeezing?" Rita asked.

"I don't know." Surely he couldn't be approaching all the adoptive parents, or word would quickly reach the police. On the other hand, if the guy was desperate enough for money, he might not be thinking straight. "Tell me what he said."

He insisted on being paid by Wednesday. "He believes we can come up with twenty thousand dollars in cash! This is crazy. My husband says we should go to the cops, but I'm terrified we'll lose Maria. I haven't slept in days."

"I'm doing the best I can," Alli responded. "There's a detective assisting me." She hoped Kevin wouldn't mind being demoted to second fiddle. "We've got a few leads. Believe me, we're doing our best."

"Thank you so much for looking into this. I heard you left the paper. Is that true?"

"Yes. I'm freelancing, but I'll find a way to stop this guy no matter what it takes," Alli promised.

"If anyone can do it, you can," Rita said.

On the other end, the little girl began demanding her mother's attention, so they brought the conversation to an end. But Alli deeply appreciated the expression of confidence.

When she joined Kevin, he glanced up expectantly. She filled him in on what she'd learned. Afterward, she said, "Since this guy must be hitting a number of families, I can't figure out why someone hasn't gone to the police."

"They probably have," he replied.

Much as she wanted the blackmailer caught, Alli felt a tick of apprehension at the possibility that her exclusive story was about to become common knowledge. "I guess all the papers know about it, then."

"Probably not." Kevin leaned back. "If it were my case, I wouldn't put out a press release until I'd made an arrest or at least issued a warrant."

That made sense. However, it still increased the pressure for her to assemble the facts quickly.

With the Wednesday deadline looming, that didn't leave much time to use the story as a bargaining tool for a new job. Furthermore, even if advance word didn't reach the papers, Alli knew how vulnerable she'd be once she disclosed her investigation during an interview. There was nothing to stop an editor from assigning one of his own reporters to duplicate her work, cutting her off completely.

Until last week, she'd have trusted the integrity of her prospective employers. After her experience with Payne, she realized how naive she'd been.

"What's going through your mind?" Kevin asked. "You look like someone just stole your teddy bear."

"It occurred to me this investigation has a very short life span," Alli said. "My best bet is probably to use it to leverage my old job back, but I'm not sure I can do that."

"Would you want it back after the way they treated you?"

"Don't forget, I worked there for five years. I love my readers and I miss my friends," she explained. "The problem is, J.J. and Ned believe everything Payne tells them. Unless he screws up badly enough to open their eyes, they're never going to see things objectively."

"I can't help you there," Kevin said. "But I have found something interesting." He indicated the screen.

"Dr. Graybar owes money?"

"He was listed as partner when his uncle opened a restaurant in West L.A. that folded in less than a year. The doc cosigned a loan as well as some leases, which put him on the hook for a lot of money."

Alli whistled. "You have to feel sorry for the guy. He might have been trying to do his uncle a favor."

"Apparently, he's not very smart about finances. He tried to recoup in Las Vegas, but he had about as much luck at the tables as he did as a restaurateur," Kevin said. "He got behind on all his payments, including rent for his office and payroll taxes."

"Isn't it illegal to use payroll withholding for anything else?" she asked.

"Absolutely. The guy was not only facing bankruptcy but also possible jail time."

"So he turned to blackmail?" It certainly looked like a motive, but Alli had a hard time picturing a physician who volunteered at an orphanage turning against his own patients.

"Here's the twist. A couple of months ago, he paid everything off." Kevin tapped on the desk. "He got caught up with his bills and made the government happy."

"Where'd he find the funds?"

"Exactly what I'd like to know. I don't see any indication that he sold property or took out a consolidation loan that could account for it."

"He either begged, borrowed or stole," Alli guessed.

"Most likely he borrowed under the table," Kevin told her. "He does have considerable income, but such a poor credit rating that he wouldn't have gotten far with a legitimate lender."

"Crooks don't lend money unless it's worth their while," she pointed out. "What could he use for security? His house?"

"Already mortgaged to the hilt," he said.

"So what did he have to offer?" It was a rhetorical question. They already knew what he must have sold: the names of patients who might lose their children if the government of Costa Buena determined that they'd been adopted illegally.

Kevin appended a query of his own. "And who did he offer it to?"

"Whoever it is, I wonder why he's moving up the timetable," she said.

"Maybe he's just greedy. My client would do anything to keep her son from being taken away and he knows it."

"Whatever the reason, we've only got a couple of days before these people have to pay," she pointed out.

"If we could get inside that medical office, we might be able to determine who on staff has access to patient records." Kevin released a long breath. "Posing as a couple might not be such a bad idea."

Alli tried to keep her expression bland. "You think so?"

"We can plan our strategy tomorrow," he said. "I do have other obligations to follow up tonight."

"That works for me," she replied, and, by an immense expenditure of effort, managed not to smile.

ALLI WASN'T SURE what to expect when she accompanied Kevin to his workplace on Monday. She kept trying and failing to imagine how the prickly detective managed his take-charge mother.

They kept matters businesslike, she discovered when Heloise arrived at the sunny two-room setting a few minutes after they did. If Mrs. Vickers had any questions about what the two of them had been doing between Saturday night and Monday morning, she kept them quiet.

"You'll need to assume another identity," she advised after they explained their plan. "You can use my maiden name, McKinley, if you like."

"Good," Kevin said. "It beats Smith or Jones."

A call came in for him. While he was tied up, Alli and Heloise retreated to her desk and put their heads together.

They both enjoyed the challenge of inventing details for the newly minted husband-and-wife team of Kevin and Allison McKinley. After a little research on the Internet, they decided the couple feared having children because of a recessive blood disorder that ran in both their families.

"How many do you want?" Heloise asked.

"Children? We only need to ask for one," Alli said.

The older woman adjusted her glasses and glanced toward the closed door of her son's office. "What about in real life?"

"You mean, do I want kids?" So Heloise *had* started thinking along those lines. "I don't believe in planning my life in advance. It's better to be spontaneous."

"That's a healthy approach," she replied, not very convincingly.

They decided that the doting McKinleys had been married for three years and that, when they found a child, Alli planned to take leave from her job as a...

"Preschool teacher," Heloise suggested.

"Me? I couldn't make a convincing case if they question me. How about aerobics instructor," Alli proposed. She'd led an aerobics class once when the regular teacher fell ill.

"But you do *like* children, don't you?"

Neither of them heard the inner door open. "Mom," Kevin warned.

"Oops. The boss is back." Heloise ducked her head. "I'd better mind my own business."

"I'd appreciate your not mentioning anything about this situation to my sisters," he said. "Not about Alli being here and not about...any of it."

"I never gossip about work," his mother assured him. "We've decided you're a financial consultant. What do you think?"

"It will certainly seem natural when I ask about confidentiality," Kevin said.

Heloise printed out the profiles they'd devised. "What are you going to do if they ask for social security numbers?"

"At our first consultation? Refuse, of course," Kevin answered. "As a financial consultant, I believe in reserving that information until absolutely necessary."

"Speaking of consultations," his mother said, "let me see if I can make you an appointment today. It's possible they won't have an opening."

Kevin's expression darkened. "They have to have an opening. We're on a tight schedule."

"I'll call," Alli offered. "I can be charming when I want to."

A cleft flashed in his cheek, emphasizing the fact that he'd shaved this morning. "And you're modest, too."

"I'm not bragging," she assured him. "It's vital to my profession."

"Really?" Kevin said. "I've known a lot of reporters I wouldn't call charming."

"They're probably not very effective," Alli retorted.

Heloise handed her the phone. "Go for it." Catching her son's quelling look, she added, "If the boss agrees."

"It can't hurt to let her try," he conceded.

Alli looked up the number and dialed. The receptionist answered with a cheery, "Dr. Graybar's office."

After listening to her explanation, the woman said regretfully that they had no appointments available for at least a month. "There's incredible demand, as you can imagine, and we spend a great deal of time with each of our clients."

"I'm sure you do. The Reverend Weatherby told me Dr. Graybar has a heart of gold!" With a catch in her voice, Alli poured out a heartfelt story of weeping at night because of her desperate longing for a child, and how the pastor had lit the flame of hope the day before.

"Today's my husband's birthday." What was one more lie among so many? she wondered. "He never complains, but I can tell he's down in the dumps. It would be such a wonderful birthday present if I could give him the hope that we're finally on our way to adopting. I wish I'd learned about you sooner, but I felt yesterday that the timing wasn't a coincidence. Some things were simply meant to be."

Listening, Heloise gave her an admiring thumbs-up. Kevin shook his head in disbelief.

"I'll see what I can do. Could you excuse me a minute? I have to catch the other line." The receptionist put her on hold.

"Well?" Kevin asked. "Are you going to bake me a cake for my imaginary birthday?"

"Darling! I'll go it one better. I'm going to give you a child!" Alli joked.

The receptionist came back on the line. "I don't believe this! That call was to cancel an appointment at four o'clock this afternoon. Could you and your husband make it in then?"

"You bet. See you at four." After completing the arrangements, Alli hung up and filled in her audience.

"You're scary," Kevin said. "You fib like a pro, and you think on your feet."

"Reporters have to do that," his mother advised. "They're always going undercover, right?"

"Actually not," Alli said. "Normally, I'm up front with people."

"You don't badger them about 'the public's right to know?'" Kevin teased.

She sniffed. "I never use that cliché."

"You manage to be pushy enough without it," he said. After explaining to Heloise that they'd met when he worked at the PD, he added, "I respected the way you did your job, but I used to think you were a royal pain."

"What a coincidence," Alli replied sweetly. "That's what I always said about you."

Kevin glanced at his watch. "I've got work to do. Why don't we meet after lunch to rehearse our aliases."

"Okay."

He vanished into his inner sanctum. While Heloise tackled paperwork, Alli picked up a copy of the morning paper folded on the secretary's desk. She hadn't had time to scan it at Kevin's.

A photograph of Payne Jacobson leaped out from page one. Drive-by Shooting Wounds Reporter, read the headline.

Despite her dislike of Payne, Alli felt a twist of concern. On closer inspection, however, the damage didn't look bad.

A bandage wrapped around one arm, Payne posed beside the smashed rear windshield of his car. One eye had taken on a discolored pouchiness, presumably where she'd punched him two days ago. This seemed to be his week to take it in the chops, Alli thought.

According to the article, Payne had been backing out of the driveway at his uncle's house—she hadn't realized until now that he lived with Ned—when he'd heard a crack. A moment later, he'd experienced a stinging sensation along his arm and noticed a trickle of blood.

Not until he got out to inspect the damage had he found the bullet hole in the glass. The article went on to explain that the police were investigating reports of a gray or blue van sighted in the area at the time of the shooting.

"My fearless pursuit of the truth must have offended some slime bag," Payne was quoted as saying. "From now on, I'll be staying with friends and taking other routes to work. So whoever did this can go crawl back into a hole."

Alli was sorry he'd been hurt. Still, what an irony that the exposé had most likely triggered the attack. Had he not stolen it she might have been the target.

When Kevin emerged from his office, she handed him the section. While he read the article, she reflected that that hadn't merely been a warning shot. Payne could have been killed. Or she could have, and the danger hadn't necessarily disappeared just because they'd turned their sights elsewhere.

She needed to stay hidden for at least a few more days. She couldn't mention it in front of his mother, though, since Heloise didn't know about their rooming arrangement.

Besides, she'd already decided that pressuring Kevin generally backfired. Tonight, if he didn't change his mind, she'd have to find somewhere else to camp out.

He finished the article. "That series is a hot potato."

"Well, it's Payne's hot potato now," she said. "If you'll excuse me, I'm going to go work on my new article." Sensitive to Heloise's presence, she avoided specifying that she was returning to his place. She even wrote down her cell-phone number for the secretary.

"When will you be back?" Kevin asked.

"Around two. That should give us a chance to practice."

He frowned. "There's no guarantee those guys won't take a shot at you, too."

"I'm on foot at the moment," she noted. "This is southern California. They'll never think to look for me on a sidewalk."

Kevin's gaze darkened. Before he could offer to do something needlessly protective, such as offer to drive her, she called out, "See you!" and hurried off.

A brisk walk carried her the half mile or so to his house, where she used the key she'd borrowed earlier, punched in the security code and fired up Kevin's laptop. On the Web, the report of the injured reporter had received extensive coverage, along with the fact that he'd been writing about Mayor Le-Mott. Klaus would really hate that, she thought in satisfaction.

Her good mood faded as she considered that Payne was gaining recognition as a crusading hero journalist. The guy had incredible luck. She wondered whether he sacrificed small animals to pagan gods.

Grimly, she made another search for job openings and printed out the few possibilities. Feeling a bit down, she grabbed a bite to eat and walked back to meet Kevin for their practice session.

With Heloise's help, they reviewed their fictional background and decided what information they should try to pry from Ms. Reed. Finally, the time came to leave.

"Well, Mrs. McKinley?" Kevin said. "Ready to go search out the child of our dreams?"

She slipped her arm through his. "Sweetheart, I'm going to make you the happiest man on earth."

Heloise made a gagging noise at the computer. But she was smiling.

Chapter Nine

Two pregnant women were skimming magazines in the waiting room as Kevin held the door for Alli. He registered the trendy color scheme and a hand-painted mural of babies at play.

Although he knew the place hid dark secrets, he was glad to take Alli inside. The news about Payne being shot troubled him. He respected her courage in refusing to cower; still, on the short drive to Graybar's office, he'd checked his mirrors frequently as a precaution.

They hadn't been followed. Kevin knew enough to spot all but the most expert surveillance.

They signed in at the reception desk. He wished he could have brought some work with him. However, he hadn't wanted to display anything that might give away his true occupation.

As it turned out, they didn't have a long wait. About five minutes later, a nurse appeared in the doorway. "Mr. and Mrs. McKinley? Ms. Reed will see you now."

Inside, the hallway forked. To the right lay a gray-carpeted corridor flanked by what appeared to be examination rooms.

The left branch might have belonged in a different building. A patterned, light-colored carpet led past a couple of plush offices to a conference room supplied with a coffee-maker and comfortable seats around a table.

The walls featured newspaper clippings about the orphanage in Costa Buena. There were also several framed photographs of Dr. Graybar, whom Kevin recognized from an online picture. The man had an intelligent face topped by thick black hair silvering at the temples.

A well-dressed, fortyish woman joined them almost immediately. "Hi, I'm Binnie Reed," she said, shaking hands. "Dr. Graybar's seeing patients, but he'll meet you later. In the meantime, let's go over some facts to help me understand how we can help you."

"Oh, thank you!" Alli gushed. "We're thrilled to be here. Did the receptionist mention it's my husband's birthday?"

"Congratulations." The counselor gave them a perfunctory smile. "Would you like some coffee? No? Well, let's talk about Kevin and Allison McKinley and how to make your family complete."

She requested their medical history, which Alli described to her apparent satisfaction. Binnie also asked if they'd considered counseling to deal with the trauma of being unable to have their own genetic offspring. Alli sidestepped that one with a mention of the pastor and his excellent counseling skills.

Ms. Reed described the home study required of all adoptive parents. "These kids deserve stable, loving homes," she told them. "I'm happy to say that our children have done wonderfully."

"How many have you placed?" Alli inquired.

Kevin, too, wanted very much to find out how many families might be vulnerable to a shakedown. The only answer they received, however, was, "We've been making matches for about six years. The demand keeps increasing, but I can't give you an exact count."

There had to be hundreds, he thought. "Can you give us an idea of the costs involved?"

"That depends on several factors." She cited the need to visit Central America, the necessity of hiring an attorney and the payment to the orphanage. "Most of our clients find their expenses range between ten and twenty thousand dollars," she concluded.

That was enough to have tapped out many people's life savings, perhaps even put them into debt. How could the black-mailer believe these parents had another twenty thousand lying around? Probably he figured if he squeezed hard enough, they'd cough it up somehow. And he might be right.

Kevin wondered how much Binnie knew about what was going on. He hadn't ruled out the possibility that she might be the blackmailer. Since the caller used a voice scrambler, the perpetrator could be a woman as easily as a man.

"Would you like to see pictures of our kids?" When they nodded, the counselor produced a photo album from a desk drawer.

Shot after shot showed adorable infants, toddlers and young children laughing at the camera and playing with their new parents. Joy radiated from them. Even Alli seemed to soften.

As he examined the images, Kevin realized that he'd always taken for granted the ability to have children if and when he was ready. Like Tara and Ralph, these parents had probably made the same assumption, then endured stages of disbelief and desperation when they discovered they couldn't reproduce the old-fashioned way. Or the new-fashioned way, either, since for them fertility treatments apparently hadn't worked.

What if he and Alli weren't pretending? What if the only way he could ever become a parent was through this agency?

For the first time, he truly identified with Mary Conners. That made him even angrier at whoever had threatened her.

"That woman looks familiar." Alli indicated one of the mothers. "Isn't she Vice-Mayor Rodale's daughter?"

"I'm sorry. I'm not allowed to identify individuals," Binnie replied.

That seemed like a good opening to raise their questions about privacy. "I presume you have permission to show these people's photos, don't you?" Kevin said. "As a financial consultant, I'm very concerned about confidentiality."

"Yes, certainly. We guard our records closely," she told him.

"Who would have access to them?" Alli put in.

"Nobody's ever asked me that before." Binnie didn't seem disturbed, Kevin noted. "In Costa Buena, I presume the orphanage discloses its records to local authorities."

"And on this end?" he prompted.

"We don't release our records to anyone unless we're required to by law," she said. "For adoption purposes, we may give information to immigration authorities and the courts. But we only display photos like these if the parents agree in advance."

Kevin decided to take a flier. "What about Dr. Graybar's business partner? Wouldn't he have access?"

"He doesn't have a partner since Dr. Abernathy retired," she explained. "However, as you seem concerned, maybe you should speak directly with the doctor."

"Sure," he said.

"Let me go see if he's available." Leaving the album on the desk, Binnie exited.

Kevin waited a beat to make sure she wouldn't overhear. "Is there some special significance to the vice-mayor's daughter having adopted?" he asked.

"I'm not sure." Rising to her feet, Alli approached one of the framed pictures on the wall. "Did you notice this?"

"That's Dr. Graybar receiving an award." At this angle, he couldn't see the people's faces very well, although he thought he recognized two city council members.

"The man standing next to him is Mayor LeMott," she informed him.

He took a closer look at the thin, mustachioed man. "So it is."

"That's Cathy Rodale on his other side," she said. "She was in line to become mayor before LeMott got elected to the council." She didn't need to explain that the members rotated that honor among themselves for two-year terms, because Kevin had learned that fact when he'd worked at the police department. "I can't understand why she stepped aside unless she'd been threatened or talked into some kind of deal. She never shrank from the spotlight before."

"You're mixing apples and oranges. I don't see what Le-

Mott has to do with—" He stopped in midsentence as the connection hit him. "He was involved in loan-sharking."

"Exactly. If anyone could provide a large sum of money, it's him."

The door opened. In came Binnie with a dark-haired man instantly recognizable from his pictures.

Kevin rose to shake hands while the counselor made introductions. The doctor, who stood about an inch taller than him, had a firm grip and regular features arranged in a sympathetic expression. Lines on his forehead revealed an underlying tension.

"I understand you have some questions about patient confidentiality," he said.

"We wondered who would have access to our records and financial data," Kevin confirmed.

"He was asking whether you have a business partner." Binnie sounded puzzled. "I didn't think Dr. Abernathy was involved anymore, but I couldn't give them a definitive answer."

"He's not. If another doctor were to join my practice, he or she would have access to the files, but naturally, I'd screen him or her carefully in advance," Graybar said. "Is that what you wanted to know?"

Alli indicated the picture. "Congratulations on your award. Are you a good friend of the mayor's?"

Binnie looked even more confused.

"What is it you two really want to know?" the physician asked.

"We're interested in adopting," Alli said brightly. "It seems we'll be in good company. I recognized the vice-mayor's daughter among your satisfied customers."

"You have friends in high places," Kevin added. "That's a tribute to your integrity."

Apparently, their comments failed to reassure him. "I need to see some ID," Dr. Graybar said.

"I'm sorry? What am I missing here?" asked Ms. Reed.

Kevin saw no purpose in continuing their pretense. Also, he didn't want to lose the chance to startle their quarry into revealing more than he intended. "We understand the El Centro Orphanage is under investigation for allegations of baby selling," he said. "Is that true?"

"What?" The counselor stared as if he'd grown two heads.

"There's been a mix-up regarding record keeping," Dr. Graybar responded. "I talked to the director of the orphanage last week and he assured me it would all be straightened out soon."

"I didn't know that," Binnie remarked to no one in particular.

"Some of the families have received blackmail demands," Alli added. "Twenty thousand dollars or they'll be reported to the authorities and could lose their children. Did you know that?"

Dr. Graybar blanched. Kevin couldn't tell whether he was registering surprise at the news or shock at being confronted.

"That's ridiculous!" Binnie said. "Who are you people?"

"Busybodies," the doctor told her. "Don't worry, they're not police. I know who they are." Dr. Abernathy must have alerted him, Kevin thought.

"What do you mean, they're not police? What do the police have to do with us?" the counselor asked.

"Binnie, would you step outside for a moment? I want to talk to our guests alone." The doctor's tone made it clear this was not optional.

"Well…certainly."

He barely waited until she'd gone. "You two are trespassing and violating my privacy, not to mention that of our clients." Graybar indicated the album. "If you reveal anything you've learned here, I'll see you in court."

Alli showed no sign of being intimidated. "We know at least two families that have received extortion demands. We're not the ones who have to worry about ending up in court."

"If someone's making trouble, the problem must have originated in Costa Buena," the man replied. "We have nothing to hide here."

"I should think you'd be eager to stop whoever's doing this," Kevin interjected.

"If you were serious about your allegations, you'd have gone to the police," Graybar snapped.

"The least you could do is hear us out!" Alli countered.

"I'm asking you to leave."

They'd learned as much as they were likely to and it seemed counterproductive to antagonize Dr. Graybar more than necessary. There was always a chance that, if he hadn't known about the blackmail, he might reconsider his position upon reflection.

"We're done here," Kevin said. "But if you're concerned about your clients, Doc, you ought to recognize that we're on the same side."

He thought Alli might argue further, but for once she took her cue from him. They walked out, passing a clearly distressed Binnie Reed in the corridor. In the front room, the receptionist smiled at them. "Did you want to schedule another appointment?"

"No, thank you," Kevin replied.

They took the stairs down two flights rather than waiting for the elevator. "That man ticks me off!" Alli said. "He acts as if we're the enemy."

"You think it's LeMott, don't you?" Kevin asked. "You think he's the guy who loaned Dr. Graybar the money."

"It sounds like the kind of thing he might do. He must have figured he could turn a considerable profit."

Kevin shook his head. "Extortion is a risky business, and LeMott has too much to lose. It doesn't make sense."

Alli couldn't disagree. All the same, the photograph linking the mayor and the doctor aroused strong suspicions.

When they emerged into the dwindling early-evening light from the bottom floor, he realized it was after five o'clock. His mother should have locked up the office by now, and he was in no mood to work on any other cases.

"We need to brainstorm," he said. "I'm not sure right now what our next step should be." The obvious choice, to make the police aware of what they'd learned, would break his promise to Mary.

"I've got an idea," Alli said as they reached his car.

"Let's hear it."

"They have early-bird specials on Mondays at the Sailor's Retreat," she explained, citing a popular waterfront restaurant. "There's a band, too."

"And we should do this because…?" He left the question unfinished.

"Dancing inspires me," Alli responded. "It clears my mind."

Kevin put the car into gear. "Are you joking? We need to sit down and review our notes."

"Correction. We need to sway in each other's arms and trust our subconscious minds to figure things out for us."

She had to be either teasing him or working some angle. "Is this your way of manipulating me into letting you stay at my house?" he demanded.

"You mean as opposed to sending me back to an apartment where two thugs may be watching for me? No, wait. Forget I said that."

He ought to be glad she was easing off, but curiosity got the better of him. "It isn't like you to back down."

"You never do what anyone pressures you to," she said. "I discovered that if I don't say anything, sometimes you come around on your own."

"Seriously?"

"It worked with my suggestion of posing as a couple," Alli said. "If I'd pressed the point, you'd never have agreed."

"Sure I would have." He didn't like the idea that she'd discovered a way to manipulate him "So you're not going to make an issue of staying at my house?"

"It wouldn't do me any good, right?"

"Right."

"Okay, I won't. I'll pack my things after dinner."

He grinned. "And I'm pleased to know that you won't be nagging me about going dancing, because you know that wouldn't work, either."

"Unfair!"

"What is?"

"You're using my own tactics against me," she protested.

"Nobody forced you to fess up."

Her eyes narrowed, but she didn't argue. They were half-way home when she said, "Okay."

"Okay what?"

"I won't nag you about going dancing."

"Great."

It *was* great. Fantastic. He'd won the right to spend the evening undisturbed rather than being dragged to some fancy restaurant.

An image flashed through Kevin's mind of a Sailor's Retreat ad that ran occasionally in the paper. Among the Monday-night dinner specials, he'd noticed the grilled-salmon dinner, which came with baked potato, fresh salad and a large slab of strawberry pie.

This was foolish. He had plenty of food in the refrigerator. So what if he'd already made too many meals of it?

For the rest of the short drive, Kevin focused on his impressions of Dr. Graybar and Binnie Reed. The counselor had seemed staggered to hear about the blackmail. Although the doctor had been harder to read, Kevin didn't have the impression he'd sold out his patients. Still, he couldn't be sure.

Maybe Alli was right. If he stopped trying to force his brain to come up with a solution, it might do the job unaided.

That didn't mean he had to go dancing. Stubbornly, he kept silent as they arrived home.

When he opened the fridge door, the leftovers didn't look any more appealing than they had a day earlier. Kevin was trying to decide what to defrost when Alli, who'd disappeared briefly, wafted into the kitchen wearing a slinky red chemise over flowing black pants.

"Going somewhere?" he grumbled.

"Just because you don't feel like dancing doesn't mean I can't go," she said.

"Alone?"

"I called Larry but he isn't home." She brushed back a tendril of chestnut hair. She'd put it up in a style that emphasized the slenderness of her neck. "I never have trouble finding a dance partner."

Kevin closed the refrigerator. "I thought we were going to discuss what happened this afternoon and map out a course for tomorrow."

She made a helpless gesture. "My brain is clogged. Not one single idea is breaking through. I'm going to clear it out using centrifugal force."

"As in dancing?" he said. "You're worse than a nag. You give a man no peace."

"You don't have to come." Alli stretched lazily, which had the effect of pressing her breasts against the thin fabric of the chemise. She wasn't wearing a bra, Kevin realized with a tingle of fascination. "If you're more comfortable at home, you should stay."

Of course he functioned best in his own territory. What man didn't? A little relaxation in front of the TV ought to help him unwind.

Kevin had a sudden image of his father ensconced in the easy chair in the family room, the remote control on one side and a bag of chips on the other. Was that what he was turning into? Middle-aged at thirty-four?

A beautiful woman stood in front of him, provocatively dressed and ready for action. Plus, the meal included strawberry pie.

"If I agree to go…" he began.

"I won't rub it in," she promised.

"No clasping your hands overhead and running a victory lap?"

"Not where you can see it." She moved forward and rested her hands on his shoulders, swaying to music he couldn't hear. "You'll be glad you came."

Her sensuous movements and the swell of her breasts beneath the fabric were bringing out an achingly pleasurable male response. Kevin knew they were playing with fire. All the more reason to remove themselves to the safety of a restaurant, he reflected.

"Take a jacket," he advised, easing away. "It turns cool in the evening."

"Not with you around," she teased. "Oh, all right. But I don't promise to wear it."

As he shrugged into his sports coat, Kevin acknowledged that, once again, she'd won without pressuring him. The curious part was that he didn't feel as if he'd lost anything.

Not yet, anyway.

Chapter Ten

They arrived a short time later at Sailor's Retreat on Pacific Coast Highway. Through a gap between buildings, Alli could see Serene Harbor, where a scattering of sailboats cruised through the dusk toward their moorings.

As she inhaled the salt air, her spirits lifted. She hadn't been kidding about the confusion in her brain.

Visiting the doctor's office with Kevin had proven an unsettling experience. Never having paid much attention to babies before, she'd been surprised by her reaction to the scrapbook. Suddenly, they'd become more than cute little figures. Through their parents' eyes, she'd seen them as real people bursting with dreams and discoveries.

She'd experienced the wonder of a baby learning to talk—a little girl discovering the joy of books on her mother's lap—a boy attending a baseball game with his father. She'd glimpsed how it might feel to share the magic of parenthood.

Had this happened because she was playing the role of would-be mother? Or had the presence of a virile male in the guise of her pretend husband stimulated some previously inactive hormonal instinct?

Her turbulent thoughts made Alli uncomfortable. She wanted to put them behind her and become her happily childfree self again.

A bit of physical exertion on the dance floor should do the trick. And if her brief flirtation with Kevin in the kitchen was any sign, it might activate some other urges that would completely take her mind off babies.

"Would you care for a table on the deck?" asked the hostess, arriving with a couple of menus beneath her arm. The tables appeared to be solidly filled, Alli realized.

"We were planning on dancing," she said.

"The band doesn't start for forty-five minutes," the hostess explained. "There's no one out there and you'll be able to hear the music when it starts. But you can wait for a seat in here if you prefer."

Alli glanced at Kevin. "Is outside okay with you?"

"Sure," he answered. "I'd rather not have to wait."

And it might be romantic, Alli thought. She decided not to say so.

When they emerged onto a wooden terrace, her soul expanded to greet the vista. Overhead, magenta and cobalt streaked the darkening sky. Across the bay, on a curving spit of land, house lights pricked the deep blue.

"What a stunning view." She pulled on her wrap, glad that she'd brought it.

"I'll send a waitress right out." Leaving their menus, the hostess departed.

"I forgot how refreshing it is to break my routine," Kevin admitted.

"Me, too," Alli said.

"I can't see you ever landing in a rut. You're too spontaneous."

"Spontaneity can be a rut in its own way," she admitted.

"How's that?" Opposite her, an overhanging lamp bathed Kevin in its glow.

She remembered their previous conversation about her father. "It can become an excuse for running away."

"From men?"

"Or from myself." She shook her head. "I don't know why I said that."

"Which part of yourself are you running from?" he pursued.

The part that wanted to drown in his dark gaze, Alli mused.

The part that wanted to lean into his shoulder and dream about having babies with him. The part that longed for someone she could depend on.

Until, at some level, he let her down.

She knew Kevin wasn't a jerk like her father. He would never disappear and leave his wife and child to fend for themselves. But there was more than one way to abandon a person.

Kevin maintained a shield around him that he only lowered for brief spans. In those moments, she glimpsed a warmth and kindness that almost beguiled her into hoping for more.

But he'd made it clear he had no desire to give her any more. She'd be a fool, and unfair, to expect it. The better she got to know Kevin, the more she understood that he was fundamentally a loner.

It was the fatal flaw that precluded any future they might make together. If someday Alli loved a man without reservation, the little girl inside had to know he would always be there for her.

Maybe she was foolish to think she even wanted to trust a guy that much. In many ways, she was a loner, too.

He'd asked what she was running away from, she remembered. "At the moment, I'm running from impending starvation." She flipped open the menu and examined the column of specials. "I'll have the ginger-grilled mahimahi. I'm paying for my own meal, by the way."

"That's not necessary. I'm treating," Kevin said.

"No, thanks. Dining out was my suggestion. If I weren't unemployed, I'd pay for yours, too."

"Generous of you to say so." He watched her with a mischievous expression.

She chuckled. "I know. Isn't it nice the way I made that offer so I don't have to actually do it?"

His face crinkled with shared amusement. And something more—something close to tenderness.

Whatever was going on tonight had to be the result of the moon rising over the bay and the sound of water lapping against the deck, Alli thought. They sat cocooned in a private world.

She realized she'd been with Kevin for almost three solid days. She couldn't remember spending this much time in proximity to a guy. Maybe she ought to be tired of him by now, but she wasn't.

A waitress came out to take their drink order. Since they were both hungry, they ordered their dinners as well.

After she left, Kevin said, "Are we allowed to discuss our investigation or does that run counter to your method of clearing the mind?"

Alli glanced at her watch. "We can review our impressions for about five minutes. Then we have to stop and let everything sink in."

"That makes sense to me, weird as it is. Which means that you're either smarter than I gave you credit for, or I'm losing my grip."

"It means you're loosening up," she said. "You're lucky I don't charge for the therapy."

From a distance, she heard the faint pulse of recorded music and pinpointed the source as a yacht at anchor. Lights blazed and Alli saw figures moving on deck. Apparently she wasn't the only one interested in dancing tonight.

Kevin's gaze flicked toward the yacht and returned to her. "So what did you make of Dr. Graybar?"

"I don't believe he's blackmailing the patients. Even though he may have financial problems, I can't picture him taking such a crude approach."

"Neither can I," Kevin agreed. "He'd have been better off declaring bankruptcy."

"Unless he owes money to a mobster," she noted.

"I'd believe almost anything about Klaus LeMott," he said. "But why loan somebody a huge sum and then try to recoup it by breaking the law? If my guess is right, that loan approached a million dollars. At twenty thousand a pop, he'd have to rip off a huge number of families just to break even. He's too smart to do that."

"Looks like we've hit a dead end," Alli concluded.

The waitress brought their drinks and salads. As they ate,

sharing a comfortable silence, darkness fell. No other couples joined them on the deck, so they had the night and the bay to themselves.

When Kevin's leg brushed hers beneath the table, Alli gave it a playful rub before shifting her ankle away. His edgy smile made her breath catch.

"Playing with fire?" he asked.

"Testing your self-control," she retorted.

"What about *your* self-control?"

"I don't have any."

He regarded her skeptically. "I'm beginning to suspect you can muster plenty of self-control when you need to."

He was right on that score. Alli liked to come across as a free spirit, but in reality she had a fierce survival instinct.

"Let's talk about something else, something we never get a chance to discuss because we're so busy running around," she suggested. "What's your favorite kind of movie?"

"Action adventure," he said. "And science fiction. How about you?"

"Thrillers with a love story where the heroine's as smart as the hero." Honesty forced her to add, "And romantic comedies with gloriously happy endings."

"As long as they're really funny?" he put in.

"Yes. And original and surprising."

They began naming specific films and debated their merits. By the time they had moved on to music, dinner arrived. Her mahimahi tasted as good as it looked.

"I'd better hurry and find another job so I can afford to eat this way more often," Alli said.

"What's your ideal position?" Kevin asked. "Have you ever considered television news? You've got the looks for it." He spoke so matter-of-factly it almost didn't sound like a compliment.

Alli knew her height and bone structure suited the camera, so she didn't bother to protest. She'd never considered newscasting as a profession, however.

"TV news is about creating an image, writing snappy

sound bites and filling up airtime. While there are some terrific correspondents, mostly you have to make mountains out of molehills to compete with the other earnest talking heads," she said. "The money's great, but the work would suck the soul out of me."

"What do you like about reporting?" he said. "I mean, other than righting the wrongs of the world. Is it a power trip? An adventure?"

"I enjoy listening to people and figuring out what makes them tick." She thought for a beat before adding, "And, truthfully, I get an adrenaline rush when I'm on the trail of something hot. Plus, organizing a story presents a real challenge. I enjoy the writing for its own sake."

"Don't you want to be rich and famous?" Kevin murmured with a trace of irony.

Alli rested her chin on her palm. "I used to want to work for a big-city paper where I could see my name in lights, so to speak, but I'm not sure that would appeal to me anymore."

"You always struck me as ambitious," he said.

"I was," Alli agreed.

"What changed?"

"I got fired."

"You mean on Thursday?"

She nodded. "It's made me take another look at who I am. You know what? I care about this community. I love the way people call and e-mail, and talk as if they know me because they've read my writing for so long. I like being able to cover little stuff as well as big stuff, to meet merchants with offbeat shops and students who win awards. For a while, I get to be part of their lives."

Alli hadn't understood the depth of her feelings until she described them to Kevin. But this was who she'd become, a member of a community, which made it even more painful that a newcomer like J.J. had cast her out.

"It's like you're part of a family," Kevin summarized. "I never thought about a reporter that way but I can see that it's true, in your case at least."

"J.J. hasn't been in Serene Beach long enough to understand," she said. "I'm not sure he's been at any paper long enough. He's famous for arriving, spending a couple of years reshaping the package, and then moving on."

"Any chance of him changing his mind?" Kevin asked. "I know you've said he buys into that kid's flashy persona, but surely he's got to recognize the truth sooner or later."

"Unfortunately, it may be much later." Alli thought about Payne's talent for insinuating himself into the editors' good graces. On the other hand, nobody got lucky forever. "I'm not giving up, but if this adoption story doesn't do the trick, I'll have to regroup."

"It's hard to regroup alone," he said.

Dance music pulsated from within the restaurant as the band got off to a rocking start. Enough serious talk, Alli decided. "I'm not alone," she said. "I'm with you and I intend to take advantage of it."

He grinned. "You're going to take advantage of me? Can I help?"

Standing up, she reached for his hand. "Come on, big guy."

"I haven't had my dessert yet." He grinned, but he rose obediently to his feet. "You're a slave driver."

She rested her arms atop his shoulders and regarded him directly. "Dance with me, handsome."

His hands closed around her waist. "I'd rather do this first." His mouth found hers with a heat and moisture full of promise.

Alli couldn't resist the pleasure spreading within her. Through Kevin's coat and slacks, her body traced the bulge of muscles as her tongue played a taunting game with his. Her core tightened with desire as his hand gripped her derriere, bringing her close enough to tease his arousal.

The scrape of the door restored her to reality. "I can come back later," said the waitress, who'd brought two pieces of strawberry pie.

"You'll leave those here, if you know what's good for you," Kevin growled, stepping away but holding on to Alli's arm.

"Yes, sir!" Smiling, the waitress scooted the plates onto their table and made her escape.

"You don't have a romantic bone in your body," Alli challenged as the door swung shut. "You could at least try to act as if you preferred me to the pie."

"I didn't drop you on the ground and lunge for it, did I?" he said. "Can I help it if I have a typical guy reaction to dessert?"

"Besides which, you figure we can always continue this later, right?"

His dark eyes glinted with humor. "I've been around women long enough to know that if I said any such thing, my life would be forfeit."

"Not your life, but possibly the use of your limbs." Much as Alli hated to back down, however, the scent of glazed strawberries *was* hard to resist. "I suppose I ought to give in just to be a good sport."

"You think I didn't notice you sniffing the breeze?" Kevin retorted.

Their eyes met. By unspoken mutual consent, they bolted to their seats and dug into the strawberries.

In no time, the pie disappeared. Then, hearing the band in full swing, they headed for the dance floor.

Alli missed the excitement of their kiss, but this was, after all, a semipublic place. Besides, she'd already assessed the danger of getting involved with Kevin and decided it didn't merit the risk, no matter how appealing he seemed.

As they entered, the music shifted to a slower piece. Alli had been looking forward to a workout, but when her companion held out his arms, she nestled into them with a sense of belonging.

Kevin's gentle strength surrounded her. Closing her eyes, she buried her face in his neck and let the song carry them once again into their private world.

The two of them moved with an instinctive rapport. *I like this man,* she thought as he whirled her between two other couples.

She liked the way he hummed along with the music, sending a vibration rumbling into her. She liked the way they could relax and put their joking manners aside. She liked his scent—civilized and elegant with a hint of musk.

She knew it was risky to think about Kevin this way. But if you never took chances, what was the fun of living?

"Hey! Wow! Imagine running into you two!" exclaimed a male voice.

Go away, she thought fiercely.

"Hello. Harry, isn't it?" Kevin responded with forced politeness.

"Larry," corrected the newcomer. "You know Adrienne, don't you?"

"For years."

Larry had a date with Adrienne? Matters were certainly progressing. Alli raised her head.

Two perky faces regarded her, Larry's freckled and friendly, his date's cheerful and inquisitive. Although she was pleased to see them together, Alli wished he hadn't picked such an inconvenient moment to show up.

There might still be hope. "Great to see you both," she said. "We wouldn't dream of interrupting your date."

"No problem!" Adrienne sang out.

"I've got a lot to tell you." It didn't seem to occur to Larry that standing in the middle of the floor forced other dancers to dodge around them. "Where are you sitting?"

With a sinking feeling, Alli muttered, "Outside."

"Great idea!" Larry waved toward one of the indoor tables. "We'll retrieve our drinks and join you."

After they had moved out of earshot, she whispered, "I don't suppose there's any subtle way to get rid of them."

"Not one that comes to mind." Kevin's arm tightened around her waist. "It's too bad we have to quit now. I was starting to get some insights into Dr. Graybar's operation, just as you promised."

"You were thinking about Dr. Graybar?" she demanded.

"Wasn't that the idea?" Before she could sputter a reply, he pulled her close and cradled her against him.

He'd been joking, she realized, embarrassed at having fallen for it, until the music and his nearness swept away all other thoughts. They finished the number at their leisure while the other couple waited beside the dance floor with drinks in hand.

"That's a great song, isn't it?" Larry said as the four of them trooped outside. He and Adrienne seemed perfectly content to have waited.

"It's one of my favorites," his date said. "I like the jazz influence."

The two of them radiated contentment. This didn't seem like a first date, so she presumed they'd spent most of Sunday together.

Alli remembered Betsy telling her that Adrienne was a kindergarten teacher who'd once dreamed of becoming a stand-up comic but had discovered her jokes were too tame. Her five-year-old audience turned out to be much more appreciative than grown-ups.

She and Larry certainly seemed to be the right audiences for each other. Before he'd met Adrienne, Alli had never seen him this comfortable with a woman other than a casual friend.

"What did you want to tell me?" she asked as they reached the table, where the waitress had cleared their plates.

Kevin switched her drink to his side. Taking a hint, Alli sank down beside him.

"Things are pretty intense at work," Larry said. "The police chief came by in person to talk to J.J. He's bent out of shape because Payne implied he's not doing his job. Apparently, racketeering investigations aren't the police department's jurisdiction."

"We know," Kevin said.

"Also, the scuttlebutt is that LeMott's attorney called to demand a retraction," Larry went on. "I think the editors turned that one over to the paper's attorney."

"How's Payne handling the pressure?" Alli inquired.

"He claims he's got evidence to back up his speculations," the photographer replied. "Do you suppose that's true?"

"He doesn't even have speculations to back up his speculations," Alli told him. "He stole those from me, remember?"

An Important Message
from the Editors

Dear Reader,

If you'd enjoy reading romance novels with larger print that's easier on your eyes, let us send you *TWO FREE HARLEQUIN SUPERROMANCE®* NOVELS in our *NEW LARGER-PRINT EDITION*. These books are complete and unabridged, but the type is set about 25% bigger to make it easier to read. Look inside for an actual-size sample.

By the way, you'll also get a surprise gift with your two free books!

Pam Powers

Peel off Seal and

Place Inside...

THE RIGHT WOMAN

she'd thought she was fine. It took Daniel's words and Brooke's question to make her realize she was far from a full recovery.

She'd made a start with her sister's help and she intended to go forward now. Sarah felt as if she'd been living in a darkened room and someone had suddenly opened a door, letting in the fresh air and sunshine. She could feel its warmth slowly seeping into the coldest part of her. The feeling was liberating. She realized it was only a small step and she had a long way to go, but she was ready to face life again with Serena and her family behind her.

All too soon, they were saying goodbye and Sarah experienced a moment of sadness for all the years she and Serena had missed. But they had each other now and that's what

She held

Printed in the U.S.A.
Publisher acknowledges the copyright holder of the excerpt from this individual work as follows:
THE RIGHT WOMAN Copyright © 2004 by Linda Warren. All rights reserved.
® and TM are trademarks owned and used by the trademark owner and/or its licensee.

YOURS FREE!
You'll get a great mystery gift with your two free larger-print books!

GET TWO FREE LARGER-PRINT BOOKS!

YES! Please send me two free Harlequin Superromance® novels in the larger-print edition, and my free mystery gift, too. I understand that I am under no obligation to purchase anything, as explained on the back of this insert.

PLACE FREE GIFTS SEAL HERE

139 HDL D7VV   339 HDL D7VW

FIRST NAME   LAST NAME

ADDRESS

APT.#   CITY

STATE/PROV.   ZIP/POSTAL CODE

Are you a current Harlequin Superromance® subscriber and want to receive the larger-print edition?
Call 1-800-221-5011 today!

◀ **DETACH AND MAIL CARD TODAY!** ◀

(H-SLPA-07/05) © 2004 Harlequin Enterprises Ltd.

The Harlequin Reader Service™ — Here's How It Works:

Accepting your 2 free Harlequin Superromance® books and gift places you under no obligation to buy anything. You may keep the books and gift and return the shipping statement marked "cancel." If you do not cancel, about a month later we'll send you 6 additional Harlequin Superromance larger-print books and bill you just $4.94 each in the U.S., or $5.49 each in Canada, plus 25¢ shipping & handling per book and applicable taxes if any.* That's the complete price and — compared to cover prices of $5.75 each in the U.S. and $6.75 each in Canada — it's quite a bargain! You may cancel at any time, but if you choose to continue, every month we'll send you 6 more books, which you may either purchase at the discount price or return to us and cancel your subscription.

*Terms and prices subject to change without notice. Sales tax applicable in N.Y. Canadian residents will be charged applicable provincial taxes and GST.

If offer card is missing write to: Harlequin Reader Service, 3010 Walden Ave., P.O. Box 1867, Buffalo, NY 14240-1867

BUSINESS REPLY MAIL
FIRST-CLASS MAIL   PERMIT NO. 717-003   BUFFALO, NY

POSTAGE WILL BE PAID BY ADDRESSEE

HARLEQUIN READER SERVICE
3010 WALDEN AVE
PO BOX 1867
BUFFALO NY 14240-9952

NO POSTAGE
NECESSARY
IF MAILED
IN THE
UNITED STATES

"Oh, right."

"He's such a jerk!" Adrienne sympathized.

"J.J. might be starting to wonder what he's gotten into," Larry confided. "Madge heard him asking Payne when he conducted the interview with the mayor that he keeps quoting from. LeMott's attorney denied they'd ever spoken."

The newsroom gossip mill was obviously running full speed. "What did Payne answer?" Alli asked.

"According to Madge, he claimed he ran into LeMott outside city hall and asked him a few questions, which didn't sound very convincing," Larry said. "To make matters worse, when J.J. wondered why he hadn't interviewed the vice-mayor, he said, 'He's been avoiding me.' He didn't even know it's a woman!"

"He's an idiot. But then, so's J.J. for not pulling him off the story," Alli commented, and then, suddenly, she realized what their next step had to be.

The others went on talking about the dissatisfaction in the newsroom. Alli listened with only half her mind.

Her reporter's instincts were baying like hounds. She could hardly wait to get started.

KEVIN OBSERVED the secretive smile playing around Alli's mouth. She'd hit on something.

It must have been the dancing. It had definitely worked a spell on him, although not one likely to help with their case. Or with his peace of mind, either.

All evening, his yearning for Alli had grown by jagged leaps. And he'd relished every minute of this feeling. He'd enjoyed prolonging the ache, something that he couldn't recall happening before. Although he'd always tried to be a gentleman, long buildups weren't his style.

He didn't intend to sleep with Alli Gardner. He'd never met a woman more utterly wrong for him. But he hadn't minded the luxurious sensuality that wove through their dancing like a glittery thread. Strangely, he found that wanting a woman and knowing he couldn't have her could be pleasurable even while it drove him crazy.

At last Larry ran out of tidbits about Payne, and he and Adrienne went on their way. When Alli smothered a yawn, Kevin suggested they go home.

"Good idea," she told him. "I've got things to do."

What things, at this hour? he wondered.

She refused to let him pay her share of the bill. Although he supported the idea of financial equality, Kevin wished she'd give in gracefully. Holding the purse strings made him feel in control of a situation and, besides, she didn't have an income. However, he acquiesced gracefully.

In the car, Alli hummed the tune the band had been playing as they left. Her throaty contralto caressed Kevin like a massage.

He reminded himself that sex would be a bad idea. Unfortunately, he felt too tired to remember why.

"What's this stuff you've got to do tonight?" he asked as he steered.

She tore her gaze away from the passing shops. "For one thing, I need to figure out what questions to ask the vice-mayor tomorrow."

"So that's what you came up with." He remembered that Mrs. Rodale's daughter was a client of Graybar's. "I should have thought of that. It's a bit late to call her tonight."

"I'd rather show up without calling to make it harder to put me off," Alli said. "She has a real-estate office but I've heard she usually works from home in the mornings. You can meet me there if you like."

"Why would I have to meet you?" Kevin asked. "We can drive over in my car."

"That's because of the other thing I have to do tonight."

"What?"

"Pack."

Oh, right. He'd evicted her. "And it's against your new policy to nag me about letting you stay."

She stifled another yawn. "Correct."

His pride ordered him to stick to his guns and let her go. But this late in the evening? And back to a place that had been stalked by thugs and invaded by Payne Jacobson?

Despite his stubborn streak, Kevin wasn't cruel. Or foolish. "It's more efficient if you stay one more night."

"I wouldn't want to inconvenience you," Alli replied.

"Don't push your luck. I gave in, okay?"

She smiled. "Thank you."

"You're welcome."

Uncomfortably, he noted that an absence of nagging meant he had to pay closer attention to Alli's needs. It might even force him to be more accommodating in the first place.

Did there have to be a downside to everything?

When they got home, he realized with a start that he no longer minded the mess in his living room. It was worth it, because it meant Alli was going to stay until tomorrow.

Kevin didn't care to examine his feelings. He preferred to chalk them up to seductive music and the unpredictable effects of strawberry pie on his nervous system.

"I'll see you in the morning," he said, and made his escape with what dignity he could muster. He couldn't fall asleep for a long while, and when he did, he found himself reaching out in his dreams for someone who wasn't there.

Chapter Eleven

Cathy Rodale lived in a neighborhood of sprawling ranch-style homes near Serene College, on the east side of town. Clipped hedges and rosebushes in full bloom separated the houses, each of which was painted in muted earth tones probably vetted by a homeowners' association.

Mentally, Alli reviewed what she knew about the vice-mayor. Long divorced, she'd raised her daughter alone and earned a comfortable living selling real estate. After serving as a PTA volunteer, she'd been appointed planning commissioner and, five years ago, won election to the city council.

Known for her energy and outspokenness, Cathy was considered by many to be a potential candidate for the state legislature. That put her directly in Klaus LeMott's path, and when they'd come face-to-face a few months ago, he was the one who'd walked away with the mayor's job.

She couldn't feel happy about that. If her daughter's adoption had been threatened and she saw a connection, Alli hoped she'd get angry enough to tell them anything she knew or suspected about her rival.

On the other hand, she might simply order the two of them off her property. Cathy was no novice when it came to avoiding the press. She'd declined to talk to Alli previously about her reasons for yielding the mayor's seat and, although she'd always acted friendly at council meetings, in private she answered only factual questions and never volunteered anything.

As usual, Kevin parked a few doors away to avoid notice. Even so, since theirs was one of only three or four cars on the street, it seemed to Alli that their footsteps echoed as they walked to the front.

She rang the bell, which chimed a classical melody. After a moment, a curtain rippled on one of the windows as if someone was peering out.

"We should have made a backup plan in case she refuses to talk," Kevin said.

"Like what? Returning disguised as Girl Scouts selling cookies?" Alli quipped.

"Like talking to her daughter first," Kevin replied.

Before she could respond, she heard the snick of the bolt and Cathy appeared in the opening. Her short dark hair, usually faultless, lay rumpled and uncombed. Instead of a designer suit, she'd thrown a short-sleeved sweater over slacks. Even so, the woman projected an air of authority that Alli knew she'd acquired the hard way during her fifty-five years.

She didn't bother with a greeting. Instead, she surveyed Kevin and said, "You look one heckuva lot better than your picture."

"What picture?" he inquired.

"The one in the paper."

"You mean the one three years ago?" Alli asked.

"Excuse me?" The vice-mayor blinked in confusion.

"Maybe we should start over."

Kevin produced one of his cards. "Kevin Vickers. I'm a private investigator."

"You're not Payne Jacobson?" Cathy said. "Why is a PI working for the newspaper?"

"He isn't. Neither am I. They fired me," Alli explained. "It's a long story, but that's not why we're here."

The vice-mayor studied them as if weighing her options. "You're not here about the investigation of Mayor LeMott?"

"We're here about threats to adoptive parents," Kevin replied. "The victims are afraid to contact the police because there's a chance they could lose their children."

"And you think I know something about this?" Her manner remained guarded.

"Your daughter adopted twins from the El Centro Orphanage," Alli said. "We don't know if she's been threatened, but we hoped you might help us."

"Who exactly are you working for?"

"Kevin's representing a client. I'm freelancing," Alli answered.

After a moment of internal debate, the woman allowed them inside. "I'm going to take a chance on you two because I don't know where else to turn."

"Thank you," she said.

They entered a large entryway with a sunken living room to their left and a dining room to the right. Straight ahead, beneath a skylight, plants ringed an atrium.

The decor suited its owner: flowing pastel colors and sleek furnishings, original paintings and sculptures, a few books arranged tastefully on a glass shelf. Alli hoped her shoes hadn't picked up any dirt, because the carpet was off-white.

"Anybody want coffee? I have a feeling we're going to need some." Cathy led them through the sunlit court into a large kitchen done in shades of amber glass, industrial steel and oak. On a peninsula counter, fragrant coffee dripped into a pot. "It's an imported blend. Would you like my specialty? It's a—never mind. You didn't come here for a mocha-frappa whatsis. Tell me what you're doing."

With his dark jacket and broad shoulders, Kevin dominated the kitchen despite—or perhaps because of—his stillness, Alli noted. She let him speak first. He outlined their investigation so far, including their meetings with Abernathy and the reverend, and the discovery that Dr. Graybar had recently repaid massive debts.

As he talked, the vice-mayor moved around the kitchen, pouring coffee and setting out sweetener, cream, napkins, mugs and spoons. Her attentive air yielded to a flare of anger when they mentioned the possibility of a connection between the doctor and the mayor.

"You think LeMott's got something to do with this black-mail business?" she demanded. "That Graybar might have sold him confidential patient information?"

"It's speculative at this point," Kevin said. "That's where we're hoping you can help put us on the right track."

"If that weasel of a man had anything to do with this, I'll make sure he'll never get elected to anything again in this town." After handing them drinks with a slightly shaky hand, Cathy perched on a stool opposite them.

"You've heard about the threats," Alli guessed. "Your daughter must have received one."

"You don't miss much, do you?" She picked up her mug, then put it down again. "Frankly, I'm so desperate I didn't know what to do. I've been at my wit's end since Friday."

"What happened?" Kevin asked. Alli took a small tape machine from her purse.

"This is off the record," the vice-mayor said.

She put the machine away. "Mind if I take some notes for background?" she asked. "I'll respect your confidence but I don't have a photographic memory."

Their hostess nodded. Glad that she'd established a repu-tation for respecting confidences, Alli produced a small pad and pen, while Kevin did the same.

"Annette and Hobie—that's my son-in-law—adopted twin boys through Dr. Graybar a year ago," Cathy explained. "They were trying to start a family, when Annette had to have a hys-terectomy. I'll spare you the medical details, but believe me, the operation was essential. After the trauma of discovering her sterility, she couldn't bear to wait years and go through all that rigmarole for a regular adoption, assuming they could find a healthy baby in this country. I'd heard about Dr. Gray-bar and I recommended she try him."

"They were able to adopt quickly?" Alli inquired.

Cathy swallowed a long draft of coffee. "A few months, that's all. And they were lucky enough to find twin boys, which was fabulous. I adore my grandsons. Everything seemed to be going so well. And now…this."

"What exactly is 'this'?" Kevin probed.

"On Friday, I had dinner at their house. Apparently, Hobie didn't want Annette to say anything, but I could tell she'd been crying. She broke down and explained that the adoption might be illegal, that they've been threatened with exposure and they had to come up with twenty thousand dollars to keep someone quiet. She asked me to loan the money to them."

"Did you?" he queried.

Cathy scowled. "No. I told them they can't go this route. The blackmailer will just come back and hit them again."

"How did they react?" Alli said.

Tears glittered in her eyes. "My daughter and I have always been close. But she couldn't accept what I told her. She acted so angry and hurt, as if the whole thing were my fault. I did promise not to go to the police, but I'm beginning to regret that. I don't know what to do. I couldn't sleep all weekend."

Cathy's high-power personality and no-nonsense approach to handling city business had earned her the nickname the "Iron Maiden" among some of the press. However, the woman sitting across the counter was no tough-as-nails lady. She was a mother suffering for her daughter.

"LeMott used to be involved in loan-sharking, so we figure he might be the one who loaned Dr. Graybar the money," Alli said. "We saw a photo of them at a city council meeting, so obviously they're acquainted, but do you know if they're closer than that?"

"It was me who recommended that the council honor Dr. Graybar's work," Cathy replied bitterly. "I'm pretty sure LeMott and Graybar hadn't met before that, but they seemed to hit it off. I saw them playing golf a few days later."

Kevin jotted a memo. "Did you see them together on any other occasions?"

"Not exactly. Didn't you used to work in the police department?" the vice-mayor asked abruptly.

"I was in the detective bureau until a few years ago," he said.

"I thought so! Lieutenant Vickers. The secretaries used to

make bets on who could snag a date with you first," she said. "No one ever collected as far as I know."

Kevin gave an embarrassed cough. "I try not to date people too close to my workplace." City hall lay adjacent to the police station.

"In that case, Alli must be missing a bet." Cathy's mouth quirked.

"You said you didn't exactly see LeMott and Graybar together," Alli reminded her. "What did you mean by that?"

"I'll show you. Hold on a minute." Scooting back from the counter, she vanished into another room.

Kevin flipped through his notebook, rereading what he'd written. He didn't need to do that, which meant he was trying to avoid a conversation. Alli could guess why.

"You sure were cruel to those secretaries," she teased. "They didn't work in the police department, so what would have been the harm?"

"I didn't want to risk having an affair go sour and bumping into the woman every time I turned around," he said. "I've seen it happen to other guys and it isn't pretty. Don't tell me you date guys where you work."

"A few times." She hadn't done so since joining the *Outlook*, mainly because she hadn't met any likely prospects. "But I never got involved enough for it to create a problem when we parted company."

"Are you sure the guys felt the same way?"

"If they did, they were gentlemen enough not to throw it in my face." From within the house, Alli heard a copy machine humming. "Sounds like she found something."

"I'm glad she's decided to trust us," Kevin said.

Alli doubted that either their personalities or their reputations deserved the credit for beguiling the vice-mayor. "I suspect she'd do almost anything to help her daughter."

"What parent wouldn't?"

Alli didn't answer. When she thought about a mother, she pictured her own mom, not herself. How would she react if she had a daughter? Say, a little cutie like Kevin's niece Fleur?

An unfamiliar twinge in the area of her heart warned that the topic had a power of its own. So maybe she was slightly susceptible to children, Alli conceded. That didn't mean she planned to rush to have one.

Cathy returned with a folder. "This is strictly confidential. If anyone asks, you don't know where this came from."

"Someone left it on my doorstep." Kevin accepted the folder. "Thank you."

Alli peered over his shoulder. Inside, she saw a hand-written list itemizing debts and creditors, with a total sum of nine hundred and fifty-five thousand dollars.

Below the list, a different, bold hand slashed an even larger number, with the annotation "In case you overlooked anything."

"I don't know what Randy Graybar's handwriting looks like, but Klaus wrote that note at the bottom," Cathy said. "I've got plenty of samples to compare it to, believe me."

"Where'd you find this?" Alli couldn't believe either man would have been careless with such an incriminating document.

The other woman gave an apologetic shrug. "I've never stooped to this kind of thing before, but I figured the day might come when I'd need something to hold over Klaus's head. A while back, I was in his outer office and I noticed his secretary had stepped out and left a pile of papers to shred. I stuffed a few in my briefcase. That was the only one that looked interesting."

"It doesn't prove he made a loan," Kevin conceded. "And it certainly doesn't prove blackmail. But it's a start."

Alli hadn't missed Cathy's remark about wanting something to hold over the mayor's head. "How did LeMott force you to step aside for the mayor's position?"

"Who says he forced me?" Her instinctive response hung in the air, unanswered. After a beat, she added, "Okay, I guess it's obvious I didn't step aside willingly."

"Did he threaten you?" Alli asked.

"Not directly."

"Care to elaborate?" Kevin said.

"He mentioned that he'd make it worth my while if I'd step

aside. I told him to blow it out his ear," the vice-mayor said. "That night, I started receiving hang-up calls at home on my unlisted number. The next night, someone rattled a window and set off my burglar alarm."

Alli wrote that down. "Did you call the police?"

"I filed a report of an attempted break-in, but I didn't mention Klaus because he hadn't threatened me," Cathy explained. "I can't go making unsubstantiated accusations without hurting my credibility."

"Did the harassment continue?" Kevin inquired.

"There were little things—well, not all that little. A broken window in my car. A dead mouse on the front porch. Nothing that pointed the finger at him, but I knew who was behind it. As soon as I announced I was withdrawing from consideration, the incidents stopped."

The sneaky way Klaus's men had invaded Cathy's property and shaken her peace of mind disturbed Alli at least as much as an outright threat. It indicated that he could be devious as well as brutal—a dangerous combination.

"One more thing," Kevin said. "Why would LeMott make Graybar such a large loan? This extortionist might not even earn that much, and he's taking a big risk of being caught."

"That puzzles me, too, if we're assuming Klaus is the blackmailer." Cathy refilled their mugs and offered more cream and sweetener. "It doesn't pan out financially. Besides, he had another, much more likely motive for making the loan."

Alli regarded her expectantly. "Which is…?"

She toyed with her cup. "I'm sure you know that the doctor's the son of a former lieutenant governor. Aldis Graybar is still a big player behind the scenes in statewide politics, so his son must have political contacts out the wazoo. He could introduce Klaus to the right people to win party support."

"Would that kind of contact be worth this much money?" Kevin asked.

"Sure, especially since Randy Graybar has enough income to pay it off eventually," Cathy responded. "Besides, Klaus surely realizes that a politician can only muscle his way ahead to a certain point. He can't win a party's nomination with hang-up phone calls and dead mice."

"Any hint that he's involved in extortion could blow his chances completely." Much as Alli wanted to believe they'd found their blackmailer, Klaus would have to be crazy to pull something like that.

"Perhaps he took the information as security and somebody else got hold of it," Cathy said. "Maybe those goons he calls guards. But if I know Klaus, and I'm afraid I do, he'd skewer the two of them if they went behind his back."

"Do you have any reason to believe Dr. Graybar would do something as unethical as turn over patient information, even to secure a loan?" Kevin asked.

"Personally? I have no idea," the vice-mayor responded. "He'd have to violate every type of medical ethics imaginable if he did."

The interview appeared to be at an end. Despite the paper she'd given them, Alli thought ruefully, they hadn't made much progress. In fact, they might have ruled out their prime candidate. "The blackmailer's moved up the deadline to tomorrow. We've got to move fast. Any ideas?"

"Tomorrow?" Cathy shook her head. "That jerk."

"We may have to take the risk of confronting LeMott directly," Kevin said. "Even if he's only an unwitting player, or if he resold the information, I have a suspicion he knows something."

"I doubt his guards will let you near him," their hostess said. "Wait! I've got an idea." She opened a drawer and extracted two tickets.

"Those would be for a baseball game, would they?" Kevin said hopefully.

Cathy managed a weak chuckle. "Sorry. They're for a political cocktail party tonight, strictly inner circle, meet and greet. I sent in my donation but I wasn't looking forward to showing up, not in my current mood. Why don't you two go. Just don't mention who gave you these."

"Thanks," Kevin responded.

"This is invaluable. We're in your debt." Alli indicated the folder. "Would it be all right if we flashed that note in the mayor's face to see how he reacts?"

"Sure. Maybe he'll have a heart attack," Cathy said. "I didn't mean that. I'd rather see him in jail than in the hospital."

Kevin studied the tickets. "The Paris Hotel. I'd better shine my shoes."

"Be careful," their hostess warned. "Even if LeMott isn't behind the extortion, he'll squash anyone who gets in his way. You might end up with a vicious enemy and no criminal charges to stick him in prison."

Her words chilled Alli. In some respects, the challenge of sniffing out clues had begun to take on the aura of a game, with themselves as hunters and LeMott as quarry. Now she recalled the sensation of a bullet whizzing by her at Dr. Abernathy's.

"If I don't get my job back, I'll have to leave town anyway," she said, as much to reassure herself as them. "Kevin's the one who's going out on a limb."

"Let's hope Hizzoner bears in mind that cops hate seeing one of their own harmed, even one who's no longer on the force," he responded. "But all the same, I may go back to wearing my Kevlar vest for a while."

"You own one?" Alli asked.

"Call it insurance. But I won't use it unless I have to. Too hot under the collar." He tucked the tickets in his pocket. "We'll put these to good use."

The vice-mayor walked them to the door. "We'll let you know how things go," Alli told her.

"It's better if you don't contact me again," Cathy said. "It won't take much to wise up Klaus."

Alli wished she could say something reassuring about Annette and her babies, but the truth was, she still didn't know if they were going to be able to head off trouble. "We appreciate everything you've told us."

She and Kevin didn't discuss the interview until they were

in the car pulling away from the curb. Then she said, "I've never seen her so friendly before."

"Neither have I. I didn't realize she knew who I was."

"She seemed to like us," Alli said. "I think she was genuinely worried for our safety." Her estimation of the vice-mayor had gone up several notches.

"She's right about LeMott. I should go to the cocktail party alone tonight in case things get ugly."

She couldn't accept the offer. This was her story and she intended to be in the thick of it.

"I'm coming, too," she said. "Don't even argue."

"You sure?"

"I can be as stubborn as you can."

"I never doubted it," he replied, and dropped the subject.

ALTHOUGH KEVIN SPENT most of Tuesday working for other clients, his thoughts kept returning to the blackmailer and the cocktail party scheduled that night. He didn't like using confrontational tactics and doubted that LeMott could be startled into making any incriminating admissions, but everything else they'd tried had drawn a blank.

What if LeMott *wasn't* the blackmailer? Who else could it be?

The only possibilities that came to mind were Binnie Reed and Dr. Graybar, or perhaps another employee at Graybar's office, since they might be able to tap into the data. Since Kevin lacked the authority conveyed by a badge, however, the doctor's refusal to cooperate made further inquiries along those lines almost impossible.

When he'd dropped Alli off at home after leaving Vice-Mayor Rodale's house, she'd promised to do further research into the situation at the orphanage. In addition to checking on the Internet, she'd planned to drop in to see the Reverend Weatherby. If she leveled with him, she'd said, maybe he'd come up with an idea.

Kevin was glad now that he'd agreed to work with Alli. Neither of them could have gotten this far alone.

Even so, it might not be enough. The clock was ticking very close to midnight, metaphorically speaking, for Mary Conners and the other parents.

That evening, he arrived home to find Alli standing in the living room, staring at the display of clothing on the entertainment shelves. "Just leave it," he said as he entered. "You can stay here until we wrap up the case."

"Thanks," Alli said, "but I'm going back to my place tomorrow. I'd pack tonight except it might be late when we come home from the meet and greet."

"What's your hurry?" Although Kevin looked forward to regaining peace and order, a little variety never hurt anyone. Besides, he'd gotten used to seeing lingerie emboldening his living room.

"I miss being alone," she said.

"You do?" A twist of disappointment caught him off guard.

She fiddled with the blanket overlying her makeshift tent. "Actually, no, and that scares me."

"Why?" Discovering he was still holding his briefcase, Kevin lowered it to the floor.

"People move on," she told him. "Nothing's permanent. I may be seeing Serene Beach in my rearview mirror—in fact, I'll have to if the paper won't rehire me. I don't want to get used to…anything."

"Do you mean *anyone*?" He didn't know what prompted him, but he had to ask.

"As in, you?" she retorted.

"We've been rubbing along fine," he pointed out. "Better than I would have expected."

"Exactly," Alli said. "It's too comfortable. The next thing you know, we'll be finishing each other's sentences."

"So you find me boring?" He should have figured as much, given her mercurial nature. She didn't appreciate stability the way some other women did.

But other women bored him. The insight stunned Kevin. What was happening here?

A wistful expression crossed Alli's face. "You're not boring," she said. "Stodgy, maybe. Frustrating. A hopeless stick-in-the-mud. But never boring."

"In other words, I've grown on you?"

"Like a barnacle," she admitted. "I guess I need my hull scraped, because I'll be leaving port soon."

He didn't understand why he felt so disappointed. He didn't want her to stay more than another few days. Everything she did drove him crazy. But in a perverse way, he'd been looking forward to their next argument.

Not this argument, though.

He remembered what she'd said about him reacting badly when he felt pressured. The same probably applied to her, so he avoided the temptation to point out the disadvantages of returning to her apartment. "There's no hurry," was all he told her, and hurried into his sanctum.

Or, rather, his former sanctum. Now it, too, radiated her presence. She'd left printouts and jottings strewn across his desk, and a sweater tossed over his seat back. A couple of her long hairs clung to the knit.

The borrowed laptop blinked at him, since she'd carelessly left it activated. He ought to remind her to shut down the machine. You never knew when some hacker would find a way in, even through a firewall.

Be careful, look twice before you cross the street, and don't accept candy from strangers. Never give your heart until you've checked out your list of required traits, with dependability at the very top. Quick-witted women with messy habits and infectious grins need not apply.

What on earth was he thinking? Hunger pangs must have affected his sanity, Kevin concluded.

"I wonder if they're going to have food at this shindig," Alli said as she entered the room.

"You're reading my thoughts," he confessed. "We'd better eat before we go."

"Agreed."

In the kitchen, a frozen pizza disappeared between them in record time. When Alli stretched her long legs beneath the table and plopped her feet on his knees, Kevin didn't object.

Tomorrow night, he'd have all the privacy in the world. All the silence, too. And plenty of leftovers if he fixed a pizza.

For some strange reason, he wasn't looking forward to the prospect.

Chapter Twelve

Alli couldn't decide what to wear. That wasn't unusual, but tonight she had so many conflicting purposes. To fit in at a political cocktail-party event. To turn men's heads. To prove to Kevin that she hadn't the slightest interest in dangling herself in front of him like those secretaries at city hall.

Except that she did.

She couldn't believe the emotion that had come boiling up when Cathy Rodale explained about that silly bet. Jealousy. It was utterly foreign to Alli and downright shameful.

That was when it hit her that she had to leave before things went from bad to worse. Before she made a mistake like sleeping with the man, for instance. Before she let herself care.

Before she started counting on him.

"Okay, this one," she said aloud, and pulled down a shocking-pink dress that draped from one shoulder, baring the other along with both arms. A moon-shaped cutout disclosed a tantalizing glimpse of hipbone, while the skirt clung to the body, reaching just below the knees. She'd found it at a secondhand shop frequented by celebrities in Hollywood.

That ought to set tongues wagging among the Orange County elite.

When she emerged from the bathroom a short while later, hair upswept and spilling over a cluster of silk blossoms, the flash of stunned appreciation in Kevin's eyes rewarded her more than amply. "Taking no prisoners tonight, are you?"

"I'm out for blood," she confirmed. She didn't mention whose.

But she didn't want to win Kevin. She only wanted to prove to her own satisfaction that she could have had him.

Alli sighed and put the whole messy subject out of her mind. She'd already filled him in over dinner about her research that day. Disturbed to learn about the blackmail and the problems at the orphanage, Weatherby had promised to get to the bottom of it through a missionary he knew who was working in the area.

"I can't promise I'll have something by tomorrow, but I'll do my best," he'd told her. "Hopefully, my friend keeps informed about the status of the investigation. As for the extortion, there's always the possibility of a corrupt official from Costa Buena, but the government cleaned up last year and the worst apples got thrown out of the barrel."

He'd also urged them to go to the police. Alli was beginning to think that might be their only option if tonight didn't result in a major discovery.

In the car on the way to the hotel, she and Kevin discussed problems they were likely to encounter. "Most likely, LeMott's already heard about our visit to Dr. Graybar," he pointed out. "Once he spots us, he'll know why we're there."

"You think he'll have us thrown out?" she asked.

"Let's hope he won't want to make a scene in front of people he's trying to impress," he replied.

Speaking of impressions, Kevin was sure to make one of his own. He'd changed into a dark suit that made a striking impression with his white shirt and dark coloring. The stubble had disappeared from his cheeks, making him look all the more touchable.

Alli voiced her greatest reservation. "We might be able to put the mayor on the spot and I might land a few good quotes, but how on earth are we going to crack this case?"

"We can't." Kevin steered south on Alsace Way. "My best hope is that we'll scare LeMott into backing off on the blackmail demand."

"What if he isn't the culprit?"

"We may be up the proverbial creek with a wet noodle for an oar."

Located below a large bluff and atop a small rise, the Paris Hotel provided a breathtaking view of the harbor. In the dark, lights from the peninsula and from moored yachts twinkled over the water. Above them sailed a three-quarters moon tinged with orange.

Kevin parked in the outer lot. "I'm not turning this car over to a valet, in case we have to leave in a hurry."

Alli glanced ruefully at her high heels. "I'd rather not do any Olympic sprinting, but I can make tracks if I have to. Are you wearing your vest?"

He shook his head. "I changed my mind. It's too uncomfortable and I doubt anyone's going to start shooting at a cocktail party."

Alli hoped he was right.

In the lobby, a discreet sign gave directions to one of the meeting rooms on the mezzanine. There, a well-dressed woman took their tickets and indicated the no-host bar. "The bubbly's free," she added.

"Great." When Kevin glinted her a smile, she beamed back.

Alli didn't mind. The lady had to be twice his age, and besides, who could blame her?

They'd purposely arrived half an hour late to avoid being conspicuous, and the play worked. Several hundred guests filled the space with chatter and an olfactory mixture of perfumes, aftershave lotions and breath mints.

Several men regarded Alli with evident appreciation. One woman raised an eyebrow dubiously at her dress. Serene Beach tended to fall on the conservative side, fashionwise.

"Don't look now, but LeMott's by the refreshment table. And guess who's with him?" Kevin said.

"Graybar?" She saw him nod. "That makes sense, if the purpose of the loan was to meet the right people. Is the former lieutenant governor here?"

"Yep. The doctor brought his daddy." Kevin nodded toward a gray-haired gentleman standing with Graybar and LeMott.

What a contrast the men made, Alli thought. The two sophisticated Graybars loomed over the scrawny Klaus who, with his narrow mustache, appeared ratty despite his expensive clothing.

As they watched, several other guests joined them, including a couple of mayors from nearby cities. Alli patted her purse, where she'd tucked the document copy that Cathy had given them. "How combative do you want to be?"

"Remember, once we show our hand, we won't have much time before they give us the heave-ho," Kevin said.

"Do we want to do this in front of as many people as possible, or not?" Alli asked.

"Let's give the man a chance to keep it secret. The goal is to encourage him to back off. Why should he do that if the cat's already out of the bag?"

Adrenaline sizzled through her. She always functioned best under pressure, and now she began getting ideas.

"I know what," Alli said. "Let's not accuse him."

"What?" As Kevin declined a waiter's offer of champagne, Alli was tempted to take one anyway, but she recognized the need to keep their heads clear.

"Instead of making accusations, let's say we're trying to alert him to a problem. Like we're doing him a favor."

"He won't believe it," her companion replied. "Still, it might help keep him from going ballistic."

"Maybe he'll ask security to walk us quietly to the door before they throw us on our butts," she quipped.

"Something like that."

"I can make it work," she told him. "Leave it to me."

As they waited to catch LeMott and Graybar alone, Alli focused so intently on what lay ahead that she blotted out everything else. The men ogling her. The possibility of being arrested for trespassing. Kevin. Sex. Okay, maybe not Kevin and sex. But most things.

It took a tug on her arm as her companion headed into the crowd to make her realize their quarry had been left unguarded. Alli stumbled and had to catch hold of him.

"Sorry," Kevin said. "I thought you were paying attention."

"I was," she sniffed. "It's these shoes."

When Graybar and LeMott spotted them, both men went rigid. LeMott took out his cell phone. Calling security, or else his goons.

"Mr. Mayor!" Alli extended her hand. "It's great to see you."

He ignored her greeting, but he did shut the phone. "Who let you in? There's no press allowed here." Dr. Graybar merely stood there glaring.

"I'm a businessman," Kevin told him. "I'm allowed to bring a date."

Given the likelihood of an imminent ouster, Alli decided to get to the point. "Obviously, we're not here to socialize. We felt you should be alerted to a situation that could create problems for you, Mr. Mayor."

"You and that rag of a newspaper are the only situation creating problems for me," LeMott snapped. His voice carried enough to make nearby conversations break off, and he bit back any further comments.

"I don't work for the *Outlook* anymore," Alli explained. "I'm freelancing."

"Sure you are," he said. "This is part of your paper's vendetta against me, isn't it? I wouldn't put it past you to try anything. Randy here told me you were spouting some nonsense about adoptions and blackmail. I presume that has about as much substance as that other junk you've been printing."

"I'm not writing those stories," she told him. "That's Payne Jacobson's investigation." It nearly killed her to say so, but given the mess he'd made, she had no desire to admit she'd played any role in the exposé.

"Payne Jacobson?" the mayor scoffed. "That kid dropped by city hall today, as if I would waste my time talking to him. Nobody could mistake that little twerp for a reporter. You're behind this. I'll give you one thing. Until now, I figured you were good at your job."

Alli might almost have taken that as a compliment, except

that it came with a very visible form of rejection: two men in gray suits, approaching fast.

So much for sidestepping confrontation. From her purse, she retrieved the paper Cathy had given them and unfolded it in view of the two men. Dr. Graybar paled. LeMott's complexion turned a mottled red.

"This loan isn't going to look good when the public finds out someone's blackmailing Dr. Graybar's patients," she said. "Did he give you names and phone numbers as security?"

"Where did you get that?" After signaling the guards to halt, the mayor made a grab and caught one edge.

Alli held on. The two of them must have made a ridiculous scene, grown-ups playing tug-of-war with a piece of paper. She was about to let go, when the thing ripped, sending her stumbling backward. Kevin's hands closed around her waist.

"This is none of your... It has nothing to do..." LeMott sputtered, but couldn't finish the sentence, so he glared at the torn scrap of paper in his hand.

"If you have any idea who's threatening those people, you might want to advise him to back off," Kevin went on. "By the way, as I'm sure you've noticed, that isn't the original."

"You can't really think I did this," the mayor snarled. "Listen to me, Detective. That reporter is using you. She's drumming up trouble to sell papers. Like I said, there's no blackmail."

"Unfortunately, I have independent confirmation that there is," he responded.

"You could ruin me." Dr. Graybar spoke for the first time. "I haven't done anything wrong. You should go to the po—" He stopped, apparently realizing that a police investigation wasn't going to help his reputation, either.

Alli gave zero credibility to LeMott's protestations of innocence. The gynecologist was another matter. "You didn't turn over the information?"

"Absolutely not."

"Did you let him examine your records in any way?" Kevin asked.

"He reviewed my financial data, but that didn't include any

specifics about my clients." Graybar frowned. "Believe me, I'm paying it all back. There was nothing illicit about this."

"Don't bother talking to them, Randy." The mayor waved to security. "I want these leeches out of here. You two ought to be ashamed of yourselves, harassing innocent citizens."

"Innocent of blackmail or innocent of shooting up Payne Jacobson's car?" Alli asked as a guard caught her arm. "Even if he is a twerp, that doesn't make it right to use him for target practice."

LeMott's jaw clamped shut. This time, he didn't try to deny the allegation. The thing that worried Alli was seeing him take out his phone again. Since security had already arrived, she hated to think who he might be summoning.

The guards deposited them outside the hotel and positioned themselves on the walkway with arms folded. "Please leave quietly. Don't make us call the cops," one of them said.

Kevin brushed an invisible speck of lint off his jacket. "Don't worry. We got what we came for."

But had they? Alli wondered.

As they navigated through the lot toward his car, she said, "Do you honestly think that did any good?"

"Probably not. The man's shameless." Kevin squared his shoulders. "But we livened up an otherwise dull party."

"I felt a little embarrassed because what he said about the *Outlook* is true, but I'm not the one who let that happen." Alli halted in the middle of the pavement. "The *Outlook*! That's it!"

Moonlight glittered off his eyes. "I hope this is the brainstorm of the century, because we need it."

She resumed walking. "Give me a minute to put my thoughts in order."

"Are you sure that's wise?" Kevin teased. "It might cramp your style."

Alli punched him in the arm. He felt rock solid. After a moment's delay, he said, "Ouch."

"Like that hurt!"

"I thought I should protest on general principle or you might hit me again."

She laughed. Being with him felt like an adventure, despite the serious issues at stake. "I won't. Thanks for watching my back in there."

"I hope you realize how entertaining it was to see you and the mayor fighting like kids over a piece of paper."

"Too bad Larry wasn't around to snap a picture." A movement several lanes over caught her attention. She hadn't noticed any other vehicles moving, and this one, she realized, was a van. "Uh-oh."

Kevin spotted it, too. "Better safe than sorry. Follow me."

She dodged behind a parked truck in his wake. Keeping low, they made their way between rows of cars.

The van continued to prowl. Passing several vacant spaces, it moved relentlessly in their direction.

Alli couldn't tell the color in the semidarkness. But when the glare of a lamppost shone through the vehicle, she noted two men in the front seat. Pairs of men didn't generally go cruising around swanky hotels in the middle of the evening, passing up available spaces.

Unless they were looking for someone.

Kevin kept darting in a stop-and-go pattern, homing in on his car. Alli hoped their pursuers didn't know which vehicle it was.

At last they reached the sedan. He opened the door with a key instead of the clicker to avoid flashing the lights.

"The next part's going to be tricky," Kevin said. "Jump in back and keep your head down in case they start shooting."

"Maybe it's time we called the cops."

"They haven't fired any shots, so it wouldn't be treated as an emergency. By the time anyone responds, we'd be dead."

"That's reassuring," Alli grumbled, and got in as directed.

From her position on the floor, the car seemed to roar like a jet as the ignition caught. Kevin eased the vehicle backward and then righted it. He must have kept the lights off, because Alli didn't catch any hint of glare.

Their safety lay in his hands. His tension radiated through the seat between them. She pictured him gripping the steering wheel, his face a mask of concentration.

There was no one in the world she would sooner trust with her life than Kevin Vickers, Alli thought. The traits she'd chided him for—stodginess and control—shone like knightly virtues in a predicament like this.

He might not be around in the future if she needed him. But thank goodness he was here now.

The tires muttered over the blacktop. A pair of headlights crossed their path, making her grip the edge of the seat.

"It's a Porsche," Kevin told her, his tone flat.

"Can you see the van?"

"It's off to our right. Still hunting."

The Porsche's lights passed out of range. In the dimness, Kevin's car rolled into the aisle.

Alli wished she could see what was going on. She didn't want to distract the driver by demanding a progress report, so she gritted her teeth and gauged their progress by the turns.

Surely they must be nearing the exit, where they'd have to stop to pay for parking. At that point, the van could hardly miss them.

"Almost there," Kevin said.

"Where are they?"

"I can't tell."

"Is that good?" she asked.

"We won't know till it's over." He sounded maddeningly calm.

How could anybody play his cards that close to his chest? she wondered. She was too excitable.

"I'm going to have to turn my lights on," Kevin added. "We're getting close to the exit."

Alli held her breath as the evening whitened by several shades. A moment later, they halted and the driver's window snicked down.

"Having a good time tonight, folks?" asked the ticket taker.

What an inane comment, she thought. No doubt the management required its employees to act friendly, but under the circumstances, the fake cheeriness grated on her nerves.

"Terrific." Kevin didn't engage the man in conversation; he simply handed over his money. "Keep the change."

"Thanks!"

Alli hoped the fellow wouldn't peer inside the car to make sure everyone was having fun. She'd need to invent some excuse for crouching here on the floor. Lost her contact lens? Too many sheets to the wind?

They pulled into the street. "Are we safe?" she asked.

"Too soon to tell. Stay down."

Behind them, she heard the squeal of tires. The van sounded unbearably close.

"They're on a parallel lane inside the lot," Kevin told her as he hit the gas. "It'll take them a minute to go through the—well, less than a minute. They took out the gate arm."

When they swerved, Alli banged her hip on something hard but didn't complain. She kept expecting to hear shots.

They rounded another corner. She tried to picture the area and gathered they must be heading toward the rabbit's warren of car dealers and auto shops south of Serene High School.

During the next series of screeching turns, she lost track of their location, and Kevin was too busy driving to enlighten her. A couple of explosive sounds behind them jolted her nerves.

Gunfire. She hoped the men were lousy shots.

At last they hit a straightaway, going fast. She guessed they'd reached Little Paris Avenue, which ran north-south.

"Uh-oh," Kevin said. "There's an event of some kind letting out at the college." Its campus lay beyond the high school.

Alli's heart shifted from high gear into supersonic. "Are we trapped?"

"Maybe not. There's a cop ahead, directing traffic."

The car slowed. Alli's pulse rocketed on, unabashed, as the sound of other engines surrounded them and headlights washed out the night.

They stopped, dead in the water. "Talk to me," she said.

"We're stuck in a line of traffic. The van's pulling off the road, but it can't get around." After a pause, he added, "It looks like they're taking a side street and leaving."

She couldn't believe they'd give up that easily. "Do you think they plan to lie in wait?"

"Their pattern has been to attack, then disappear. After all, they know who we are and presumably can find out where I live."

"Don't you keep your address a secret?"

"I try. But I can't keep it off the water bill. If the mayor hasn't already looked it up, he could do so tomorrow."

She uttered a couple of profanities. "We still can't prove he's behind this, can we?"

"You said you had an idea," he reminded her.

"Oh, right." In the heat of the moment, she'd forgotten. "I still need to work out the details."

"Care to clue me in?"

Before she could answer, the traffic opened up and they started forward. "We'll need my laptop," Alli replied. "That's the important part."

He digested this information. "We'll have to swing by my house and pick it up. Then we should spend the night somewhere else."

"Any suggestions?"

"I refuse to put my family or your friends at risk. That means we're checking into a motel."

One room or two? Since they'd be working together for hours, what was the point of incurring additional expense?

Alli decided not to mention it yet. Kevin had too many other things to think about.

And so did she.

Chapter Thirteen

Kevin parked in back by the garage and accompanied Alli inside. He was doubly grateful for the alarm system, which guaranteed they wouldn't find any unexpected visitors.

"Don't turn on the lights," he warned. A low-burning bulb between the kitchen and the front room provided enough glow to find their way without bumping into the furniture. Beyond that, they'd have to rely on the flashlights he kept handy throughout the house.

"You're prepared for anything, aren't you?" Alli said as he handed her one.

"It's a sensible earthquake precaution."

"Don't tell me you have a week's supply of canned food in the garage!" she sputtered.

"And a gas camp stove," he said. "Did I mention the thirty gallons of bottled water?"

"Please don't."

During the chase, he noticed, her hair had tumbled from its perch and that tantalizing pink dress had plastered even more tightly to her curves. Her body radiated an excitement that was almost tangible.

He suspected it would quickly become tangible if he touched her. So he didn't.

"Keep it quick," Kevin warned. "Grab the laptop and let's head out of here."

"You think I'm running around town like this for who knows how long?" She indicated her disheveled state.

By now, he knew better than to argue. "Throw a few things into a bag and bring them with you. Don't try to change here."

"Okay."

"I'll gather the information we've found. We wouldn't want it falling into the wrong hands."

Although the alarm company would summon the police if someone broke in, that might take fifteen minutes. In the meanwhile, LeMott's men could clean out his desk.

"Right," Alli said, and took off.

They worked quickly and silently. Kevin picked out a change of clothing, as well as toiletries. No sense in being any more uncomfortable than necessary.

As he worked, he replayed the chaotic scene at the hotel. Policemen were trained to control a situation, not provoke their opponent to see how hot the fireworks burned, so it had felt odd to him.

The weird part was that he'd enjoyed it. He liked seeing the arrogant LeMott go ballistic. Alli's chutzpah had tempted him to lead a couple of cheers.

They'd unquestionably stirred things up. One way or the other, push would come to shove tomorrow.

After that, with Alli gone and the blackmail deadline past, things ought to settle back to normal. Kevin should have relished the prospect, assuming they both survived unharmed, but instead it made him feel let down.

His own gear collected, he kept watch through the window until Alli finished packing. A pair of powerful headlights cruising down the street sent his adrenaline pumping, but as it rolled by, the vehicle turned out to be an SUV.

At last Alli appeared. Ignoring his orders, she'd changed into jeans and a tank top, with her hair falling provocatively about her shoulders. He decided not to bother complaining.

Kevin activated the alarm, locked the door after them and led the way to the car. He didn't speak until they were on their way.

"Now let's hear your idea," he said.

"Remember when I first moved in? You suggested we

might use the spyware to play a trick on Payne. Much as I hate tipping my hand about this story, I don't see any choice."

"You're going to write down the truth?"

"Well, not all of it," she murmured.

A practical problem reared its head. "What are the odds he'll be working at this hour?"

"I don't know the odds, but I don't need to. At this very moment, Payne's sitting at his desk wearing an expression of sheer despair," she said gleefully. "He hasn't been able to produce sources for his quotes or come up with a new angle for a follow-up, either. Larry says J.J.'s losing his patience."

Kevin scowled as he realized what she'd implied. "You called Larry while I was waiting?"

"I can talk and pack at the same time," she responded blithely. "I figured he'd be on duty tonight, so I decided to pick his brain."

"You didn't tell him what you're planning, did you?" Heading west across town, he kept watch for suspicious vehicles.

"He asked what was up. I told him it was better if he didn't know."

"Good, because you might want to rethink the whole plan." Much as Kevin disliked LeMott, going to the press could have all sorts of repercussions if they were wrong. "We don't know for sure that the blackmailer isn't some crook from Costa Buena, or one of Graybar's employees."

"Don't worry." Alli shot him a conspiratorial grin. "I'm going to make sure even Ned Jacobson wouldn't be daft enough to print this story."

"How?" Kevin had begun to doubt that the loose cannons at the *Outlook* would hesitate at anything.

"I'll cite unnamed police sources. After the way Payne screwed up with his speculations about LeMott, Ned will insist on learning the names in advance."

"And when he can't provide them?"

"He'll have to phone the PD, ask about the blackmail investigation and find a name he can quote," Alli explained.

Kevin began to follow the logic. "When the police learn

that the newspaper's looking into this and that the payoffs are due tomorrow, it will either tip them off if they didn't already know about the case or light a fire under them if they've been dawdling."

"I just hope we're not too late to keep our people from losing their life's savings," Alli said.

He considered what she'd suggested. Not a bad idea, although it risked giving away her story to that creep Payne. Still, it avoided entangling either of them with the police, but was that entirely honest?

Kevin shook his head. "We can't do this."

"Why not?"

"I promised my client not to tell the cops," he reminded her. "I know it will be you—indirectly—rather than me, but this has become a joint investigation. I'm responsible for whatever happens."

Alli weighed his comment for a moment. "She made that request last week, right?"

"So?"

"Maybe she's changed her mind. The least you can do is call and give her the option." She wriggled sideways on the passenger seat so she could face him. "You might point out that we won't use her name. The police will never even find out you and I are involved, so they can't quiz us about our sources."

It was a calculated risk, but Mary might go for it. "It's worth a try." Having reached the west side of town, Kevin turned north into a modest section of Serene Beach that held several motels. "So you're really okay with giving up your exclusive?"

She rested her head against the seat. "It kills me. After all this work, I'm handing the whole thing over to my worst enemy. I won't even have anything special to dangle in front of another paper. Don't you hate having to do the right thing when it deprives you of something you really want?"

He nearly chuckled at her rueful tone, but was too busy watching for a place to hole up. "Are you going to mention LeMott by name?"

"I'll have to."

"But if he isn't the culprit, whoever's doing this won't back down," he pointed out.

"Let's hope the cops can move faster than we've been able to. Otherwise the parents are going to be shafted," Alli concluded. "I'll have given away my exposé for nothing and Payne Jacobson will once again come out smelling like a rose."

"That's rotten," he said. "But…"

"But what?"

"It's the…" When he paused, she joined him for the rest of the line: "…right thing to do."

Alli smacked her hands against the dashboard in a drumroll. Kevin picked up the beat on the steering wheel.

He remembered what she'd said earlier, that before long they'd be finishing each other's sentences. They seemed to be doing it already, and more.

He couldn't for the life of him see what was wrong with that.

THE FIRST THREE PLACES had posted No Vacancy signs. "That's the problem with June," Kevin said. "Too many people in town for weddings and graduations."

"Why don't they all stay home?" Alli joked. "How inconsiderate." She was in a surprisingly jolly mood, considering the circumstances.

"Darn right." He pushed northward into a seedy area close to the freeway. "Hey look, it says Vacancy." The aging neon sign advertised the Slumber Well Motel, whose name had been shortened by nonfunctioning light bulbs to the Slum We Motel.

"The word *No* is probably burned out," Alli grumbled.

Kevin halted in front of the office. "I'll find out."

He emerged shortly afterward. "They had one room left, and we got it." As he strapped on his seat belt, he added, "Hope you don't mind."

"Sharing with you?" She shrugged. "Not a problem. You can protect me from the cockroaches."

"Are you dissing our lovely accommodations?"

"I hear the rats around here have bodyguards."

Kevin drove along the side of the building. "They provide cable TV. What more could you ask?"

"In this location? Bulletproof windows."

They unloaded the car quickly a few units away from theirs. "Is it safe to leave it here?" she asked.

"It would be hard to spot from the street," Kevin noted. "Besides, if we leave the car too far away, we wouldn't be able to escape in a hurry."

"There's a cheery thought," she muttered.

"Besides, if LeMott's men see it, they could stake it out no matter where we park," he said.

"Cheerier and cheerier."

Inside, the place smelled of stale cigarette smoke and spices, a giveaway that a previous tenant had cooked on an illicit burner. When Alli thumped the worn bedspread, she half expected dust to rise into the air.

She took out her phone. "I'll call Rita to see if she's heard from the blackmailer again."

"And I need to call Mary—I mean, my client—about alerting the police." After taking out a change of clothing, he vanished into the bathroom with his cell.

The Hernandez phone gave five rings before a machine picked up. Alli left a message. "I need to update you about what I'm doing," she said. "Please call as soon as you receive this, no matter how late."

Her partner must have reached his client, because she heard the deep rumble of his voice from the bathroom. She didn't need to make out the words to catch the concern with which he spoke.

Alli sat on the bed next to his open suitcase. How had he managed to roll his underwear so smoothly and fold a spare shirt with precision while packing by flashlight? The man needed a woman to muss his hair and unbutton his collar, she thought.

The realization that she'd checked into a motel with Kevin Vickers sent a tingle through Alli. Here on neutral territory, who made the rules? Were there any?

Yanking her thoughts away from temptation, she opened the laptop and set it on a small table. The only chair available rocked a bit on its uneven legs as she began typing, but soon she was concentrating so hard she forgot the inconvenience.

She'd never intentionally created an irresponsible story before. It was a challenge to write a lead so awkward it might convince someone that Payne Jacobson had penned it.

To figure out what to include, Alli reviewed the information they'd gathered during the past few days. There were Costa Buena's investigation into the orphanage, threatening phone calls, terrified parents and a shortened deadline. She also included the connection to Dr. Graybar's orphanage service and his loan from Mayor LeMott.

Much of the information she would never have used in a real story because it was speculative. But her name wasn't going on this one. She nearly goofed and wrote Payne Jacobson at the top before remembering that he was supposed to think she'd transmitted this by accident.

Instead, she left it without a byline. She didn't always put one on her rough drafts, anyway.

Inventing quotes from unnamed police sources proved to be fun. Alli gave one of the officers a tendency to use malapropisms and another a habit of speaking in exclamation points.

She'd felt certain Ned would recognize that the quotes had been invented. Maybe he'd finally wake up and see his nephew for a fraud, but she wouldn't be foolish enough to bet on it.

She pictured the assistant managing editor's shock of graying hair and customary stern expression. He'd intimidated her when she started working at the *Outlook*. However, he'd also impressed her with his high standards.

The one thing he'd never displayed was a warm heart. Although he'd respected Alli's abilities, that hadn't been the case with another young reporter who'd arrived a year later. He'd raked the woman over the coals when she failed to ask the hard questions of her subjects, so relentlessly that she'd quit after a few months. Yet she hadn't made nearly as many errors—nor such serious ones—as Payne.

Ned might not recognize it, but Alli considered that she was doing him a favor. The sooner he snapped out of his nepotistic daze, the better for him and the paper.

The bathroom door clicked. Kevin emerged in gray slacks and a hooded black pullover. In these casual clothes, he looked younger than usual.

However, seeing him reminded Alli that she couldn't use this story if his client objected. "What did she say?"

"She tried to borrow the money from relatives, but they don't have it," he explained grimly.

"She must be upset." Judging by his glower, so was Kevin.

"She was in tears. I had to reassure her that no matter what happens, the authorities aren't likely to swoop down and grab her son without lengthy legal proceedings."

"What did she say about notifying the cops?"

When he stood behind her chair, she sensed his gaze sweeping the screen. "She feared any publicity would make the situation worse, but I persuaded her she has nothing to lose. I hope the cops jump on this one, although catching a blackmailer can be tricky."

"I should think they'd especially resent the fact that he's portraying them as bogeymen who steal children. Wait! That would make a great quote!" Alli typed rapidly, putting these words into the mouth of one of her unidentified policemen.

Kevin sat on the bed beside her. "It looks like you're having fun."

"It's a little scary how much I'm enjoying it," Alli admitted. "When I hear about real reporters who invent their stories, I feel disgusted. It's the worst kind of lying, because it tarnishes an entire profession."

"But this is more like a game?" he surmised.

"It's working out that way." She couldn't help smiling. "I'm making the piece as outrageous as possible. My sources all have funny mannerisms in their speech."

"Don't carry it too far," Kevin warned. "Payne can't be that stupid."

"That remains to be seen." She couldn't bear to gut her beautiful fake prose.

He helped her outline the rest of the article. Since there was no telling which parts might make it into print, they agreed to soft-pedal Dr. Graybar's role and use innuendo regarding LeMott's possible access to the adoption data. There was no point in naming a suspect when implications would suffice.

"I'll refer to the mayor's alleged past as a loan shark. Of course, Payne might plug in the stuff he's already run to make the mayor look like the villain," Alli said.

"Which he might be."

"He's certainly no angel," she agreed, although the journalistic recklessness left her uneasy.

She stretched her shoulders, which ached from the uncomfortable chair. Reaching over, Kevin massaged the knots with strong, gentle hands.

When he lifted her hair out of the way, his fingers caressed the long strands before returning to her muscles. "Ready?" he murmured close to Allie's ear.

She nearly answered, "Getting there fast," before she realized he was referring to the article. "Uh, I think so. Want to read it over before I close it online?"

"Sure." Looping his arms around her, Kevin brushed his cheek against hers as he scrolled through the story. His warmth enclosed them both. By the time he said, "Fire away," Alli had nearly melted.

Taking a deep breath to regain her composure, she dialed the server. Once she was on the Internet, she closed the story. It seemed to Allie that there should be bells and kazoo noises, or at least a notice that said "Spyware at work." But to all outward appearances, nothing happened.

"How fast does this work?" Kevin asked.

"It pops up immediately," she said.

"I wish there were a way to find out if he's reading it. He might have gone home by now."

"Hey! I thought I was the impatient one in this crowd."

"There's a lot riding on this."

The only way to do that would be to ask Larry to go over to Payne's desk, but that was likely to give away the tactic. And Alli didn't want her friend to risk attracting too much attention.

The sight of the blinking cursor started to annoy her. It felt like a traitor, so she angled the screen away.

Her watch showed a few minutes past nine. That didn't leave Payne much time to surprise his uncle with the story and make his calls. "This could be held over another day," she admitted.

"Let's not agonize over things we can't control," Kevin advised. "By the way, did you talk to your contact?"

"She wasn't home."

"Probably out robbing a bank," he quipped.

"I'm sure she was tempted."

Kevin stretched out on the bedspread. He'd taken off his shoes somewhere along the line, Alli saw. "I don't know about you, but I've had a long day."

"Wimping out on me?"

"Why? Were you expecting me to do something else tonight?" he asked playfully.

He looked different than usual, more relaxed. The way he'd pushed up his sleeves and rumpled his hair made him hard to resist.

"My back is itching like crazy." Alli moved from the chair to the edge of the mattress. Never mind that she was playing with fire. Even cheap motels came with extinguishers, didn't they? "It's this bra. They must hire sadists to design the hooks so they dig into your skin."

"I didn't think you were wearing a bra under that sexy pink dress." Kevin lifted the back of her tank top and began lazily scratching her. "Not to mention this tank top. Where do you hide the straps?"

"They do make strapless bras," Alli said.

"I'm trying not to think about that." His palms smoothed upward, lifting the bra's fabric and scratching the points beneath the hooks that she could never reach. "Does that help?"

"It's fabulous."

She was still sitting up, while he lay beside her. They

hadn't gone beyond the point of no return, or even the point of questionable return.

She could leave it that way. Kevin wasn't going to push her. Yet bit by bit he'd lowered the barriers until almost none remained.

Alli didn't have to make a decision to cross the line. She simply knew instinctively the time was right.

With a quick motion, she lifted her tank top over her head and tossed it to the floor, revealing the strapless construction. "It's a marvel of engineering, isn't it? Keeping a space station aloft is nothing compared with this."

Kevin smoothed his fingers to the front and outlined the rim of the bra. "Thanks. Now I can see what I'm doing."

"Always happy to oblige." She might have carried off the blasé attitude except for the moan that escaped her.

Kevin responded by raising himself until his mouth met hers. The kiss connected them with a sizzle, sending a rush of desire through Alli.

He prolonged the kiss, teasing her with his tongue as he peeled away the bra. When he bent to take her nipples between his lips, she could hardly bear the tension welling inside her.

She tugged upward on Kevin's jersey. He shrugged it off over his head, baring an impressive chest. After exploring his sculpted muscles with her palms, Alli swung her hair across his bare skin.

His breath quickened. Down her ribs, his thumbs seared a path to the waistline of her jeans, where he worked the snap. Together, they stripped them off and lay side by side, basking in the whisper of skin against skin.

With the heel of her hand, Alli rubbed the center of his slacks. She enjoyed the deep groan that tore from his throat.

"Woman, anyone would think you meant to seduce me," Kevin murmured.

"Oh, I thought you were doing that to me."

"It crossed my mind."

"What's crossing your mind now?"

"This," he said, and pulled her atop him.

Her bare breasts pressed into his chest as he kissed her again. Below, only a few wisps of fabric separated them.

When their mouths parted, Alli traced a line along his stomach with her tongue. Removing his slacks, she tantalized him until a gasp warned that he couldn't hold out much longer.

"Alli." Kevin half whispered her name. "I have to ask—did you bring any—I don't have protection."

"I'm on the prevention plan."

"Really?" He quirked one eyebrow. "You never struck me as the cautious type."

"That's why I'm on it."

If she'd meant to say anything more, she never got the chance. After rolling her onto the bed, Kevin removed her panties. Then his mouth brought her to the brink of losing control.

When he tucked into her, Alli cried out with the sheer pleasure of his long, hard entry. She relished his burnished skin, his chuckle of delight, the perfect way he fit against the length of her.

"Let's do this all night," she said.

He didn't answer. He was too busy rocking in and out of her, pausing only to watch her reaction and give them both a chance to savor the experience.

They skirted the edge of a cliff. Alli clung to Kevin's strength, yearning for this ecstasy to last forever, but their sheer velocity carried them too far.

She felt them tumbling through a waterfall, sunlight and magic glinting around them. She gripped him as if she might spin away and get lost entirely, and he anchored her through all the brilliance and the glory.

Afterward, ripples of color sparkled through Alli's awareness, blending with the heat of Kevin's body. Curled against him with his arms holding her tight, she registered the amazing fact that they had just blasted through paradise.

This was the man she'd considered stuffy and stiff-necked—Kevin, whose picture she'd saved for three years because she couldn't bear to throw it away. Kevin, who'd sneaked below her radar because she knew how utterly impossible it was for her to fit into his life or for him to fit into hers.

With all the worry about drive-by shooters, she'd missed the real danger. If she wasn't careful, she might fall in love with him, and she knew what that would mean, because she'd grown up loving a man she couldn't have.

Alli refused to go there. Not even now.

Chapter Fourteen

Lying under the covers with his arms around Alli, Kevin tried to figure out what had hit him. He'd always considered her sexy, but that didn't explain the surge of passion that had awakened a new tenderness in him.

While making love, his pleasure had come as much from her response as from his own. He'd anticipated her every move and relished every gasp. Only when he'd felt her release had he soared until they became one.

If only he had words to describe what had happened. He wanted to relive the experience again and again—except that to do so might deepen his need instead of satisfying it.

Did Alli share his amazement? Kevin wondered. Was she willing to take the next step with him? Maybe it was worth trying.

He drew her closer. "Incredible."

She brushed a kiss across his temple. "Those secretaries at city hall don't know what they're missing."

A laugh burst out of him. "I should hope not!"

"You're every woman's fantasy male. It was great." She sounded sleepy, contented—but hardly as if he'd turned her world upside down.

"We should talk," Kevin said.

"We can't."

"Why not?"

"Guys never want to talk after sex," she told him. "It's too weird."

"That doesn't make sense."

"You always like to have meaningful discussions after orgasm?" she challenged.

"That's not what I meant." Sure, the green-apple scent and the silky texture of Alli's hair spilling across his chest could easily carry him into a stream of driftwood and dreams. "The thing is, I wanted to know…"

Whether they were starting a journey together or whether they'd soon be parting ways, Kevin thought. Yet he wasn't ready to ask the question that bluntly.

"We've made love. That changes things," he said, instead. "You agree, right?"

"Don't tell me you're turning possessive." The way she snuggled into him took some of the sting from her words. But not all.

"Of course not. What makes you think that?" he plied, a little annoyed.

"Because you usually insist on taking charge, so I assume that's what you're doing now."

He wasn't taking charge. He was simply trying to steer the conversation to where he wanted it to go. "Unfair," he said. "I didn't push you into anything tonight."

"Of course not. What we did was terrific." Alli covered a yawn. "Can we go to sleep now? I'm exhausted."

"Sure." He could hardly conduct a conversation alone, could he?

"Good night."

"Night." Kevin tried to lie still so as not to disturb her. Gradually, her breathing grew regular.

Obviously, he'd mistaken her response to him. Whatever new vista he'd uncovered tonight, he'd gone there by himself.

He pulled the blankets over them both. Nice and warm. He ought to doze off with no trouble at all.

People made love all the time, and nothing resulted from it. No epiphanies, no shared dreams, no happy futures. If Alli hadn't been affected in more than a superficial way, Kevin didn't intend to dwell on it.

Why had he imagined this bed to be comfortable? The

mattress was hard and the blanket so small it barely reached his feet.

He was going to be stiff in the morning, and in the wrong places. All because of one lousy motel with inferior beds.

Growing more irked by the minute, he closed his eyes and waited for sleep to claim him.

ALLI HAD EXPECTED to lose consciousness immediately. Instead, although she pretended to doze, she lay there wondering what Kevin had meant about things having changed.

Maybe she should have given him a chance to explain. Maybe she ought to start trusting him more.

But she didn't want to. Only fools made the same mistake over and over.

A cell phone rang. "Is that mine?" she asked.

"Must be. Mine's on vibrate." He sounded wide awake.

Drowsily, she extricated her limbs from the covers. By the time she reached the phone, she feared the caller might have hung up, but the line remained open.

The voice that answered Alli's "Hello?" had a thick quality as if from crying. "This is Rita," she said.

"Thanks for calling back!" Alli sat back on the bed, aware of Kevin's gaze playing over her naked torso. She'd never been uncomfortable about nudity. "Has the blackmailer called?"

"Yes. He phoned to arrange about the money."

"Did he give you any details?"

"No. I had to tell him we can't raise that much. What does the man expect? We're not rich." Rita sounded torn between tears and anger.

"What was his response?"

"He said we'd better come through or we'd regret it. I told him we could only find ten thousand and he said that might do as a down payment."

"A down payment?" Alli hoped the Hernandezes wouldn't fall for that. "What's to stop him from demanding more and more? It could go on indefinitely!"

"What should we do?" Rita wailed.

"I know there's at least one other victim who can't pay." A new angle occurred to her. "That means that if he carries out his threat to even one of you, he'll have to notify the authorities. Yet if he rats out one family, everybody's shafted, whether they paid or not."

"You don't think we should pay him anything?" Rita asked. "That's what Jose wants. He says we should save our money for a lawyer."

"I'm no expert," Alli conceded. "But one way or the other, I think the police are going to find out about it, and they'll notify Immigration and Child Services. So your husband's probably right."

"The guy seemed in an awful hurry," Rita said thoughtfully. "He got so frantic he forgot to tell me where to send the ten thousand and I didn't think of it until he'd hung up." She paused briefly before adding, "Somebody spoke to him in the background, a woman. He clicked off before I could hear much."

Alli pulled out a pad. Anything Rita had heard might be helpful in establishing the man's identity. "What language did she speak?"

"English."

"Did she have an accent?"

"Standard American, if there is such a thing."

That was good news, in a way. Someone in Costa Buena would most likely have spoken Spanish. "Could you make out her words?"

"She said, 'Who are you talking to?' No, wait. First she addressed him by a name, or I think it was a name. It sounded like Ardee."

"Ardee? Are you sure?" Alli wrote the name down.

"Now that I think about it, yes. I don't know why it didn't register with me sooner," Rita said. "I was so upset it didn't quite sink in that she might have spoken a name. I don't even know if it's his last or his first. "

"Still, it's something." Alli quizzed her for a while longer but nothing else turned up. Apparently the extortionist had rung off before his companion could grow too curious about what he was doing. "I'll see what my detective friend makes of it. In the meantime, please call me again when he lets you know where to send the money."

"Okay," Rita said. "But we won't really pay him."

"Good." Alli hoped the man's other victims would resist, too.

After they finished, Kevin leaned forward, the covers falling around his waist. "What's going on?"

She explained the situation. "I'm trying to remember Dale's and Bruce's last names." Slowly, they surfaced from the far reaches of her subconscious. "It's Dale Fox. And Bruce...Merckle. The mayor's bodyguards. It doesn't sound anything like Klaus LeMott or Randolph Graybar, either." She felt disappointed. "I guess we can rule them out, unless one of them conned a woman into thinking his name is Ardee."

"I've got a funny feeling about this." Kevin wrapped his arms around his knees.

"You've figured out who's behind it?" That would be an amazing break."

"Just a suspicion." He shook his head. "It's too far-fetched. I need to think some more." Flopping back onto the pillow, he closed his eyes.

"Uh-oh," Alli said as another consideration hit her.

His eyes flew open. "Uh-oh what?"

"That article I sent to the paper. It practically fingers Mayor LeMott. What if we're wrong?"

"What if we're not?" Kevin retorted with maddening logic. "Besides, if the blackmail didn't originate in Costa Buena, then somehow or other the information had to come from Dr. Graybar's office, so we weren't wrong about that."

"Anyone might have poked into his files. A member of the cleaning crew, a nurse—who knows?" In the excitement of faking the story and under the pressure of trying to help the parents, she'd shoved aside her doubts. Now they returned full force. "I can't risk letting the paper run a story when I have evidence it may be totally off base."

"You said they wouldn't run it," Kevin pointed out. "You said Payne's uncle is sure to kick it back and make him call the police."

Uneasily, she wondered why she'd been so certain of that. "The way they've been acting lately, you never know."

"And you're suffering from a guilty conscience," he said.

"I guess I am."

"Toward Klaus LeMott? His goons have been taking pot-shots at us."

"Not them." In fact, if it weren't for the shooters, she wouldn't be sitting here naked in a motel room with a lot of wonderful memories and a splendid view of Kevin's bare chest.

However, stretching the truth was one thing, but shattering it into tiny pieces was another. She had too much pride. And, for her friends' sakes, she didn't want to contribute to the *Outlook's* self-destruction.

"After what Rita said, I'm less and less sure the blackmailer is connected to the mayor," she admitted. "Since our goal was to scare him off, the story won't serve any purpose and it might hurt the paper."

He didn't argue further. "What are you going to do about the situation?"

"Fess up," Alli responded.

"You're going to call the paper and admit what you did?" Kevin regarded her dubiously.

"It's not as if I have anything to lose. They already fired me." Of course, an admission of wrongdoing might hurt when she needed to get a recommendation for her next job. Still, at least if the editors believed her, they'd also have to believe that Payne was stealing her stuff. "I've got to try."

"Be my guest." Lying back, Kevin closed his eyes again. Contemplating the mystery of Ardee, she supposed.

Alli dialed the newsroom number. One of the copy editors answered. When she gave her name, he said a friendly hello and transferred her to Ned.

"What is it, Gardner?" the editor asked.

"Did Payne turn in a story about a blackmail scheme?" She

purposely left the type of scheme vague in case her laptop hadn't transmitted the story after all. No point in giving away her investigation unnecessarily.

"How did you hear about that?"

So the scheme *had* worked. "I wrote it. He stole it out of my computer," she said. "Listen—"

"I've had enough of your games," Ned snapped. "One of your buddies is spying for you, isn't he? That must be how you learned about the story."

"Oh, for heaven's sake!" she burst out. "I'm trying to do you a favor. It's a dummy story. I've found new evidence that indicates LeMott has nothing to do with the extortion. I'm calling to ask you to drop the whole thing until you can check it out thoroughly."

"You mean, until you can take it to another paper?" he retorted. "Get this through your head—You're out, Payne is in, and you should learn to live with that." He slammed down the receiver.

Ned had gone over the edge, Alli thought. He'd committed so completely to the support of his nephew that he'd become irrational. Her attempt to help had succeeded only in stimulating his protective instincts.

"Unbelievable," she said.

"He's not buying it?"

"He accused *me* of spying on Payne. How do you like that?"

"I guess this means there's no chance of stopping the article." Kevin didn't sound terribly unhappy about it.

She hated to see the paper make such a huge mistake. Such a massive screwup could harm everyone's reputation, and it provided a disservice to readers as well. "I wonder if I could find J.J.'s number at home. I ought to alert him."

"Alli!"

"They can't do this!" she complained.

"And you seriously think you can stop them, short of planting a bomb in the printing presses?" he said. "Give it up."

Her fighting nature pushed her to carry on the fight, but she knew already she would lose. J.J. would listen to Ned, not her.

Maybe once Ned calmed down, he'd see the need for caution. He'd always been a stickler for doing things right. She had trouble believing his blind spot for Payne had grown that large.

"I'll bet he'll cut the story to a few paragraphs mentioning only the blackmail angle," she said. "They can leave the rest for a follow-up. Maybe they'll be satisfied with knowing they've scooped the competition."

"They'll also have scooped you in your own investigation, and with your help," Kevin reminded her.

"Did you have to mention that?"

"I don't feel as charitably toward that paper as you do," he returned. "I hope they make fools of themselves."

He seemed to take the subject personally, even though it didn't affect him or his case. "You resent the way they treated me?"

"You bet I do." He patted the bed beside him. "Since there's nothing more you can do about it, why don't you come here and get some sleep."

She considered asking whether sleep was really what he had in mind, and decided against it. Her mood right now was anything but romantic. "What about this Ardee business?" she asked. "Did you have any further thoughts about who the blackmailer might be?"

"I'll tell you in the morning," he said. "I want my subconscious to work on it during the night. It may be nothing."

"But you know somebody named Ardee?" Alli persisted.

"Not exactly."

"Stop being so vague!" she ordered. "I want the truth!"

He chuckled at her vehemence. "So do I. Still, I can't say anything until I mull it over."

Dissatisfied, she curled up and let him cover her. The bed dipped as he lay down alongside.

Alli tried to relax, but she kept expecting Kevin to explain, or for the phone to ring again. It might be Ned demanding more information and offering an apology. Or Rita, telling her that the blackmailer had provided details about where to leave the money.

When the phone finally rang, however, it was J. Edgar Hoover. While he was explaining where to find Jimmy Hoffa's body, she figured out that she must be dreaming.

EARLY-MORNING LIGHT filtered through the thin curtains, revealing what the darkness had hidden last night: a spiderweb in one corner of the room and a burned patch on the carpet. There were probably plenty more flaws as well. However, Alli didn't bother to look for them.

Kevin slept beside her in a tangle of sheets. It took a great deal of control not to run her hand across his exposed skin, but she decided to let him sleep.

She was tempted to turn on the laptop and access the newspaper's Web site to see if the story had run. However, she was leery of the thing while that bug remained in place. Besides, the beeps and hums would wake her companion.

After ducking into the bathroom, she took a quick shower and dressed, leaving her hair to dry naturally. When she emerged, since Kevin hadn't moved, Alli pocketed the key and went out quietly.

She'd seen a newspaper stand in front of the motel last night. Heading there, she noted the rumble of traffic from the nearby freeway, so steady it turned into white noise.

A few doors down, a family was piling into a station wagon bearing Arizona license plates. She guessed they'd be heading to either Disneyland or the beach.

When she reached the newspaper vending case, a headline leaped out from atop the stack of papers: Mayor Linked to Adoption Scheme?

Alli's heart sank. Ned had not only run the thing, he'd played up the most incendiary, and probably erroneous, angle. The use of a question mark didn't compensate.

As she'd expected, Payne's byline appeared prominently, along with a thumbnail photo of him. His uncle had gone all out.

Anger washed away her dismay. True, she'd set up this debacle, but for heaven's sake, she'd warned Ned!

After digging coins from her wallet, Alli extracted a copy.

They'd run her story almost word for word, she saw as she read. The only addition was a puny quote from last night's watch commander suggesting that the paper call the detective bureau in the morning. That wasn't confirmation, it was a brush-off.

"This thing has red flags all over it," she muttered to no one in particular. "The cops must be furious." Not to mention LeMott.

He already believed Alli was still working for the newspaper. He'd probably blame her for this piece, too, despite the fact that her name wasn't on it. And, in a way, he'd be right. Worse yet, whoever Ardee was, he'd believe the police were targeting the mayor and that he had a clear field.

The hum of an engine accelerated toward the motel along the street. Despite the other traffic, the sound caught Alli's attention.

She should have been paying heed to her surroundings, she realized with a jolt, and looked up.

A gray van barreled toward her along the road. In a few seconds, it would arrive directly in front of the motel, separated from her only by the width of a driveway and a landscaped buffer.

And she was standing here with not one shred of cover.

Chapter Fifteen

Inside the parking lot, the station wagon full of kids and parents turned a corner, right into harm's way. Waving frantically, Alli shouted, "Go back!"

The sharp report of a gun made her dodge. As the station wagon halted, she gazed wildly around for cover, then took off running toward the side of the building. The tourists sat gaping, obviously confused. She hoped no one had been hurt.

Two more shots rang out before the van gunned its engine and lurched forward. Alli turned in time to see it heading into traffic. Escaping again, she thought in disgust.

Unexpectedly, a black-and-white police cruiser emerged from a side street directly in the vehicle's path. With a bang and the crunch of breaking glass, the van smashed into it, inflating air bags and sending both vehicles into a skid. Across four lanes of traffic, cars screeched and swerved to miss them.

The front window of the station wagon rolled down. "What was that?" asked the woman.

Alli pointed at the van. "They fired at us."

"Wow!" cried one of the kids. "Can we get out and see?"

"Absolutely not!" roared the father. The kids chorused their displeasure, but at least no one appeared harmed.

From the cruiser, two officers emerged with guns drawn. Dale and Bruce stumbled out of the van with hands in the air.

Bruce, the one with the wiry orange hair, had a grating

voice that carried quite a distance. "We weren't doing nothing," he whined at the policemen.

"She's the one you ought to lock up." A furious Dale pointed toward Alli. "Did you see the lies she wrote in the paper about our boss?"

"Dale, shut up," Bruce said.

Onlookers gathered as the officers disarmed and handcuffed the men. Toward Alli along the sidewalk loped Kevin, his shirt untucked and his feet sockless inside his shoes. "I thought I heard shots. Are you all right?"

"I—think so." She indicated the tableau on the street. "They nearly shot me."

Violent shivers overtook her. If Kevin hadn't gathered her in his arms, she didn't know what she would have done.

KEVIN PREFERRED not to leave Alli alone while she was upset. Although the officers shouldn't have left two witnesses in proximity, where they could possibly contaminate each other's testimony, he drove Alli to the police station. In all the confusion, no one seemed to notice.

As they waited to be interviewed, a cup of coffee helped restore her equilibrium. She calmed down a little when he reminded her that Dale and Bruce were finally behind bars.

The scene in front of the motel wouldn't be cleared for hours, he knew, as crime-scene investigators searched for the bullets and police contacted as many witnesses as possible. Drive-by shootings were a rare event in Serene Beach, and this one had endangered bystanders as well as the intended target.

Target. That meant Alli. Lovable, crazy, incredibly sexy Alli. She had walked into the path of those bullets and he'd done nothing to prevent it.

When she left the motel room, Kevin had heard the door close behind her. However, he'd been too sleep-dazed to respond. Why hadn't he remembered that the van might be lurking? Why hadn't he stopped her?

A man ought to protect the woman he cared about. Not because he was a former cop or because he had outdated notions about women being helpless, but because he'd rather risk his life than see her get hurt.

Kevin knew better than to mention that idea, since Alli had made it clear last night that she didn't want to be crowded. He confined himself to supportive words and trips to the coffee machine.

Finally, someone led them each to a separate interview room. Although he'd missed the actual shooting, Kevin related to the investigator how the van had been hunting them and why.

Since his client had given permission, he filled in the blanks about the blackmail scheme. By the time he finished, several detectives had entered the room, including his replacement as bureau lieutenant, an old friend named Brad Zucker.

"So tell me," Brad said, "does this reporter friend of yours have anything to do with the story in the *Outlook* this morning?"

Having read the front section while waiting to be questioned, Kevin knew the whole sorry mess had made it into print. "She called and begged the paper not to run it," he said. "You can't blame her for that garbled nonsense. Were you aware of the blackmail, by the way?"

"I can't comment on an ongoing investigation," Brad replied, which meant yes.

There was one point Kevin hadn't mentioned in front of the other investigators. "Can I talk to you alone?" he asked.

The officers glanced at the lieutenant questioningly. He nodded. "Sure. Guys?" They scraped back their chairs.

"Not in here." The room could be observed from outside, and Kevin had reasons for keeping his comments private.

"My office okay?" Brad inquired. "I guess I won't need to show you where it is."

"I vaguely remember." They were both kidding, since it used to be Kevin's office.

As they walked to the detective bureau, the hubbub of the station felt familiar and reassuring. "How's Alli doing?" he asked.

"Still going over the facts," Brad said. "Those reporters can be pretty observant."

"She's good at her job," Kevin told him. "You'd be surprised how easily she persuades people to open up."

"I'm not even going to ask how you two hooked up, although I can assure you the rumor mill's running overtime
around here."

"Our mutual interests coincided." Kevin didn't add any
more until they'd settled into the office with the door closed.

The place hadn't changed much, except for a bit of extra
clutter and a framed photograph on the desk. Although he
couldn't see the people in the picture, he knew they must be
Brad's family.

"What did you want to tell me?" the lieutenant asked.

"We learned something new last night about the blackmailer," he said. "Something I didn't want to mention in front
of anyone else."

"Why not?" Brad watched him guardedly.

"Because it concerns a former member of this department."

To ALLI'S CHAGRIN, she got the shakes a couple of times during her interview. Each time, she calmed down by force of will
and continued talking.

Seeing no point in holding back, she explained about the
adoption probe. A phone call to Rita gained permission to use
her name as a witness, so Alli passed it along.

Afterward, she found Kevin waiting for her in the hall, discussing the Angels' chances in the coming season with Brad
Zucker, whom she'd often contacted in the past regarding
stories. She decided to go directly to her questions.

"This blackmail case," she said, "were you looking into it
already?"

"No comment." His smile failed to appease her.

"Hey, we've given you a bunch of stuff we've dug up ourselves," Alli said. "The least you can do is tell me what's going
to happen to the parents. They're scared to death they'll lose
their kids."

"I'm not in the business of ripping children away from their
families," he answered. "If Costa Buena wants to demand the

babies back, they'll have to initiate the process on their end. Then it'll be up to the feds and the courts. As long as the parents aren't accused of a crime, they don't fall into my jurisdiction."

"This could drag out for years, couldn't it?" Although she supposed that might come as a relief, it could also prove an expensive legal battle.

"I presume so."

After a beat, Kevin addressed her. "Ready to leave? We need to check out of the motel."

Something tickled the back of her brain. "Not quite. You told the cops everything, right?"

He nodded.

"That means you told them who you suspect Ardee is," Alli continued. "It's my turn. What did you come up with?"

He and Brad exchanged glances. It was just a quick flick of the eyes, but sufficient to put her on guard.

"That's confidential," the lieutenant replied.

"I'm afraid so." Kevin wore the cagey look he used to assume in the old days—generally right before he tossed Alli out of his office.

"I'm part of this investigation!" she declared.

"Not officially, you're not," Brad responded.

"I have a request," Kevin told him before Alli could do more than sputter in protest. "She's earned special consideration. How about a promise to give her first crack at any developments in the case before you release them to the rest of the media?"

"I can't hold back the fact that we've arrested the mayor's bodyguards, because that's public record," he said. "As for any future exclusives, will they help get rid of that incompetent clown who took your place?"

"I hope so," she responded.

"Then I can assure you this department will cooperate with you fully," Brad said.

"You've got my cell number, right?" she asked.

"You bet."

He walked them to the lobby. On the drive to the motel,

she tried to wheedle more information out of Kevin about Ardee, but he kept repeating that it would endanger the investigation to tell anyone, even her.

"You've turned back into Detective Hardnose!" she railed. "I thought we were partners."

"You heard Brad. As soon as he finds anything, you'll be the first to know." He kept his expression bland.

She couldn't believe that she'd slept the whole night in this man's arms without incurring frostbite. Yet, she reflected, she'd never felt happier to see anyone than when he'd grabbed her on the sidewalk and kept her from collapsing.

"We're still working together, though, right?" she said.

He didn't immediately answer. Alli narrowly resisted the urge to punch him in the arm.

"Sure," he answered at last. "Hopefully this case will be wrapped up soon, but there's more between us than that. And if there's any way I can help restore your job, count on me."

There's more between us than that. What exactly? she wondered, and bit her lip to keep from asking.

She wasn't ready to have this conversation. She preferred keeping things light, hanging out with Kevin as they chased clues, snuggling with him without having to make commitments. They'd play it by ear. That suited her fine.

"The reverend was going to try to find out more about the orphanage," she said. "I'd better call him."

"Whatever you say, keep it general, okay? The less the public knows about an ongoing investigation, the better," Kevin advised.

"Okay."

When they arrived at the motel, few signs remained of this morning's shooting, only a remnant of yellow crime-scene tape and some shards of glass. Alli hoped the Arizona family hadn't been detained too long, although perhaps the kids had found witnessing a crime more exciting than a day at the beach.

When they entered the motel room, the scents and the rumpled bed reminded her vividly of last night. Apparently they didn't affect Kevin, because all he said was, "We'd better get moving. Checkout time's in twenty minutes."

"Could you be a little less romantic?" she snipped.

He paused on his way to the bathroom. "Sorry. I'm not very good at that sort of thing. Maybe I could buy you some flowers later?"

"Forget it. A gift should be a surprise. And it has to come from the heart."

He disappeared, returning a moment later with his shaving kit in hand. "As I said, I'm weak on the fine points of courtship."

Her annoyance dissipated. *Courtship* was such an old-fashioned, endearing term. And reassuring, because it indicated he hadn't slotted last night in the category of short-term pleasures.

"A rematch would be nice," she said.

"Tonight?" he asked hopefully.

"If it happens." She closed the laptop with a snap.

"Spontaneously," he filled in. "Right?"

"You're catching on, Detective."

They finished packing with ten minutes to spare. Impatient to contact Weatherby, Alli dialed his number.

The church secretary put her through. "Miss Gardner," the minister said cheerfully. "I was going to call you."

"I hope that means good news." She prepared to take notes.

"As a matter of fact, yes. I talked to my missionary friend and also to the director of the orphanage. It appears they'd installed a new computer system and lost some of their records. When the authorities decided to audit, they interpreted the absence of data as a sign of wrongdoing."

She jotted down key words as he spoke. "It was a computer error?"

"They had to go back and find hard copies of documents, which was very time-consuming. They're better at nurturing kids than at maintaining paperwork," the minister said. "For a while, it looked like they were going to be charged with illegal buying and selling because they couldn't prove they'd obeyed the law. But they resolved the whole thing on Friday."

"It's over?" she inquired.

"They've been completely cleared. My friend says he posted it on a Web site where he writes about his experiences as a missionary. I think he called it a blog."

"Short for Web log," Alli filled in. "Kind of an online diary for the public to read."

"Yes, well, he updated it on Saturday, although I'm not sure how many people knew to look for it," Weatherby said, and gave her the Internet address. "I hope you'll help put out the word. This should end that terrible blackmail business."

"Except for anyone who's already paid," Alli responded. "But the police are working on that." She explained briefly about the morning's developments. "Thank you so much for checking it out."

"Glad I could help," he said.

By the time she clicked off, they had to hurry to reach the front desk on time. Once they were in the car, she told Kevin what she'd learned. "You can reassure your client, and I'll call Rita."

"The missionary posted the information Saturday?" Kevin repeated as he steered. "That's interesting."

"Why?"

"Because on Saturday night the blackmailer called his victims and moved up the demand date."

"That's why he was in such a hurry!" Alli smacked her forehead. "That creep! He was hoping to grab the money before people found out there wasn't a problem."

"Call Brad with this, will you?" he said. "I promised to keep him apprised."

She put in calls, first to the lieutenant and then to Rita, who was elated. "When they catch that jerk, I'm going to sue him for intentional infliction of emotional something or other," she declared.

"Give your little girl a big hug for me."

"You bet!"

They parked in front of Kevin's house. "I've got to clean up before I go to work," he said. "Which reminds me, I need to check in with my secretary."

His mind was obviously running ahead to other obligations. So should hers, Alli thought, and reluctantly faced the
fact that she had no further excuse to stay here. "I'll pack the
rest of my stuff."

"There's no hurry. You still need to use my computer until
you have yours fixed," he pointed out.

He was leaving open a world of possibilities. Alli forgave
him for the lack of flowers or their equivalent.

"Okay!" she sang out. "I'd like to start writing even though
I have no idea whether I'll find a place to publish it."

"Brad hated Payne's article, by the way," he said as they
got out. "I made sure he knew you tried to prevent it from
being printed."

"You didn't tell him I wrote it, did you?"

"Of course not."

They were allies again. Alli couldn't have asked for more.

They'd reached the front porch, when she noticed a movement at the side of the house. "Kevin!" She caught his arm.

He stood stock-still. Alli saw why a moment later.

They hadn't been cornered by another set of thugs. They'd
been caught with suitcases in hand by his mother and two sisters, who were gaping as if they'd just arrived in a spaceship.

Chapter Sixteen

During Kevin's senior year in high school, when he'd been squeezed by the pressure of applying to colleges, taking SATs and seeking scholarships while keeping up his grades, he used to have dreams in which, one by one, every single thing unraveled.

He'd overslept his tests, filled out the wrong applications, missed deadlines and arrived at school naked. Those had been the worst nightmares he'd ever experienced...until now.

Okay, he might be exaggerating. There were worse things than being caught in an awkward situation by the three people whom he'd always tried to keep in the dark about his personal life. Like showing up at school with no clothes on—although he wasn't entirely sure about that.

"Hello, there," he said to the three accusatory faces. "Something I can help you with?"

"It's no use playing innocent," his mother replied. "Do you know how worried we've been?"

He tried to ignore a tinge of guilt as he unlocked the door and tapped in the security code. "I'm sorry you were upset. I should have called."

"Somebody was shooting at you!" cried Betsy. "We heard it on the radio."

"They mentioned a former *Outlook* reporter and we knew it had to be you," said Barbara, who was carrying the obligatory casserole. "Are you okay, Alli?"

"I'm fine, thank you."

The women formed such a tight knot at the door that for a moment it didn't look as if anyone would navigate inside. With a jolt, Kevin realized that, when they did, the evidence before them would prove damning.

"Let's keep this outside." He swung to face the women while blocking the doorway with one arm. "The place is a mess."

"Your place is never a mess," Heloise pointed out. "Did those thugs break in and tear it up? What's going on?"

Alli ducked beneath his arm—not an easy task, given her height—and scooted past him. "Just let me tidy up," she offered. Apparently, she realized how compromising the situation would appear.

He should have figured he couldn't keep his family outside. They knew him so well they coordinated without visible effort. Betsy poked him in the stomach and, as he instinctively recoiled, Barbara pushed him out of the way.

His mother marched inside and halted with a gasp. He knew exactly what she was staring at.

When Kevin dared to peek, he discovered the scene looked even worse than he'd remembered. Before they left, Alli must have disarranged her clothing and tent while packing, so that now her lingerie and the blankets looked as if they'd been tossed around during an orgy.

"I see," said Heloise, which was literally true. "You didn't think to mention that Miss Gardner was living here?"

The use of her surname did not bode well. He wanted to speak up and clear the air, except that he didn't know what to say. What *was* their relationship?

"I'm not exactly living here." Alli glanced at him in mute appeal.

"That's not how it looks to me," said Heloise, unable to tear her eyes from the dangling lingerie.

"You moved in with a woman and didn't tell us?" Hurt laced Betsy's voice, as if he'd rejected his family by leaving them in the dark. "I'll bet practically everybody at my party knew except us!"

"Nobody did," Kevin said.

Heloise folded her arms. "This has to be serious, because you never lived with anyone before, even Lisette. I hope you're not planning to shortchange everyone by eloping. Alli, I realize you don't have any family locally, so please count on us to help with the wedding."

"What wedding?" She glanced at him, clearly stunned by this leap of imagination.

"Don't let my son put you off too long." His mother's gaze played over the suitcases. "I can see you two had a fun time at that motel they mentioned on the radio. Not that I'm a prude, but I realize young people don't always think ahead. Alli, take my word for it, you don't want to walk down the aisle past the third month, because by then everyone can tell."

"Tell what?" she asked.

Barbara, who'd gone into the kitchen to refrigerate the casserole, returned in time to hear the end of her mother's statement. "You're pregnant? Oh my gosh! I'm so jealous. I've been wanting another baby, but Betsy's been giving me a terrible time about it."

"I have not!"

"You're afraid Mom won't have time to babysit for the triplets!" returned her older sibling.

"That's not true!" Betsy squawked.

Kevin held up a hand for silence. When his sisters continued squabbling, he roared in his officer-in-charge voice, "Stop right there!"

Everyone froze.

"Alli is not pregnant," he announced. "We are not getting married. We are not living together or contemplating doing so. We have been working on a case and it is now nearing completion. She is going to pack her belongings and return to her own apartment now that it's no longer being staked out by criminals. Taking my laptop with her, if she so chooses," he added, remembering belatedly that he'd promised to let her use it.

"But—" Heloise began.

"You're sure she isn't…?" asked Barbara.

"No romance, no wedding bells, no baby," Kevin reiterated. "Everybody got that?"

Three heads nodded.

"Thank you for the casserole," he said. "Goodbye. Heloise, I will see you at work. I presume you still work for me?"

"You can't fire your own mother!" she wailed.

"I wasn't suggesting that." He breathed a sigh of relief as the trio made their departure. He'd exerted his authority and everyone had backed off. Temporarily, anyway.

His stomach reminded him that it was lunchtime. Maybe that casserole hadn't been such a bad idea.

"Alli?" he called. "You hungry?"

She emerged from his office with his and hers laptops. "Go ahead and eat. I'll be on my way."

"On your way where?" He hadn't meant to rush her.

"Home." Reaching the entertainment center, she began pulling down underwear with a series of vicious yanks.

"I thought you were going to stay." What had he missed?

"I work better alone." Flipping open her suitcase, she stuffed garments into it willy-nilly, apparently trying to set a new world record for wrinkles.

"You can't pack that way," Kevin told her.

"Watch me." She crammed in even more. "I'll fold the blankets and put them away if you like."

"Don't bother. I'm going to have them cleaned." They needed it after dragging on the carpet. "Are you angry about something?"

She paused while hauling her stuff toward the back door. "What makes you say that?"

"You were planning to stay here and work on your article." He didn't understand why she'd become so prickly.

"What I really need to do is look for a job." Alli avoided his gaze. "It could be anywhere in the country, so maybe I'll move in with my mom in Texas to cut expenses."

Where had this come from? One minute she'd been happily planning to finish her exposé, and the next she was moving out of state.

"You owe me more of an explanation than that," Kevin said.

At last her eyes met his, but he still couldn't read anything beyond the fact that she was annoyed. "You said it. We were working on a case and we're done. Unless you plan to clue me in about Ardee."

"I told you, I can't." Was that what had touched her off? But she'd appeared to accept it while they were in the car.

Kevin hadn't liked fingering someone he knew and respected. If not for Ralph Durban's financial stresses, he might have joined the man's security firm. Until last night, Kevin had assumed those problems were resolved.

But the mention of his nickname, R.D., had raised a red flag. Could it be a coincidence that Ralph and Tara were planning to adopt, and knew Binnie Reed?

Once Kevin's brain had begun turning over the possibility of Ralph's involvement, he'd gradually assembled the pieces. He should have realized before that an ex-policeman would have researched the orphanage on the Internet, which meant he must have come across the Costa Buena investigation.

Yet Ralph hadn't mentioned any problems at the party on Saturday night. He'd even gone out of his way to reassure his wife.

Exactly how he'd gotten his hands on the other parents' data, Kevin didn't know. But when he'd mentioned Ralph to Brad, the lieutenant had confided that police were already investigating complaints by former clients about embezzled funds.

That he would stoop to stealing was bad enough, but to extort money from desperate families turned Kevin's stomach. He felt as if Ralph had betrayed him personally, and he could tell Brad had had the same reaction. Officers formed a brotherhood. They weren't supposed to switch sides and join the crooks.

Maybe the official investigation would clear Ralph. But the more he thought about it, the less Kevin believed that. Still, he'd given his word to Brad not to tell anyone, even Alli, until the investigation was complete.

The clunk of the patio door shutting jolted him from his thoughts. He cut across the kitchen and wrenched it open.

Halfway through the yard, Alli glanced back. "I'll return this in a few days." She hefted his laptop.

"No need to hurry."

"I don't plan to."

He wanted to add something personal, but he had an instinctive reluctance to air his private business where the neighbors could hear. Besides, no doubt she'd demand that he say something spontaneous and from the heart.

While Kevin tried to figure out how to do that, she disappeared into the garage.

Retreating indoors, he registered the hollowness of his footsteps on the linoleum. The air hinted of Alli's fresh scent and, when he went into the living room, he noticed her blankets lying forlornly on the floor.

In the entertainment center, a couple of DVDs jutted out from their orderly lineup and last week's edition of *TV Guide*, which he would have discarded on Sunday if it hadn't been hidden from view, stood propped against the set. A few minutes of picking up restored the house to normal.

Kevin could scarcely tell that anyone had been here. That should make him feel great.

Instead, it left him very, very empty.

ALLI OUGHT TO BE jumping for joy. She was back in her comfortably messy apartment, she had a laptop to work on, and an endless stream of Internet job sites awaited her.

She kept reminding herself how great it was to be free. Unlike other job seekers, she had nothing tying her down. Anywhere a likely prospect turned up, she could move in the blink of an eye.

Instead, she couldn't concentrate. She missed Kevin's house. She missed his teasing smile and the way they played off each other.

"Well, what did you expect?" she said aloud to the empty room. "That he was going to stand up to his entire family for you? And say what?"

She was the one who'd avoided any discussion about the

future. And Kevin had reacted to the situation in accordance with his nature.

In other words, he'd gone back to being a lone wolf.

"Okay, so you made love," she continued to her invisible audience. "And he said that changed things, and you started hoping he meant it. So what are you using for brains these days, recycled aluminum?"

Alli knew she was being irrational. She didn't even *want* a wedding or a baby. True, she could definitely get used to having Kevin rumple her sheets. He looked so darn cute in the morning with stubble on his face and his usually perfect hair flopping onto his forehead.

And his arms around her felt safe and loving. A woman could nestle into a guy like that, and unbutton his shirt while she was doing it. Unsnap his pants. Tackle him onto the bed and...

Wait. Stop. Rewind to former scenario.

He was a louse. Not exactly a louse, but a disappointment. Like every other guy, he'd failed her in a pinch. Just because she'd insisted on keeping things light didn't mean he had to disown her in front of his entire family—well, almost his entire family, except for his father and the dog.

How could she be such an idiot? She ought to be enjoying a time in her life filled with possibilities.

Like unemployment? Like running around the country scrounging for work?

Alli buried her face in her hands. The computer beeped a protest as her elbow hit the space bar.

"Even inanimate objects are turning against me," she lamented. "I can't stand this. There has to be somebody out there more miserable than I am."

She picked up the phone and called Larry.

"The mood around here is what you might call Early Funereal," he said. "Alternating with Advanced Hysterical. The police say Payne got the whole story wrong. None of the officers will admit having spoken to him except the watch commander who told him to call back in the morning."

Alli relished every word. "I guess he blew it."

"J.J. called Ned into his office this morning. Nobody could hear what they were discussing, but Ned's been snarling at people ever since and J.J.'s pulling out what's left of his hair. Rumor has it you called Ned last night. What gives?"

"I told him not to run the story."

"You knew about it?" he asked in surprise.

"Sort of." Alli wasn't sure how much she dared disclose at this point. "Please don't tell anybody."

"Okay." After a beat, he added, "No wonder you said it was better if I didn't know what you were up to."

"Believe me, I never planned this big a mess," she responded. "I was trying to do the paper a favor against my own best interest, because there are other people I wanted to help. But the whole thing backfired."

"Big time," he confirmed.

"What's Payne doing?"

"Keeping his head down. Nobody knows what's going to happen, but according to one of the front-desk clerks, there's been a parade of suits in and out of the publisher's office all day."

"Suits" translated to lawyers. LeMott's, Graybar's or the newspaper's? she wondered. Probably all three.

"No matter what happens, I doubt I'll be rehired," she said gloomily.

"I wouldn't recommend popping in here today," her friend concurred. "Obviously, the paper's going to have to run a retraction. J.J.'s put a couple of other reporters on the story to try to fix things."

There went what remained of her exclusive, Alli thought. She wasn't putting a lot of confidence in Brad's promise to notify her first of any major developments. "I'm sure they'll do a competent job."

"We heard someone fired shots at you," Larry added. "I tried to call earlier but your phone was turned off. You weren't hurt, were you?"

"I'm fine." Except for a broken heart and a cloudy future, she mused. "I turned off my phone while I was being interviewed at the PD."

"It's weird that the same guys who went after Payne went after you too," her friend commented. "Uh-oh. Ned's glaring at me through the glass." A clear divider separated the photo department from the newsroom. "He's paranoid about people being on the phone unless he knows who they're talking to. I'd better go."

"Catch you later," Alli said, and rang off.

She'd expected hearing about the chaos in the newsroom to make her feel better, but it didn't. She wished she could be there with her friends, helping fix things and joining in the gossip.

"Find a job," she muttered. "Get a life."

For the next hour, she researched via Web sites and updated her résumé. At last, driven into the kitchenette by hunger, she heated canned soup in the microwave.

While she was eating, the phone rang again. Alli's heart leaped. She didn't want to hope she'd hear Kevin's voice on the other end, but she did.

Her spirits sank when a female voice asked for her. "This is me," she replied.

"It's Betsy Vickers," said her caller. "I got your number from Mom at the office. Please don't tell my brother I called."

"Okay." Curiosity tugged at her. "Can I help you with something?"

"First, I want to apologize. We didn't mean to barge in on you. We were just worried about Kev." She sounded nervous.

"I understand." Alli waited impatiently, sensing more to come.

"Also, I've been worrying about this blackmail business with the orphanage that was in the paper today," Betsy added. "Mom mentioned you were looking into the situation, but she didn't know any details and she doesn't dare bother Kev about it. I hoped you wouldn't mind if I asked you."

"Why?" Alli inquired.

"You met my friend Tara Durban, right?"

"Sure." She had a clear recollection of the blonde who'd put them on track to the Reverend Weatherby.

"I was afraid her adoption might be in danger. She and her husband have waited so long for this."

"From what I've heard, the orphanage is in the clear."

"I hope so. Their marriage isn't...well, they've had a few problems. Money trouble, I guess, and who knows what else. Tara said R.D.'s been acting secretive. She hopes a child will bring them closer."

R.D. The initials rang a bell. Alli's heart nearly skipped a beat. Maybe the name Rita had heard wasn't Ardee, after all.

It might be a coincidence. Or it might not.

"Betsy," she said. "I have a small favor to ask of you, too."

"Sure, I'd be glad to help. What is it?" her caller asked.

"Tell me about Ralph Durban."

Chapter Seventeen

Returning to work that afternoon helped Kevin take his mind off how empty his house felt without Alli. After sorting through the new jobs that had come in, he called Mary Conners to tell her Costa Buena had dropped the accusations against the orphanage.

"You mean we're safe?" Judging by her tone, she could scarcely believe it.

"Your adoption was legal. You don't need to worry."

She released a long breath. "I can't tell you how grateful I am."

"I'd recommend you contact the police to offer testimony as a victim. However, it's up to you." Kevin gave her Brad's name and phone number, adding, "He's an old friend."

She took down the information. "I might get in touch if they don't have enough other witnesses, but right now I want to move on with my life."

He wished her well and rang off. If only his own life could be sewed up so tidily, he mused. Why had Alli given him the cold shoulder this morning? And why did it make him feel bereft?

He refused to call her. She'd disrupted his life so thoroughly that he needed time to adjust to her absence. Maybe they should meet after a few days, when, with luck, they could settle into a less intense relationship.

But they wouldn't have the chance if she zoomed off to Texas. He didn't understand her hurry. She was too impulsive, which meant he ought to be glad to let her go.

But he wasn't.

The phone rang in the outer office. A moment later, Heloise came in. She hated using the intercom.

"It's Miss Gardner," she said formally.

Kevin's mood lightened. "Thank you." He waited until she closed the door to answer. "Hi."

"I know who Ardee is," Alli said without preamble.

Her husky voice tickled his nervous system, even though he knew this call wasn't personal. "Oh?"

"It's Ralph Durban." Score one for her, he thought. "He's in financial trouble and he probably learned about the orphanage's problems when he researched it for him and Tara."

"You win the brass ring." Seeing the perils ahead, Kevin added, "The paper can't print this information yet. It would be obstruction of justice."

"I haven't got a paper," Alli reminded him. "And I haven't received any official attribution, either, just a hunch."

"What are you going to do about it?" He hoped she'd have the sense to leave the heroics to the police.

"Since I guessed the important part, how about telling me the rest?"

He figured he owed her that much, but only as a friend. "It's strictly in confidence."

"You ought to know by now I'm smart enough to realize that," she grumbled.

"Sorry. It's the ex-cop in me." He hoped Brad never found out what he was about to reveal. "The police already had Ralph under surveillance for suspected embezzlement."

"Of what?"

"Funds he'd been handling for some clients. The minute he makes a wrong move in the extortion case, they'll nail him."

"Have they figured out how he got the data on the parents?" she demanded.

"Not as far as I know." That was the big question mark for Kevin, too.

"Well, I have." She stopped.

He knew she was waiting for him to ask how. Frustrating

er seemed more entertaining than appeasing his curiosity, so e said, "You ought to tell Lieutenant Zucker."

"No offense, but he'd screw things up," she responded.

He bristled but tried not to show it. "How did you reach hat conclusion?"

"Because the cops will never be able to prove a connection. Even if they guess who Ralph must have swiped the ames from, they'll get stonewalled."

Much as he wanted to argue, he'd developed a respect for Alli's effectiveness. "Who is this connection?"

"If you want to find out, you'll have to help me."

Uneasiness pooled in Kevin's stomach. "Help you do what?"

"I need some muscle," Alli said.

Aside from the insulting reference to him as mere brawn, e objected to her putting herself in the line of fire all over gain. "You're not crazy enough to go after Ralph!"

"Certainly not. I'm going to confront his source."

"Wasn't this morning's shooting enough for one day?" Vorry for her safety sharpened Kevin's tone.

"Why do you think I'm calling you?"

Although he had way too much work demanding his attention, and furthermore disliked the idea of serving as Alli's enorcer, Kevin couldn't allow her to face a possible felon unaided.

"Tell me what you suspect," he said. "If I concur on your pproach, I'll help you."

"It's not up to you to sit in judgment. You should help beause, until this case is resolved, we're partners!" she retorted.

"If we're partners, level with me." He considered his logic mpeccable.

She apparently didn't. "Meet me in front of Dr. Graybar's ffice in ten minutes," she snapped, and hung up.

Kevin smacked one hand onto the desk so hard his palm tung. Papers scattered into the air and coffee slopped onto is mouse pad.

In flew his mother. "What's going on?" She surveyed the ness. "This isn't like you, Kevin."

"What isn't?" he muttered.

"Acting emotional." She collected the fallen papers. "I'l fetch a towel for your desk."

"Thanks." Rising, he noticed a wet patch of fabric cling ing to his thigh. On top of everything else, now he had a cof fee stain to show for his ill temper. "I have to meet Alli," he said. "She's likely to get killed."

"Then why are you still here?" demanded Heloise.

He didn't stick around long enough to formulate an answer

WHEN KEVIN PULLED INTO the parking lot, Alli's spirits lifted She'd never been a coward, but even she found the prospec of marching into the office of a doctor who hated her guts intimidating.

Besides, it excited her that he'd come when she asked. I meant...actually, she didn't know what it meant, but it felt good

"Glad you showed up," she told Kevin as he joined her on the sidewalk. "What happened to your pants?"

"You're bad for my wardrobe," he muttered. "And my tem per." He shrugged. "I don't know why I'm here. My case is wrapped up except for the final report."

"You're here to see justice done," she told him. "Besides you'll be helping Brad, in the long run."

"He may not think so when he finds out we acted withou consulting him," Kevin pointed out.

"You didn't act. I did," she said. "You're along for the ride.'

"And to provide the muscle." He gave her an ironic smile

"I was speaking figuratively, but I like the literal aspect too." As she rubbed her hand over his forearm, memories tin gled to life of his powerful build poised above her in bed.

She hoped for a rematch, and soon. Assuming they were still speaking to each other when this was over.

"Let's get this show on the road before somebody builds a planter around us and adds fertilizer," Kevin grumbled.

She should have known better than to expect romance from the dour detective. "Nicely put," Alli said, and entered the building ahead of him.

On the third floor, they faced rippled-glass doors bearing the doctor's name. "Hold on," Kevin said.

"Why?"

"You haven't told me precisely who or what you suspect." He slanted her a dark look. "We're going to be intruding in the office of a guy who may already plan to sue us, not to mention that we're interfering with a police investigation. I have a right to know the details."

If he hadn't acted so arrogant on the phone, she'd have told him earlier. "Okay." Alli had promised to keep Betsy's part in this a secret, so she weighed her words. "According to a source, Ralph cheated on his first wife. In fact, Tara's the one he cheated with."

"How does this affect the adoption business?" Kevin asked.

"It shows his character," Alli explained. "Based on that, I drew the conclusion that—"

A noise from within alerted them barely in time to step aside. The doors parted, ushering out a young woman. Standing in plain view inside the office, Binnie Reed spotted them through the open doorway.

The counselor's jaw tightened in anger. Alli knew she had to act in a hurry or lose the opportunity to press her cause. Leaving the explanation unfinished, she launched her way inside, with Kevin right behind.

Binnie quivered with rage. "Call security," she told the receptionist.

"You don't want to do that," Alli advised. "It would be better if we talked in private."

"Nobody's talking to anybody. You're leaving," came Dr. Graybar's deep voice as he joined them. In his white coat, with a patient's chart in one hand, he might have stepped from a TV screen.

The receptionist hesitated, one hand on the phone.

Alli hated to make a scene in front of the patients. "Honestly, we should talk somewhere else."

"What's the point? Everybody who hasn't read this morning's newspaper has heard about it," the doctor answered bitterly. "You've made a hash of my reputation entirely without cause. And now we've got to deal with this terrible situation at the orphanage. Heaven knows what's going to happen."

"It's been resolved," Alli said. "The orphanage is cleared."

He regarded her suspiciously. "How do you know?"

"The Reverend Weatherby told me. You can check with him yourself."

His scowl softened. "Well, that's good news. Now, what do you want?"

"We came here to talk to Ms. Reed," she told him.

After a moment, the doctor gave a curt nod. "You've got five minutes," he said, and led the way to the conference room.

Stepping inside, Alli hoped she hadn't figured wrong. She would certainly owe Binnie one heck of an apology, and she'd have made a complete fool of herself. But sometimes a reporter had to take a risk.

Thank goodness for Kevin. She appreciated that he trusted her enough to offer support even without knowing the whole story.

"What's this about?" the counselor demanded.

"Tara Durban says you're having an affair with her husband." Alli hadn't talked to Tara. It was a bluff, a big one.

She'd put together the facts that Ralph had financial problems, that he knew about the investigation in Costa Buena and that he had a history of marital infidelity. She'd speculated that he must have figured out he could access data on vulnerable parents by seducing the counselor.

Her guess had hit home, she saw when the color drained from Binnie's cheeks. The woman clenched and unclenched her hands a couple of times without speaking.

"I'm sorry?" Dr. Graybar shook his head. "I don't understand what this has to do with anything."

"Ralph and Tara Durban are prospective adoptive parents," Kevin replied coolly. He didn't look happy, probably because, indirectly, they were revealing the identity of the blackmailer before the police had closed in on him.

But she could see from the set of his jaw that he'd followed her line of reasoning. Probably he was disgruntled because he hadn't thought of it first.

If Brad and Kevin had leveled with her, Alli would have had to respond in kind. Having figured out Ralph's identity on her own, however, she considered herself under no such obligation.

"Mrs. Durban says her husband and Ms. Reed carried on their affair right here in the office after hours," Alli fibbed, outlining the scenario she'd hit upon as most likely. "She left him alone while she went to the bathroom. He used that time to copy the names of some adoptive parents from your records."

Binnie gasped. "I can't believe he'd do that!"

It took a moment for Dr. Graybar to absorb the implications. "You think this man is the blackmailer?"

Alli nodded.

He turned to his employee. "Is this true? You're the one who leaked those names?"

Binnie glanced desperately around as if for inspiration, but none came. "I don't know what Ralph did. I can't believe he called those people and tried to extort money. It's horrible."

"You had sex with a man here—worse, a client—and left him unsupervised with access to patient records?" Dr. Graybar demanded.

She pressed her lips together and lowered her gaze. It was answer enough.

"If you try to warn Mr. Durban in any way, you'll be charged as an accessory," Kevin interposed. "This is a police matter."

"I won't," she whispered. "Oh, Dr. Graybar, I'm so sorry. I've never done anything like this before. I don't know what came over me."

"We have strict policies against that kind of conduct," he reminded her. "Not to mention the negligence involving patient records."

"I'll submit my resignation." Binnie fought tears. "What else can I do?"

"The police need you to testify against Ralph Durban,"

Kevin said. "I'll give you the lieutenant detective's number. Call him now and volunteer the information. He may not charge you with anything if you contact him of your own accord."

"You won't tell him you forced my hand?" she asked.

"We're just trying to get this case resolved." Now that Rita Hernandez and Kevin's client were off the hook, Alli could spare a measure of sympathy for Binnie. Ralph had obviously been a skilled manipulator.

Dr. Graybar stared grimly into space. "This is unbelievable," he muttered to no one in particular. "A breach of privacy like this, in my office."

"I'm sorry we suspected you of being involved," Alli said.

"I am involved, indirectly," he replied. "Are you going to publish this whole mess in your story?"

"It depends on what the police say," she admitted.

The doctor grimaced. "This didn't have anything to do with Klaus LeMott then, after all?"

"As far as we know, he's in the clear," Kevin confirmed. "At least, in the matter of the blackmail."

"I assure you, my dealings with him have been strictly ethical," Graybar responded. "I'm repaying every penny of that loan."

"Sorry for the misunderstanding," Alli said.

The two of them stayed until Binnie placed the call to the detective. Then they slipped away.

"It's ironic. If LeMott had kept a leash on his bodyguards, he'd be off the hook. What an idiot," Kevin noted as they took the elevator. "Listen, why don't we finish discussing this over a bite to eat?"

His casual tone rubbed Alli the wrong way. Couldn't he at least suggest a candlelit dinner? "It's five o'clock. I'm not hungry yet."

Her edgy tone must have given away her mood. "Are you mad at me for some reason?" Kevin asked.

"No. Yes. Never mind! I wouldn't want to be seen having dinner with you. It might give your mother and sisters the wrong idea." The words tumbled out before Alli could stop them.

"What wrong idea would that be?" he inquired as they reached the parking lot.

She knew she ought to make some sassy remark and walk off. Brazen it out, the way she always did. Put on the tough veneer that kept the rest of the world at bay.

She couldn't. This was Kevin. He'd hurt her too much.

"The wrong idea that you and I mean something to each other," she blurted. "After all, our case is over. We're not living together and we're not planning to, as you pointed out."

A furrow creased his forehead as if he were trying to read fine print flashing by at high speed. "What's this got to do with grabbing a burger?"

"Seeing us together might give somebody the wrong impression," she griped. "Like Heloise, Betsy and Bitsy."

"That's Boopsy. I mean, Barbara."

"Right. They might think I'm pregnant. Or that I'm your girlfriend. They might mistake me for someone they could welcome into their family and expect to see in the future. Somebody they might teach to make casseroles and wrap up food in aluminum foil. They might even let slip the secret of where to buy those 'From the kitchen of' labels."

"But you hate acting domestic." He sounded utterly confused.

"That's right, I do." Alli fought through defiant tears. "Obviously, I'm not cut out to stick around. I'm not the ooh-Kevin kind of woman. I never made a bet that I could get a date with you. I don't throw my precious hands in the air and get the vapors when some kid sits on your face. I'm clearly not your type." A phrase that particularly rankled came rolling out. "No romance, no wedding bells, no baby."

"Whoa," Kevin said. "You want a baby?"

"No!"

"Alli, where is this coming from?" He reached for her arm, but she backed off. Across the parking lot, a couple of people glanced in their direction. She ignored them.

"Do you ever stop to think how lucky you are?" she pressed. "You have this wonderful home. You have a loving family, even if they overdo it once in a while. Women throw themselves at you. I guess it becomes a huge burden, doesn't it? You'd rather be alone. Okay. I'm leaving you alone."

She half ran to her car, embarrassed by the drops burning tracks down her cheeks. What was wrong with her? She'd just made a scene in front of the man she'd come dangerously close to falling in love with.

It was a good thing she'd wised up in time. She'd told him off, too. She ought to be proud of that.

She'd unloaded a burden, Alli mused as she hit the gas and screeched away. Any minute now, she was going to feel light as a feather.

Any minute.

THE RED SPORTS CAR streaked across the blacktop and disappeared into traffic. Easing into his sedan, Kevin wished he understood what had upset Alli. He'd responded to her request for muscle, hadn't he?

In his car, he noticed a paper coffee cup she must have left on the way back from the police station, and which had somehow escaped his notice earlier. A small wad of lined paper, apparently from her pad, lay crumpled on the dashboard.

In addition, he thought he detected a small object wedged between the seat back and passenger-seat cushion. As he extracted a ballpoint pen, his hand brushed the upholstery and found it warm.

For one heart-twisting moment, it seemed like residual body heat. Then he realized it must be from the sun.

Kevin deposited the leftovers in a nearby trash receptacle. As he got back in, he suddenly realized that he'd removed the last traces of Alli except for the faint scent of green apples.

When he reached home, he sank into one of the swivel chairs that had served as a yurt support and wondered what the odds were of the Anaheim Angels making it into the pennant race this year. And how many lifetimes it would take before he stopped seeing the tears running down Alli's face as she told him she was leaving, and wishing he'd stopped her.

WELL, THAT WAS GREAT. She'd completely blown it in front of Kevin. He was the last man on earth to sympathize with a weepy, out-of-control woman. For heaven's sake, the guy was allergic to excess.

If she'd kept her cool, Alli thought, they might have shared a few more days or weeks of fun before failing finances forced her out of town. She would have been the first to advise a girlfriend that it was stupid to give up fabulous sex after a single night.

The man had haunted her dreams and her desk drawer for three years. She'd finally gotten him in the sack, an accomplishment that would have wowed 'em at city hall. And what had she done? Gone sentimental, like that ditzoid hanging around him at the party Saturday night.

This gloomy creature blowing her nose into a tissue wasn't the real Alli Gardner. She ought to be out tossing back a beer with the photographers. Shooting the breeze with Larry. Dancing.

Glumly, she discarded the tissue and wandered to the refrigerator. Since she hadn't gone to the supermarket, there was almost nothing in it. In the freezer, three pint-size ice-cream containers yielded a combined few scoops of butterscotch, chocolate–peanut butter and pistachio-mint.

She ate on the living-room couch, digging in with a soup-spoon. The worst part was that she could hardly taste the flavors.

It was all Kevin's fault.

When she was done, Alli watched a couple of game shows, then switched between channels to catch the news. Several stations carried footage of the police hauling Dale and Bruce to the lockup. They also flashed the picture of Payne from Monday morning and trumpeted the tale of the hard-driving reporter who'd nearly become a martyr. None of them mentioned Alli.

At least nobody used the adoption story, probably because they hadn't been able to confirm the *Outlook*'s screwed-up information. By now, Brad must be closing in on Ralph, she thought. With Binnie's help, an arrest should come soon.

That was some consolation, anyway.

Alli fell asleep on the couch, barely remembering to click off the set. When she awakened in the morning light with a view of empty ice-cream containers on the coffee table, she realized she was once again free to be a slob. No more Mr. Clean.

She waited for a twinge of satisfaction that never came.

When her cell phone rang deep within the sofa, Alli grubbed around in the cushions. The darn thing must have fallen out of her pocket during the night and gotten shoved down there.

Finally, she retrieved it. "Gardner," she rasped.

"It's J. J. Morosco," came the editor's voice. "I'm sorry to hear you got shot at."

"That was yesterday." Old news, by anyone's standard.

"I would have called sooner, but it's been hectic," the editor said. "I'm still trying to sort things out. Could you do me a huge favor and drop by? I have a few questions I don't feel comfortable asking over the phone."

The temptation to suggest he take a flying leap nearly overwhelmed Alli's better judgment, but not quite. She still needed his recommendation for her next job. "I'm not dressed."

"Whenever you can get here would be fine," he replied. "See you in an hour."

She took her time showering, picked a cherry-red suit with a short skirt and applied enough makeup to make herself look twenty-nine again. Morale counted.

Remember, you're the one who cracked the adoption case and nailed LeMott's goons. You're a winner, even if you don't feel like one.

Buoyed by her pep talk, Alli retrieved a pair of high heels from the closet, the better to tower over J.J. For good measure, she grabbed her laptop on the way out.

You never knew when it might come in handy.

Chapter Eighteen

Alli paused in the *Outlook*'s lobby to glance over Thursday's paper, which lay on the front counter. A retraction of the adoption story dominated the left side of page one. It disowned the unattributed police quotes and apologized to Dr. Graybar and the mayor.

On the right, a photo showed yesterday's arrest of the bodyguards. The headline, with uncharacteristic restraint, identified the men only as drive-by shooters. Not until the third paragraph were they revealed to be in the employ of Klaus LeMott.

J.J. appeared to be learning caution belatedly. He might get lucky, however. With his aides in the slammer and his own reputation on the line, LeMott was unlikely to file libel charges for yesterday's story. She doubted Dr. Graybar would, either, given Binnie's culpability.

The desk clerk signed her into the building. "Are you coming back to work?" she asked.

"Not as far as I know." Alli didn't dare assume anything of the kind.

"Too bad." The young woman gave her a sympathetic smile. "I hope they change their minds."

"Thanks." Alli was touched. It hadn't occurred to her that staff members outside the newsroom cared about her.

Upstairs, when she stepped out of the elevator, the subdued level of noise struck her at once. A few ringing phones and quiet conversations replaced the usual clamor. In the quasi-silence, she could hear the tap of keyboards and the squeak of her own shoes across the linoleum.

A couple of reporters nodded or smiled. Madge Leeky shot her a thumbs-up, to which Alli replied in kind.

She didn't see Larry, which was just as well, because she didn't want anyone to know he'd been helping her. As for Ned, he hunched over his desk, glowering. Payne was nowhere in sight.

She approached J.J.'s office and, in the absence of his secretary, gave a warning knock before entering. "How's it hanging?" she asked, trying for her usual cockiness.

"Thanks for coming." The editor rose to shake hands and waved her into a chair. "I was hoping you could clear something up for me."

So much for any lingering optimism about a job offer. "Sure."

"One of the copy editors mentioned that you called Ned on Tuesday night."

"Sure did."

"May I ask why?"

Alli would have preferred to let the matter die, but she wasn't about to lie, so she took the plunge. "I called to tell him to kill the blackmail story because it was off base."

J.J. blinked a couple of times. "How did you know we were running the blackmail story?"

"Because I wrote it."

He went stock-still. Apparently he expected her to fill in the blanks, or else he was in shock, because he didn't say anything. Neither did Alli. Let the guy stew for a while. He deserved it.

"You wrote the story?" the editor managed to say at last.

She nodded.

Dryly, he commented, "That wasn't your usual level of reporting."

"It wasn't reporting," she told him. "It was fiction."

He seemed to have trouble breathing.

"I thought the cop who used malapropisms was particularly funny. Guess I've got a gift for dialogue," she said. "Care to see the original?"

His head bobbed stiffly.

Setting her laptop on his desk, Alli opened the file and turned the computer so he could see. "There it is."

J.J. read the piece slowly. He must have gone over the *Outlook*'s account with a fine-tooth comb yesterday, so he probably recognized that it was nearly the same. "I don't understand."

"Where's Payne?" she asked.

He glanced into the newsroom. "I sent him to the garden club."

She nearly choked. "He's covering the garden club?" That was an assignment fit for a student intern not a reporter. "Well, while he's gone, I'd like to show you something. Follow me."

Closing the laptop, she went out. J.J.'s footsteps followed.

At Payne's desk, she perched the laptop atop a stack of papers and plugged it into the network. Opening a blank file, she instructed the editor, "Write something."

"Me?"

"Doesn't matter what. Anything."

As he frowned at the screen, Ned came over, trailed by a couple of copydeskers. Madge joined them, too, watching wordlessly.

The editor typed, "This is J. J. Morosco." When Alli closed the file, a small window appeared on Payne's screen. "Click on that," she said.

The editor tapped the mouse. A file opened on Payne's screen.

It read, "This is J. J. Morosco."

She heard a collective release of breath. Ned coughed. J.J. stared at the screen.

"It's spyware," Alli told them. "It works whether I'm writing at that desk over there—" she indicated the empty one where she used to sit "—or at home, or even at the Slumber Well Motel."

"This is a trick," Ned responded.

He'd picked the wrong time to open his mouth. The editor turned on him and, in front of everyone, said, "Did Ms. Gardner phone you Tuesday night and tell you not to run the story about the extortion scheme?"

"She made some wild accusation about Payne stealing it from her," he blustered. "I'd had enough of her excuses."

"I told you it was a dummy story," Alli said. By now, no one in the newsroom was even pretending to work. "I told you I had evidence that LeMott wasn't involved with the extortion, and that you should wait until you could check the whole thing out."

"I supposed she'd learned we had a scoop and she wanted to beat our time with another paper," Ned protested.

"This adoption story," J.J. said. "You made the whole thing up?"

"No," Alli replied. "It's an exclusive I've been working on. It went completely against my interests to clue you guys in, but the blackmailer was putting the squeeze on a couple of families and I couldn't wait."

"Why didn't you call the police like any normal person?" Ned scoffed.

"Because I'd promised my source I wouldn't." It might not be entirely true, but Alli refused to bring Kevin's vow to his client into the discussion. "If I'd gone to the cops, I'd have had to involve her. So I decided to tip you guys off via Payne's spyware so you'd call and alert them."

"You set us up to run a story full of speculation just to tip off the police?" J.J. asked incredulously.

"I never figured Ned would run this obvious mess the way it was. I assumed he would make Payne check it out." To clarify, she added, "At the time I wrote this, I honestly believed LeMott was behind the extortion. Later that night, I received new information, so I tried to stop the story."

"Who *is* behind the extortion?" Ned inquired.

"The police are closing in on him now," Alli said. "I turned my information over to Lieutenant Zucker and he promised me advance notice when they catch the guy. Beyond that, I'm not at liberty to say."

Ned's lip curled. "That makes a nice excuse. The way I see it, you embarrassed this paper with your irresponsible reporting and now you're pretending to have an exclusive that doesn't exist. You can't even tell us who the blackmailer is."

"Wait." J.J. held up one hand. "This is a lot of detail for me to sort out. Ned, nothing she's said excuses you for running this article. Nor does any of it excuse Payne for stealing, which he's obviously been doing."

"She probably rigged that thing." Ned regarded the laptop with disdain. "She could have fixed it to send files to his computer so it looks like he did it."

Alli's stomach churned. Once again, her attempt to clear her name was being twisted and used against her. Fat chance that J.J. would start believing her over his assistant managing editor.

The knot of staff members behind them, which had grown to include half the newsroom, responded with angry muttering. "He swiped my piece on the new fire-ant threat two months ago," said Jane Breyer, one of the younger reporters.

"He asked me about a story I was working on that I hadn't discussed with anyone," grumbled Armand Ginastero, who covered the court beat.

"I heard him repeating a joke a friend e-mailed me ten minutes after I saved it in a file," put in Millie Linowitz, a feature writer.

The editor stared at them in dismay. "Why didn't anyone tell me?"

"Why should they?" Madge spoke up. "Every time Alli complained, Ned called her a liar and you believed him."

"Yeah, and you fired her," added Pedro Ruiz, the education specialist. "Why should we run that risk?"

"I've gone back to writing my stories by hand and carrying them with me whenever I leave my desk," Jane confessed. "Even to the ladies' room."

"Me, too." Spots of red appeared on Armand's cheeks. "Not to the ladies' room, though."

For once, Ned had nothing to say. Alli wished she could capture this moment on video to show Kevin. He'd love every minute of it.

At the back of the newsroom, a door opened from the employee staircase. Payne Jacobson stomped in, his designer haircut mussed and a brownish patch marring his suit front.

"That is the last time I waste time on that stupid garden club!" he bellowed. "Can you believe they were conducting a session on composting? It stank! Some of the stuff even flew up and hit me. I told them where they could stick their asters!"

Catching sight of Alli and the assembled news staff, he broke stride. Pale eyes narrowing in suspicion, he said, "What's she cooked up now?"

"You. In my office," J.J. ordered.

Ned faced his boss defiantly. "I should be part of this."

"Fine. You come, too."

They marched off. Alli figured she'd been dismissed, but her former colleagues surrounded her like a cheering section and it would have been rude to leave. Besides, she hated to miss the drama playing out behind the glass in J.J.'s office.

"Thanks," she told the others. "If you guys hadn't spoken, that would have been the end of it."

"I'm sorry we've been silent so long," Madge said. "We're a bunch of gutless wonders."

"You're not," Alli replied. "You sent me information I needed."

"Well, the rest of us are," Millie put in. "I figured you were strong enough to take care of yourself but that wasn't fair."

"He'd better hire you back," added Pedro.

"Do you already have another job?" Armand asked.

"It's only been a week," she reminded them. "I've hardly gotten started."

"Let's hope you don't have to," Madge said fiercely.

Raised voices from J.J.'s sanctum distracted them. When Ned reared to his feet and headed out, the staffers began to edge toward their desks, the way they always did when trouble threatened. Then, one by one, they stopped and held their ground.

The assistant editor ignored them. He took one look at his desk, grimaced as if it were covered with sludge, and marched out of the newsroom.

"Do you think…?" Millie let the question hang in the air.

Before anyone could answer, Payne slunk out. A gamut of expressions, all ugly, ran across his thin face as he regarded them.

"Get fired?" Madge asked. "Let me be the first to say good riddance."

"Laugh while you can," he sneered. "While you're stuck in this backwater, I'm going to be hitting the big time. I've been planning on moving up for quite a while."

"Where are you moving up to? The Liars' Club?" Pedro quipped.

Payne tried to think of a retort, failed, and stomped out in his uncle's wake. No one spoke until the newsroom secretary appeared with a couple of boxes.

She peered from one vacated desk to the other. "They left already?" Heads bobbed. "I guess I'll have to pack their stuff for them," she said, and grinned. "Oh, Alli, the boss wants to see you."

"Go for it!" Madge said. "He'd better be offering you a job." The others added agreement.

"I guess I'll find out." Part of Alli wanted to punish J.J. for his mistreatment by leaving him with his major stories in disarray. But the momentary satisfaction would never compensate for what she'd be giving up, and it would hurt these friends who'd rallied behind her.

The group hadn't completely dispersed a few minutes later when Alli came back out. Knowing that J.J. could see her, she refrained from clasping her hands overhead.

The editor had apologized earnestly enough to satisfy Alli's pride. He'd also reinstated her with back pay plus a bonus.

He'd made mention of considering her for the assistant managing editor's post, but Alli had declined without hesitation. Her heart belonged on the front lines, she'd told him.

"Well?" Madge asked. "How'd it go?"

"Not well." She paused to let the implication sink in before adding, "I'm afraid you're going to have to put up with me again."

As her colleagues showered her with hugs and congratulations, she wished Kevin were here to experience this moment. She wanted to see his dark eyes light up with satisfaction.

But Larry returned from an assignment just then, and her fellow staffers repeated the tale for his benefit, even embellishing to emphasize Ned's villainy and Alli's heroism. An accounting representative arrived with documents to sign, and the publisher called to invite her to lunch for the first time ever.

It was midafternoon when she settled at her computer. The reporter who'd been assigned to cover the shooting arrests had requested her help, and she was glad to pitch in.

When her cell phone rang, she answered promptly. "This is Lieutenant Zucker," said the detective's voice. "We've arrested Ralph Durban in connection with the extortion case."

"Fantastic!" She opened a computer file to take notes.

"I'm giving you a heads-up like I promised," he said. "With the mountain of paperwork involved, I doubt we'll issue a press release to the rest of the media until, say, tomorrow morning. How's that?"

"You're an angel," she responded. "By the way, I'm back at the *Outlook*."

"What about the little creep?"

"Long gone."

"That's good news." He wasted no further time on small talk. "Here's how the arrest went down."

She typed the facts into the computer at top speed. Rita Hernandez had helped the police by setting up a payoff with Ralph. A policewoman had made the actual drop, and—although as an ex-cop he should have known better—he'd risked exposure to retrieve it a short time later.

Not only had Durban been caught in the act, but his fingerprints had been lifted from Binnie Reed's computer keyboard and personal files. She and Dr. Graybar were cooperating fully.

A short time later, as Alli thanked Brad and closed her notes on the computer, her thoughts returned to Kevin. If only she were going back to his house tonight.

They could eat dinner together and savor the day's events. Never having lived with a man before, she'd never imagined how much satisfaction came from simple pleasures like talking things over at the end of the day.

If only she hadn't ruined everything. But anyway, men never stuck around. Counting on them was a good way to get your heart broken. Alli supposed she should congratulate herself for having known that from the beginning.

She found it no consolation whatsoever.

ON HER WAY HOME Friday night, she picked up a bucket of fried chicken. It was enough to last all weekend.

She wasn't in a mood to go out. For one thing, her co-workers had been celebrating with her so heartily that she needed a break. A bunch of them had taken her out on Thursday night, and several editors had treated her to lunch today in honor of the scoop that had restored honor to the *Outlook*'s front page.

She'd landed a complete exclusive on the blackmail arrest, complete with quotes from victims and witnesses. There'd been details on the now-resolved investigation in Costa Buena, praise for the adoption service from the Reverend Weatherby and plenty of background details to add texture. The TV stations, which had jumped on the story this morning, were forced to play catch-up.

That afternoon, Alli had covered Ralph Durban's arraignment and turned in a story for Saturday's paper. As for the shooting case, ballistics had matched a gun recovered in the motel drive-by to a bullet fired at Payne. LeMott, although not yet named as a suspect, had resigned as mayor, leaving Cathy Rodale a shoo-in at the next council meeting.

On the Internet, Payne's fall from grace and subsequent dismissal had turned his reputation as a crusading journalist into mockery. He'd fired back a post to one Web site claiming he intended to write his story and sell it to a publisher. A second letter writer had asked who he planned to steal his memoirs from.

Inside her apartment, Alli plopped the aromatic bucket on the coffee table and changed into jeans and a purple blouse. Then she turned on the TV to check the latest newscasts.

There she caught a glimpse of Ralph Durban being escorted to his arraignment that afternoon. Although, in person, his linebacker's build and cropped hair had given him a tough air, on the little screen he simply came across as a punk.

The camera cut to Tara Durban's tearful face. "This is an awful way to find out he was cheating on me," she said. "I guess I should have guessed that if he did it to his first wife, he'd do it to me."

"What's your next step?" the interviewer asked.

"I'm going to see a divorce lawyer on Monday," she responded.

People were breaking up all over, Alli thought. Like her and Kevin. Well, not Larry and Adrienne, who'd seemed quite cozy together when she joined them for a drink last night. And the Hernandezes, who'd called to wish her well after they saw her byline and learned she was back at the paper. Some people got lucky.

When the doorbell rang, she gave a start. She hadn't been expecting company.

Alli muted the TV. "Who is it?"

"You can smell fried chicken all the way down the hall," came Kevin's voice. "I don't suppose you bought any extra for a starving pal, did you?"

She squelched the unworthy impulse to throw open the door and leap into his arms. She already looked foolish enough for making a scene in front of the doctor's building on Wednesday. Besides, he had probably come to retrieve his portable computer.

After brushing a few crumbs off her blouse, she unlocked the door. He stood with his head tilted and a welcoming smile playing around his lips.

"Good to see you," Kevin said.

"You came from work." She indicated his suit.

"Hope you don't mind. I'm a little rumpled."

As far as she could see, he didn't have a crease on him. "Your laptop's on the desk," Alli responded. "The paper's having mine debugged."

"Glad they gave you your job back." He sauntered in. "Terrific story today. I knew Brad would keep his word." His gaze fixed on the coffee table. "You aren't planning to eat that alone, are you?"

"Help yourself."

As he tucked into the chicken, Alli wondered what was going on. Surely Kevin didn't think they could go back to being friends—if they'd ever qualified for that term—after what they'd experienced.

But then, he hadn't given his heart. She wasn't even sure he had one.

They exchanged wry comments about the TV news as they ate. Afterward, he cleaned up and stowed the leftover chicken in the fridge.

The man overwhelmed her kitchenette, almost glowing against the dinginess of the worn decor. "I'll get the computer," she said.

"I didn't come for that," he told her. "Keep it as long as you like."

"Why *are* you here?"

"A couple of reasons." He fell silent as he surveyed the modest surroundings. This was the first time he'd been in her apartment, Alli realized, and wished she'd tidied it. Better, she could have painted the walls and bought new curtains. Or, best of all, hired a bulldozer.

"You can answer anytime," she said.

"What? Oh, my reasons." Kevin cleared his throat. It was his first hint of nervousness. "You're not really attached to this place, right?"

"I've seen better."

"The couch would come in handy, but it needs

reupholstering. Why don't we start with the coffee table?" he suggested.

"Start what?"

His mouth quirked mischievously. "Don't tempt me."

If he hadn't said that, Alli might never have done what she did. But the chance to tempt Kevin was impossible to resist. And she might never get this chance again, because given how long he was taking to get to the point, they'd still be having this conversation by Christmas.

She caught his arm and tugged him toward the couch. "You think it needs reupholstering?"

"I didn't mean to criticize…"

With a yank, she grabbed his lapels and pulled him on top of her. The couch creaked in protest as they landed.

Kevin braced one hand in time to keep from hitting her too heavily. Even so, there wasn't a dime's worth of space between them.

"What it really needs," Alli gasped, "are new springs."

"They don't seem that bad."

"They will be when we get done." Then she brought his face down to hers and kissed him.

Chapter Nineteen

Kevin hadn't planned to make love to Alli. He'd had no idea how she might react when he showed up. Or how he might.

Now his instincts took over with a ferocity that astonished him. Since they'd already become lovers, he would have expected to prolong the second time, but he couldn't wait and she clearly didn't want him to.

Their clothes went flying. The lack of space on the couch made for some awkward positions and a possible permanent crimp in his left knee; still, sheer joy spread through him as her tongue invited his to explore and his hands cupped her firm bottom.

When he entered her the moan that slipped from him mingled with hers.

Alli moved rhythmically beneath him. Kevin was almost afraid to add fuel to the flames for fear he'd go up in smoke.

"We should take this easy," he said when he lifted his head.

"Over," she commanded.

"What?"

"I'm flipping you."

"Do you really think that's a good—"

Mercifully, she didn't tilt toward the coffee table, because they'd both have landed on the floor. Instead, she gave a push that rolled them halfway up the back of the sofa, which shifted precariously on its rear legs.

"Ohmigosh," Alli muttered as they teetered in the air.

A front-page photo of him and Alli being carried out on stretchers, beneath a headline that read, Sexual Ecstasy Ends in Agony, flashed through Kevin's mind. They would never live it down.

On the other hand, did he care? Let the newspaper readers eat their hearts out. He was almost disappointed when they slid back onto the cushions.

He helped Alli complete her climb atop him in a more cautious manner. Lying beneath her, Kevin enjoyed a splendid view of her long body. He cherished the flow of her hair and the wild light in her eyes.

"You're magnificent," he said, and proceeded to demonstrate that he was equally skilled at claiming her from this angle.

Abandoning a last attempt to rein in his desire, Kevin matched her intense thrusting. Watching Alli lose control thrilled him until they soared in each other's arms, suffused in a glorious brilliance.

A final explosive burst wiped out everything except an incendiary realm of white light. He felt as if he had been reconfigured right down to the cellular level.

Despite the narrowness of the couch, neither of them seemed inclined to stir afterward. Kevin lay holding her atop him, relishing the pressure of skin on skin, until the kinks in his back threatened to turn into a medical emergency.

Alli rolled away. Sitting on the edge of the couch, she flipped her hair out of her face. "What did you mean earlier? About starting with the coffee table?"

"I'm sorry?" Kevin couldn't think of anything—didn't want to think of anything—except the sensations lingering in his body.

"You said the couch needed reupholstering, and then you mentioned the coffee table." She collected her clothes from where they'd landed: on the floor, a chair and a lampshade.

"Look out the window," he said.

"Why?"

"Just try it."

Going to the front window, she peered between the blinds.

"Kevin!" Dodging back in alarm, Alli exclaimed, "There's a van down there!"

"A green van," he said. "Not gray."

"Right, but—you mean that's yours?"

"That's right. I rented it for the weekend." This wasn't the kind of conversation a man wanted to have lying down, particularly not with metal coils digging into his ribs. Stiffly, Kevin maneuvered into a sitting position. "Would you mind if we didn't take the couch? These springs are shot."

"Take it where?" Alli asked.

He'd conducted this conversation backward, Kevin reflected. "I was hoping you'd move in with me. You said gestures of affection were supposed to be spontaneous. I figured I should rent the van before I asked so we could get started at once if you agree."

She turned her panties right side out before putting them on. "You planned ahead to act spontaneous?"

"Something like that." He tried to stop the words that sprang to his lips, because they would be too revealing. But that was the point, wasn't it? "I haven't been sleeping well since you left. I was afraid you'd leave town and I'd never see you again. Then when I saw your byline in the paper this morning and realized they'd rehired you, I got so excited I couldn't work."

"And your response to these strong emotions was to rent a van?" Alli sat beside him, looking splendid in nothing but her underpants.

"That's not all I did," Kevin said. "But I'm a man of action, not words. I'll have to demonstrate."

"Okay." She folded her arms across her bare breasts.

It wouldn't take much to inspire a rematch of their lovemaking. "Not here," he managed to say, reminding himself that he had a plan. "Let's load the van and head out. We can retrieve the rest of your things later."

Alli shook her head. "I'm not ready to decide about moving in with you."

"Fair enough. Let's go for a ride."

She shrugged into her bra. "To where?"

"It's a surprise." He ignored a crumpled spot on his jacket as he put it on. In a way, he kind of treasured it, because that was where Alli had grabbed him.

"So surprise me," she said.

"Whenever you're ready." Kevin watched her get dressed, and, despite his impatience, enjoyed every minute.

As THEY WENT OUT to the car, it impressed Alli that Kevin seemed willing to accept her ratty furniture in his spotless house. *She* didn't even like most of the scarred old stuff.

But he hadn't suggested anything long-term. True, it was early—only a week had passed since they first got shot at, which might be said to mark the beginning of their bond. Still, unless he intended more than a temporary arrangement, living together would be too dangerous.

She could easily start to count on him. To trust that he'd always be there. To believe in fairy tales, and end up with a sack of cinders.

As she plopped into the van's passenger seat, Alli observed two boxes almost lost in the cargo space behind them. One bore the name of a local bakery. The other came from Paris Avenue Toys 'N Stuff.

"What's this?" she asked.

"You'll find out." He grinned.

She wanted to give him a shove because he hadn't answered her question, but she found him almost irresistible. Alli wrapped her arms around herself protectively. Maybe she could hold on to her heart that way.

"This better not be a long drive," she said.

"Don't worry."

A few minutes later, they halted in front of his parents' two-story house. Alli glanced at the boxes with a wrench of disappointment, realizing they must be for his family. She'd been hoping for something romantic.

"Should I come in with you?" she asked.

"It would help."

Help with what? she wondered, but kept silent as she picked up the toy box. He took the baked goods.

The last time Alli had mounted these steps, she'd been gleefully contemplating an evening of fun. Now she felt a little lost. Where did she fit in to these people's lives?

She really liked the Vickers family. She wished she and Kevin were a real couple. However, they weren't, as far as she knew.

He rang the bell once. Without waiting for an answer, he escorted her inside.

Heloise, a napkin stuck in her waistband, stopped in the dining-room archway when she spotted them. "Oh, hi!" she said. "We're nearly finished. You should have told me you were coming."

"I didn't know," Kevin replied. "Besides, we already ate."

Behind his mother, around the table, sat his father, Betsy and Barbara and their husbands and children. Under the table, Mindy snapped up morsels.

Everyone greeted the new arrivals with warmth, but also a measure of uncertainty. Obviously, their visit had aroused speculation.

"I brought a few things." Kevin placed the bakery box on the table. "This is to celebrate the fact that I've asked Alli to move in with me, although she hasn't given me an answer."

"I remember when people didn't admit such a thing to their parents, let alone announce it," his father said.

"Don't make an issue, Frank," warned his wife.

"Just pointing out the obvious," he grumped. "If you ask me, our son ought to grab this young lady while he has the chance. 'Moving in' doesn't cut it."

"That brings me to my point." Opening the box, Kevin lifted out a wedding cake. Pink and blue flowers ornamented the single layer, surrounding small plastic figures of bride and groom.

Alli hadn't expected the sudden ripple of longing. She'd never played bride as a kid, never fantasized about lace and flowers and walking down the aisle. Until now. She hoped this wasn't Kevin's idea of a joke.

"The other day when Mom and my sisters found out Alli had been staying with me, I should have told them to mind their own business," he said, adding, "No offense intended. But what's between us is private. If you're in a hurry for a wedding cake, here it is. Enjoy it now."

"I hope it's chocolate," said one of the boy triplets.

"It is," Kevin confirmed. "With butter-cream icing. But never mind that. Alli's very special to me. If she wants a cake, we'll get whatever flavor she prefers. Where's the other box?"

Had he meant that? Was it his roundabout way of hinting that he wanted to marry her? Alli's heart was beating so fast, she forgot she was holding the box until everyone turned toward her.

Startled into motion, she handed it over, giving the children their first clear view of the logo. "Toys!" shrieked Fleur. Her brothers poked their parents urgently, obviously hoping to be the lucky recipients.

Kevin extracted a green baby jumper appliquéd with a whiskered bunny, followed by a package of baby bottles, a bib, a pacifier and a receiving blanket. "I had no idea what to get, so I asked the clerk to pick these out. If anyone's eager for a baby shower, let's throw one right now and get it out of the way," he said.

"Alli, are you…?" Betsy left the question hanging as she caught the negative headshake.

"No, but I am," Barbara said.

A stunned silence fell over the room at this news. "You are?" cried Heloise. "Oh, honey! That's fabulous."

"And you told Kevin first?" Betsy squawked.

"I didn't know," their brother protested. "My point was that Alli can decide if she—if we—whatever. I just wanted everyone to back off. Barbara, congratulations. I guess this stuff's for you." He handed the baby things to his sister.

"I can certainly use them," she responded. "I gave my things to Betsy."

"The triplets wore them out," her sister admitted. "I'll throw you a shower, Barb."

Heloise turned to Alli. "You're a good influence."

"I don't deserve the credit." She laughed. "I think Barbara's husband gets that."

Ernie cleared his throat. "I did my share."

Happy chatter filled the room. A baby on the way! Alli didn't exactly envy Barbara, but that little jumper was adorable. She wondered how you fit those tiny arms and legs into it, and how it would feel to hold such a small, precious person in her arms.

"Can we eat cake now?" asked Barbara's daughter, Rebecca.

Everyone turned to Alli, wordlessly asking permission. A wave of emotion nearly rendered her mute, a wonderful sense of acceptance and belonging, as if it really was her wedding cake.

"Sure," she managed to answer. "Let's dig in, if Kevin doesn't mind."

"That's why I brought it," he said.

Beneath the frosting, the cake turned out to be chocolate with a stripe of raspberry filling. "It's like jam!" burbled the boy whom she recalled had adopted the name Monster.

Afterward, Alli hated to leave, but Kevin appeared to have further plans, so she said goodbye and accompanied him out. Heloise walked them to the door.

"That was an excellent cake," she told her son. "For the real one, you'll need at least four tiers, what with all the guests we'll be inviting."

"Mom!"

"I mean, if and when." She squeezed Alli's arm. "We do promise to call before we come over from now on, too."

Alli didn't bother to remind her that she wasn't living with Kevin yet. "I hope it'll be often." Feeling the man beside her flinch, she amended, "Not too often."

"I understand." Heloise winked.

Kevin didn't speak as they drove away. Alli barely had time to register where they were headed when they arrived at his house. "I thought we'd stop here to open the other box," he said.

"What other box?"

From behind her seat, he plucked a small red gift bag she hadn't noticed. "This one."

Excitement curled through her. She didn't want to expect too much, though. It might be something typically Kevinish, like a personal organizer. "Fine with me."

When they reached the entrance, he tapped in the security code—1776—and said, "That's the new one."

"Since Wednesday," Alli surmised.

"Right."

"I'll never keep them straight," she said.

"I could change it once a month if that's easier," he offered.

"Sounds reasonable."

The living room had a forlorn air with only the chairs and the pristine entertainment center. "You really do need a couch." After a moment's reflection, she added, "But not mine."

His shoulders gave a twitch. Alli could have sworn they sagged. She realized he'd interpreted her remark to mean she was declining his offer.

"I meant, mine's too ugly," she clarified. "We'll have to buy a new one."

Kevin caught his breath. "You're saying yes?"

She wanted to say yes to a whole lot of things, she realized. "How could I hold out?" Although tempted to add more, Alli couldn't, perhaps because she was afraid to.

Kevin had taken a noble stand in front of his family, making up for the way he'd acted on Wednesday. But the cake and baby gifts had only been tokens. Asking her to move in didn't mean he felt ready to be tied down.

She'd almost forgotten the red bag until he removed a velvet jeweler's box. "This is for you."

Her throat tightening, Alli accepted it gingerly. Too long for a ring box, she noted. But she couldn't expect anything like that at this point, anyway.

Gently, she pried open the box. Inside sparkled a diamond-eyed seagull in flight, suspended from a gold chain. "It's beautiful."

"It reminded me of you." Slipping one arm around her

waist, Kevin stood so close she could have buried her nose in his shoulder. "Seagulls are free. They're a little messy, too— forget I said that. If you want a ring one of these days, we can pick that out together. But you said a gift should be a surprise and it has to come from the heart. And this did."

Tears slipped from her eyes. The gift told her what she needed to know: that he'd held back because he thought *she* didn't want to be tied down.

"Did I do something wrong?" he asked.

"You did everything right." Alli fumbled with the chain until he intervened, his fingers lingering against her skin as he fastened it around her neck.

"It might be too soon to make a commitment. Still, I thought we could make a commitment to make a commitment," he explained.

"Like moving in," she finished.

"It's my nature to plan things." Kevin nuzzled her hair as he spoke. "But I'm enjoying following my instincts."

"What do your instincts tell you?" She could hardly breathe.

"That I can't put you in a box like a gift tied up with ribbon," he said. "That life is supposed to be messy. That I love your strength even when you drive me crazy." He paused before adding, "And that you'd make a terrific mother one of these days. I promise not to pressure you, but I don't promise not to drop hints."

It might be fun to have a little boy with a cheeky air like Kevin's. And a smart-mouthed little girl to keep him in line.

"That's okay," Alli answered, "because one of these days I might take them."

He swept her into his arms and she nestled close. When they finally released each other, they wandered through the house discussing which of her possessions to bring and which to donate to charity.

By the time they reached the bedroom, they'd finished talking. Kevin took his time undressing her and they made slow, tender love that she wished could last forever.

HER CELL PHONE RANG at about 10:00 p.m. Alli, who'd brought it to the bedside in case of an urgent news development, grabbed it fast. Kevin stirred drowsily.

"Gardner," she said softly.

"Alli? It's Heloise." His mother cleared her throat apologetically. "I didn't want to disturb my son, and you gave me your phone number, so I hope you don't mind. I couldn't go to sleep without finding out whether you said yes."

"I did." She touched the seagull resting against her throat.

"Oh, good! I won't disturb you further. I just love happy endings."

"So do I. Good night." That was amazing, Alli thought. His mother called *me*.

She'd been drawn into a precious circle. Kevin might resist it, but she understood now that it wasn't a coincidence he'd stayed so close to home. He was a man who belonged in a family.

And he'd made it clear he wanted one with her.

After she rang off, Alli lay basking in his presence beside her. Even in sleep, he exuded a rock-solid steadiness.

Her hand closed around the seagull. He'd said it symbolized freedom, because he knew that was something she needed. But she also needed a nest to come home to, and now she'd found it with a man who would be here tomorrow, and the morning after that, and for all the mornings to come.

Then Kevin woke up and reached for her, and she forgot everything except him.

*Welcome to the world of American Romance! Turn the page
for excerpts from our August 2005 titles.*

A FABULOUS WIFE
by Dianne Castell

JUDGING JOSHUA
by Mary Anne Wilson

HOMEWARD BOUND
by Marin Thomas

THE ULTIMATE TEXAS BACHELOR
by Cathy Gillen Thacker

We're sure you'll enjoy every one of these books!

A FABULOUS WIFE
by Dianne Castell

A FABULOUS WIFE *is the first of three humorous books about three women in Whistlers Bend, Montana, who are turning forty and how they're dealing—or not dealing—with it. You'll love this new miniseries from Dianne Castell, called* FORTY & FABULOUS.

Watch for A FABULOUS HUSBAND,
coming in October.

Sweat beaded across Jack Dawson's forehead. His stomach clenched. The red LCD numbers on the timer clocked backward. Thirty seconds to make up his mind before this son of a bitch blew sky-high…taking the First National Bank of Chicago and him along for the ride.

What the hell was he doing here? Forty-one was too old for this. He was a detective, a hostage negotiator, not a damn bomb expert…except when the bomb squad got caught in gridlock on Michigan Avenue and the hostage was an uptown financial institution.

He thought of his son graduating…by the sheer grace of a benevolent God…next week in Whistlers Bend, Montana. He couldn't miss that. Maggie would be there, of course. Had it really been ten years since he'd seen his ex? She hated his being a cop. *At the moment he wasn't too thrilled about it, either.*

He remembered Maggie's blue eyes. Maybe it was time for a change.

Always cut white? He held his breath, muttered a prayer, zeroed in on the blue wire…and cut.

JUDGING JOSHUA
by Mary Anne Wilson

In Mary Anne Wilson's four-book series
RETURN TO SILVER CREEK, *various characters
return to a small Nevada town for a variety of reasons—to hide, to come home, to confront their pasts.
In this second book, police officer Joshua Pierce finds
himself back in the hometown he was desperate to escape—and is now unable to leave.*

Going back to Silver Creek, Nevada, should have been a good thing. But going home was hard on Joshua Pierce.

He stepped out of the old stone-and-brick police station and into the bitter cold of November. The brilliance of the sun glinting off the last snowfall made him narrow his eyes as he shrugged into his heavy green uniform jacket. Even though he was only wearing a white T-shirt underneath, Joshua didn't bother doing it up as he headed for the closest squad car in the security parking lot to the side of the station.

Easing his six-foot frame into the cruiser, he turned on the motor and flipped the heater on high, waiting for warmth. Two months ago he'd been in the humid heat of an Atlanta September, without any thoughts of coming home. Then his world shifted, the way it had over a year ago, but this time it was his father who needed him.

He pushed the car into gear, hit the release for the security gate, then drove out onto the side street. He was back in Silver Creek without any idea what he'd do when he left here again. And he *would* leave. After all, this wasn't home anymore. For now he was filling in for his father, taking life day by day. It worked. He made it to the next day, time and time again. And that was enough for him, for now.

He turned north on the main street, through the center of a valley framed by the rugged peaks of the Sierra Nevadas soaring into the heavy gray sky to the west and east. Here, some of the best skiing in the west had been a guarded secret for years. Then the word got out, and Silver Creek joined the skiing boom.

The old section of town looked about the same, with stone-and-brick buildings, some dating back to the silver strike in the 1800s. Though on the surface this area seemed like a relic from the past, if you looked more closely, the feed store was now a high-end ski-equipment shop and the general store had been transformed into a trendy coffee bar and specialty cookie store.

Some buildings were the same, such as Rusty's Diner and the Silver Creek Hotel. But everything was changing—even in Silver Creek, change was inevitable. You couldn't fight it, he thought as he drove farther north, into the newer section of town where the stores were unabashedly expensive. He'd tried to fight the changes in his life—all his life—but in the end, he hadn't been able to change a thing. Which is why he was now back in Silver Creek and would be leaving again, sooner or later.

He could only hope it would be sooner.

HOMEWARD BOUND
by Marin Thomas

Marin Thomas hails from the Dairy State—Wisconsin—but Texas is now home. It's a good thing, because there is never a shortage of cowboys—and never a shortage of interesting men to write about, as HOMEWARD BOUND shows!

'Just like old times, huh, Heather?"

The beer bottle halfway to Heather Henderson's mouth froze. Her heart thumped wildly and her muscles bunched, preparing her body for flight. If the voice belonged to whom she assumed, then she was in big trouble.

Longingly, she eyed the bottle in her hand—her first alcoholic drink in over two months, and she hadn't even gotten to take a sip—then lowered it and wiggled it against her Hawaiian skirt. After sucking in a deep breath, she slowly turned and faced her past.

Oh, my.

At six feet two inches, minus the black Stetson, the mayor of Nowhere, Texas, didn't exactly blend in with the gaggle of bikini-clad college coeds in her dorm celebrating end-of-year finals—luau-style. Even if he exchanged his western shirt, Wranglers and tattered cowboy boots for a pair of swim trunks, he wouldn't fit in—not with his stony face and grim personality. "Hello, Royce. Your timing is impeccable…as usual."

Eyes dark as chunks of coal stared solemnly at her from under the brim of his seen-better-days cowboy hat. His eyes shifted to the bottle peeking out from under her costume, and his mouth twisted into a cynical frown. "Some people never change…. Still the party queen, Heather?"

Obviously he believed she'd held a bottle of beer in her

hand more than a textbook since enrolling in college four years ago. She hated the way he always assumed the worst of people. Then again, maybe he was right—some people never changed. *He* appeared to be the same brooding, arrogant know-it-all she remembered from her teen years.

"I'm almost twenty-three." She lifted her chin. "Last time I checked, the legal drinking age in Texas was twenty-one."

His gaze roamed the lobby. "I suppose all these students are twenty-one?"

Rolling her eyes, she snapped, "I see you haven't gotten rid of that trusty soapbox of yours."

The muscle along his jaw ticked and anger sparkled in his eyes—a sure sign he was gearing up for an argument. She waited for her body to tense and her stomach to twist into a knot, but surprisingly, a tingle skittered down her spine instead, leaving her breathless and perplexed.

Shaking off the weird feeling, she set her hands on her hips. "So what if we're breaking the no-alcohol-in-the-dorm rule? No one's in danger of getting written up."

"Just how do you figure that?" he asked.

THE ULTIMATE TEXAS BACHELOR
by Cathy Gillen Thacker

*Welcome back to Laramie, Texas, and
a whole new crop of cowboys!
Cathy Gillen Thacker's new series
THE McCABES: NEXT GENERATION evolved
from her popular American Romance series
THE McCABES OF TEXAS.
Read this first book of the three, and find out why this
author is a favorite among American Romance readers!*

Come on, Lainey. Have a heart! You can't leave us like this!" Lewis McCabe declared as he pushed his eyeglasses farther up on the bridge of his nose.

Besides the fact she was here under false pretenses—which she had quickly decided she couldn't go through with, anyway—Lainey Carrington didn't see how she could stay, either. The Lazy M ranch house looked like a college dorm room had exploded on moving day. Lewis needed a lot more than the live-in housekeeper he had been advertising for to bring order to this mess.

"What do you mean *us?*" she asked suspiciously. Was Lewis married? If so, she hadn't heard about it, but then she hadn't actually lived in Laramie, Texas, since she had left home for college ten years before.

The door behind Lainey opened. She turned and darn near fainted at the sight of the man she had secretly come here to track down.

Not that she had expected the six-foot-three cowboy with the ruggedly handsome face and to-die-for body to actually be here. She had just hoped that Lewis would give her a clue where to look so that she might help her friend Sybil Devine hunt down the elusive Brad McCabe and scrutinize the sexy Casanova celebrity in person. "Brad, of course, who happens to be my business partner," Lewis McCabe explained.

"Actually, I'm more of a ranch manager," Brad McCabe

corrected grimly, shooting an aggravated look at his younger brother. He knocked some of the mud off his scuffed brown leather boots, then stepped into the interior of the sprawling half-century-old ranch house. "And I thought we had an agreement, Lewis, that you'd let me know when we were going to have company so I could avoid running into 'em."

Lewis shot Lainey an apologetic glance. "Don't mind him. He's been in a bad mood ever since he got done filming that reality TV show."

Lainey took this opportunity to gather a little background research. "Guess it didn't exactly have the happily-ever-after ending everyone expected it to have," she observed.

Brad's jaw set. Clearly he did not want her sympathy. "You saw it?"

Obviously he wished she hadn't. Lainey shrugged, not about to admit just how riveted she'd been by the sight of Brad McCabe on her television screen. "I think everyone who knows you did."

"Not to mention most of America," Lewis chimed in.

Bachelor Bliss had pulled in very high ratings, especially at the end, when it had taken an unexpected twist. The success wasn't surprising, given how sexy Brad had looked walking out of the ocean in only a pair of swim trunks that had left very little to the imagination when wet.

"You shouldn't have wasted your time watching such bull," Brad muttered, scowl deepening as his voice dropped a self-deprecating notch. "And I know I shouldn't have wasted mine filming it."

Lainey agreed with him wholeheartedly there. Going on an artificially romantic TV show was no way to find a mate. "For what it's worth, I don't think they did right by you," Lainey continued.

She had heard from mutual acquaintances that Brad Mc-Cabe's experience as the sought-after bachelor on *Bachelor Bliss* had turned him into not just a persona non grata where the entire viewing public was concerned, but also into a hardened cynic. That assumption seemed to be true, judging by the scowl on his face and the unwelcoming light in his eyes as he swept off his straw cowboy hat and ran his fingers through his gleaming dark brown hair.

HARLEQUIN

AMERICAN *Romance*®

is delighted to bring you four new books
in a miniseries by popular author

Mary Anne Wilson

RETURN TO
Silver Creek

In this small town in the high mountain country of
Nevada, four lucky bachelors find love where they
least expect it. And learn you can go home again.

DISCOVERING DUNCAN
On sale April 2005

JUDGING JOSHUA
On sale August 2005

*Available wherever
Harlequin books are sold.*

HARRTSC0705